THE MERCY STEP

UNCORRECTED PROOF COPY

THE MERCY STEP

Marcia Hutchinson

Abuja – London

First published in 2025 by Cassava Republic Press

Abuja – London

Copyright © by Marcia Ann Hutchinson, 2025
By agreement with Pontas Literary & Film Agency

A CIP catalogue record for this book is available from the National Library of Nigeria and the British Library.

ISBN: 978-1-913175-74-0
eISBN: 978-1-913175-75-7

Distributed in Nigeria by Yellow Danfo
Worldwide distribution by Ingram Publisher Services International

Stay up to date with the latest books, special offers
and exclusive content with our monthly newsletter.
Sign up on our website:
www.cassavarepublic.biz

Twitter | TikTok: @cassavarepublic
Instagram: @cassavarepublicpress
Facebook: facebook.com/CassavaRepublic
Hashtag: #TheMercyStep #ReadCassava

Undercover

It's squid-ink black, warm and quiet. All the outside sounds are muffled. Sunlight shines orange, almost red, dimly filtered under the soft, heavy, crimson blanket. I'm playing my game, counting my fingers and toes, marvelling at how they work, flesh bone and blood, see-through fingernails peeping out into the world.

I'm curled up, legs crossed, knees tucked under my chin, sucking my thumb. My eyes are closed. I've grown accustomed to my own little make-believe world. No one is allowed in, no matter how much they tappety-tap tap at the door.

It's just me and Mummy. Mummy and me. Tee hee hee.

I can hear Mummy's voice drifting down as she sings. Mummy sings like a lark, all swooping and fluttery. I'm close to Mummy, in her lap, face pressed up against Mummy's chest, hearing the kettle-drum heartbeat that drowns out the world outside with its regular, soothing thumpety-thump.

Sometimes, after Mummy has eaten, her belly gurgles like the emptying of a bath; loud liquid, squeezing through a small opening. I wish we could stay here forever and ever wrapped-up warm and safe. But I know that I'm going to have to come out and face the music sooner or later.

For now I can dream and imagine a world with fairies and glow worms and people without edges who laugh like flowers and sing like birds. Sometimes I can feel the tension of other, deeper voices but I curl up tighter and squeeze my ears completely shut and the other voices are sent away.

I flex and extend my toes delighting in the way that the soles of my feet alternately crinkle and stretch. I'm discovering my limbs for the first time, testing my strength and finding my range.

I'm impatient but I know that wishing won't make it happen. Nothing before its time. The world can wait until I'm good and ready to make my entrance. Regal, poised and battle ready. Armed with my shield and buckler. Well, fingers and toes to begin with. The rest, I know, will come.

One snow-cold day, with little notice or fanfare, it is time. Mummy is moaning. I try to ask her what is wrong but the words do not form. The moaning gets louder, bouncing around inside my skull until it gets tight and too suffocating and I shit myself.

Oh oh, not good, not the way I had planned this. Quite frankly embarrassing. This will not do at all.

I have to pull it back, recover my composure. All dressed up for the play, ready to make my 'Ta-da' entrance, then tripping over my too-big shoes. I've got to style it out, to get the audience laughing with me, not at me.

The jumper is being pulled over my head, but the neck is too tight and it's stuck. I can't hear and I can't see. I'm being squeezed by the turtle neck. My eyes are held so tight they're getting all bloodshot. I'm going to look like I've been crying, damnit. My little heartbeat is thundering in my ears, ten to the dozen. I can't think straight. I want to shout 'Stop. Not yet. I'm not ready, wait, wait until I'm...'

I'm imprisoned. The blanket is now a strait jacket inside a cell, inside a prison. But it's alive and pulsing like too many rubber bands cutting off my circulation. Underneath the brown skin I'm turning blue. No one said it was going to be like this; endless, squeezing, screaming torture. It's a bloody outrage.

The ink and the squid are merging, the fleshy tentacles constricting the life out of me. And finally the jumper is over my head and I'm furious. How dare they! I did not agree to this, I did not consent. I want to tell them, 'you do not have my permission.' I want to write an angry letter to *The Times*, signed 'Disgusted of Bradford' but I can't speak and I don't know how to write.

Me and the squid and the ink have slithered on to Mummy's legs. My eyes still squeezed shut, my legs kicking in fury. *I want to go back*. I want my warm blanket and my squid-ink and my diluted sunshine. I want calm and red-orange and the gentle rocking from side to side when she walks, carrying me in the cradle of her hips. Safe, secure, protected. But I know there is no going back. And for the first time in my life I cry. Valves shut like doors slamming, others swing open and blood gets diverted. I will have to circulate it round my body all by myself now with no help from Mummy.

The high pitched shrill wail of grief, pain and anger; of lungs suddenly press-ganged into action, sucking in harsh cold air and stripping the oxygen from it. Alveoli blow up like little balloons as, for the first time, outside oxygen crosses into my blood. This breathing malarky is hard work. This is going to be my life from now on. No one will breathe for me. No more swoosh and gurgle. Mummy's heartbeat is no longer in my head. I dare not open my eyes. I dare not look at the new world order. Bring back the orange and yellows and reds.

I'm lying on Mummy's chest on the outside now.

Mummy and me. Boo hoo hoo.

1

Knock Knock

It's thigh-deep snow outside. December 1962, the coldest winter of the century. Mercy has come too early. They are alone. Mummy is too weak to walk. But after the four left Back Home and the two born here, this is her seventh child and she knows the routine. The cord is still attached, thick twisting and pulsing, a sturdy rope attached to a lifebelt, connecting them forever. Mummy waits until the plate-sized, liver-coloured, afterbirth slithers out, following Mercy like a shadow. Mummy can't reach the scissors, so she leaves it still attached to Mercy, but not to her. She can't leave Mercy because it's too cold. There is no phone and Mummy is too tired to shout for the neighbours. Wrapped in a towel they wait, while Mercy plans how to get back to the perfect make-believe world inside her mother.

*

The door slams. 'Liv,' he shouts. 'Ah wheh you deh?' He's dog-tired from the foundry. Ready for a hearty meal. He finds them in the bedroom, blood and guts everywhere, mattress ruined. He looks at Mummy, sweaty and tired, clutching another pickney. He uncrosses Mercy's legs and peeps between them.

Another girl.

*

The upstairs bedroom, on the first floor at the back of the old Victorian house, faces north so the February light is cold and anaemic. The paraffin heater standing to attention in the middle of the room throws out almost as much poisonous fumes as heat. Mercy has barely left this dark, damp space since she came into the world six weeks ago.

Daddy is tall, very tall, a proper giant. But also skinny, sinewy with muscles like knotted ropes. There is a wisp of a moustache, and between thick black eyebrows the bridge of his nose is pronounced and his nostrils flare out. Cheek bones look like they have been cut with a machete and the whites of his eyes are slightly yellow.

If he took off his hat you would see that his hair comes to a dramatic widow's peak at the front with deep recesses at either side. The trilby makes him go on forever. The grey double breasted jacket swings open to reveal a pale blue shirt and the matching suit trousers which flare out before coming back in, to a turn up at the ankles. They are held up with a belt and, to be on the safe side, a pair of black elastic and leather braces.

He takes a pack of cigarettes out of his jacket pocket; Capstan Full Strength. He taps the box twice on the side of the cot before grasping the little gold strip between his thumb and forefinger and circling it to open the pack. He takes out a cigarette and places it between his lips in the corner of his mouth.

Long fingers fish into the left hand trouser pocket and wrap around a chrome cigarette lighter, two inches square with slightly rounded corners and etched with paisley pattern markings, blackened with the oil from his fingers. With a practised thumb, he flips the lid and a small leaf-shaped flame hovers, flickering yellow at the top.

He leans forward, cups his hand around the cigarette, inhales and the tip catches fire. The cigarette glows red and the paper begins to burn. He sucks more deeply and then blows the blue-grey smoke out of the side of his mouth, away from the baby. He picks her up.

'Shhhh', he says, 'Hush noh pickney. Yuh madda soon-come, soon-come.'

'Eeeyaah, yaaah.' Right in his face. Her cheeks reddening, her eyes shut tight, her mouth a trembling oval. The cry hammers on his head. Where did this one come from, this screaming bundle, weeks early, angry and demanding? He puts her back down in the crib and stares at her, astonished at the intensity of her cry. The two of them face off. She will not stop. He cannot bear it.

'Shut up,' he says in a low, threatening whisper. 'Shut up.'

The sound penetrates her soft skull. Loud and insistent.

Knock-knock. Knock-knock.

'Shut-up. Shut up.'

This isn't right.

Mummy opens the bedroom door to see Daddy bending over the crib. What is he doing?

'Shut up', he says rhythmically, 'shut-up', knock-knock, 'shut-up' knock-knock.

'Lord have Mercy,' she screams. 'Sonny, leff de baby.'

She can't run or even walk quickly. She has to hold on to the furniture to get over to the crib. He is so intent on his task that he barely hears her, the cigarette lighter held like a pen in his right hand, the corner pointing at Mercy.

'Shut up.' Knock-knock. 'Shut up.'

She swoops and pulls Mercy out from under him.

'Puppa Jesus on the Cross,' she cries, as she puts the baby to her chest. Mercy's head jerks to the left, automatically rooting for the breast: the milk and the warmth and the slightly curdling smell.

Mummy gazes down at her, her thumb gently brushing the bruise blooming on Mercy's forehead.

2

New Monya

Still winter; snow piling ever higher. Ploughs heave, push and struggle against it. Radio cackles with news about shutdowns and black-outs. Cars are buried in the drifts. Occasional footsteps crunch but mostly no one goes anywhere. It's light even at night from the reflections bouncing off the crystalline snow. The bedroom is old and cold and the air is thick with paraffin and cigarette smoke. Not ideal for a sickly baby.

It's deathly quiet outside and also inside Mercy's chest. She makes a noise. Mummy smiles at her, but Mercy is drowning, not gurgling. Mummy looks closer at her watery eyes.

Puppa Jesus. Sick Pickney.

Mummy rubs her chest with Bay Rum, but it doesn't help. Mercy won't take the breast. She is barely breathing. The skin on the inside of her lips is turning blue; arms and legs all floppy.

Quick-quick time, Mummy wraps Mercy up in towels, herself in a woollen coat, hat, scarf and boots, and takes her to the hospital. Bradford Royal Infirmary. The green and white bus is struggling, skidding and sliding up Toller Lane, churning up slush; it can't manage the hill. Mummy has to get off and walk through undulating snow to Duckworth Lane to get a second bus to the hospital. She keeps patting Mercy, singing to her and praying.

'Not my will but thine. Jesus tek the case. Have Mercy, keep her breathing Puppa Jesus.'

By the time they get there, Mercy is blue-lipped and floppy, barely swallowing sips of air. It's not enough.

The white nurse in the starched uniform says, 'When they come in looking like that, they don't usually live.'

Mummy wails and the nurse tells her to calm down.

The Doctor listens to Mercy's tiny chest and shakes his head. 'New Monya,' he says. The nurse takes Mercy from Mummy, dropping the towel on the floor. Mummy watches as Mercy is whisked behind the swing-doors which say, 'No Admittance'. She picks up her good-good towel and heads home.

They put Mercy behind glass. Every other day Mummy comes to visit and every other day Daddy comes. But they are not allowed to hold Mercy or even touch her. Mummy tries to sing to Mercy but the nurses tell her it is forbidden and Mercy doesn't even know she is there. Mummy can only stare and press her hands up against the thick green-blue panes.

*

The cord is stretched thin, like a violin wire, made of drawn out guts, all the way from the hospital to the home. It takes everything that Mercy has to keep it vibrating, to keep the music going between her and Mummy. It's more like a high pitched wail than chamber music because Mercy is not Mozart. But she does her best to keep the connection.

Her senses are starved, nothing to see but white walls, nothing to eat but milk and then bland baby food, nothing to touch but the blankets, but there is sound. Not the machines, they are boring, but the people. They change every day; they have names like Sheila and Doreen and they talk in low sing-song voices. She can make out words and knows that they have meaning. Mercy wraps her mouth around 'eela and 'oreen and they come to coo and listen to her when she says the words which are their names. Words have power, they can make people stay, they can make them bring their friends to listen to the wonder baby who can barely breathe, but yet say hello and 'bye' and 'tea'. She listens very carefully but she can never hear Mummy.

She keeps fighting for every burning breath. It takes months and months, all the way to spring with birds chirping at the windows and daffodils pushing up the infirmary flower beds, then the long days and short nights of summer.

Slowly her lungs get better.

3

Mississippi

High sided with chrome bars and a mattress covered in flower printed plastic, the cot makes a squishy noise when she moves. She's made it into double digits. At ten months old, Mercy hasn't got the hang of walking yet but she can pull herself up and wobble onto her flat little feet. The wallpaper is covered in blousy fading pink roses. In the damp corners it has started peeling, revealing sickly porridge-coloured plaster underneath. The curtains are purple satin, swooping and dipping where some hooks are missing. The light, such as it is, that comes from outside is watery from being diluted too many times.

She is not tall enough to see over the bars but she can look through them with her wide round eyes in her wide round copper brown face. Her wispy hair is tied up in ribbons. The fluffy terry nappy makes her look bow legged.

Mercy is holding court. Mummy's friends are standing around marvelling at her.

'My word!' says Sister Norman. 'An' she just turn ten month old!'

Mummy smiles her big-toothed smile, compère to the stars.

She clears her throat. 'Say Elephant, Mercy!'

'E-le-fant', says Mercy slowly, pronouncing every syllable, twinkling her eyes at them all.

Oohs, ah, coos and chucking of her apple cheeks duly follow. Mercy is so excited at their reaction that she bounces up and down on her little legs and shakes the bars with her hands and squeaks.

'Say Petroleum Jelly,' says Mummy.

'Pe-tro-lee-yum Je-lly.' She's just warming up.

Another round of applause. The audience is rapt.

'Nevah,' says Miss Mary, 'I nevah hear a baby talk before dem can walk,' and she picks her up and Mercy snuggles into her neck; it smells of sweet sweat and talcum powder. Miss Mary's baby Joy is the same age as Mercy but she hasn't said a word yet, she just stares at Mercy with her unblinking, knowing eyes.

Miss Mary plonks her back in the cot. And now- Dun-Dun-Duuun! for the Finale.

'Say Mississippi!' says Mummy.

Mercy pulls herself up to her full height, looks around the room eyeballing them one by one.

'Mi-ssi-ssi-ppi'! Slow and clear consonants and vowels. Flawlessly executed. Rah Rah Rah!

The room erupts. Mummy gets to her first and lifts her up high out of the cot. She throws her in the air and catches her. Mercy stretches out her arms to grab Mummy's cheeks but misses and grabs her big teeth instead, trying to climb back in through Mummy's mouth. While she was away, the cord became as thin as gossamer, invisible to everyone but Mercy, but she held onto it and she used it to find her way back home. She pulls Mummy in for the most delicious hug-and-cuddle. Her head is patted, fingers are pulled, and her chubby little legs are squeezed. She is in her rightful place. The centre of attention, being reminded that she is the cleverest of them all. There is general agreement on that point, even from Miss Mary. Joy finally blinks, or is she slowly cutting her eye at Mercy?

4

Missing

Mercy is thirteen months old. Talking and walking she can do with relative ease. Her bowels are now firmly under her control. Home is cold, dark, damp and full of people. As well as Daddy, there are Ruby and Janie. Ruby is slim, dark, severe. Any efforts to teach her to smile have been wasted. Janie is entirely circular. Her eyebrows are constantly raised in surprise, lips flare like tulip petals. Her eyes are two wide innocent circles, planted too close to each other in her perfectly round face. Janie is not very bright, even now she can't say *Petroleum Jelly*, never mind *Mississippi*.

*

Mummy is missing and Mercy is wretched. She searches the house from down in the cellar to the middle floor where the strangers live and upstairs to the bathroom. All those stairs are not an easy obstacle to overcome when your legs are as short as Mercy's, not to mention the bulging, and quite frankly malodorous nappy in the way.

But Mercy is not to be deterred. She eventually finds Mummy in the toilet, but the door is locked. Mercy can hear Mummy groaning in there but she can't get inside. To be so near and yet so far is torture.

All she can do is hammer on the door and scream, 'Mummy, Mummy, Muu-maay.'

Mummy begs her to wait, but patience is not Mercy's strong suit and the waiting goes on *forever*. What is she doing in there? After Mercy has screamed herself hoarse, and banged so hard on the toilet door that she has begun to strip the skin off her knuckles, she hears the latch click back.

Mummy is still sitting, sweating on the toilet. Mercy clings to her leg and looks up at a drained face. Mummy looks like an angel with her apple cheeks and big teeth and wispy eyebrows. A tired angel, but an angel nonetheless.

Nothing needs to be said because Mercy knows. Mummy is crying, her pain refracted in every tear. Did Mercy do this? Eject the new one from her old home? Mummy rests a tired hand on her belly.

Mirror-neurons fire and Mercy ignites with the pain of Mummy's loss. The one that got away. Mummy holds Mercy's face, a hand on either side of her cheek and they lean forehead to forehead. Mummy's tears drop onto Mercy's face and mingle with her own and roll around her mini apple cheeks and into her mouth. She can taste the briny mix of salt and sadness from both their tears.

'I loss this one,' says Mummy.

5

Evie

It happens again, just a few months later. Mercy can tell Mummy is different; softer, rounder, plumper. This time she grows and swells and sighs a lot. Daddy mutters that she 'ah bring belly a-*gain*'. But she still goes to work and she still cleans the house. She still cooks and irons, prays every night and goes to Church every Sunday.

She still finds time, (though not enough) to pick up Mercy, and balance her on her hip when she cooks and she still reads the Bible to her. Mercy wraps her arms tight around Mummy's neck to see if she can cross the barrier and become one with Mummy again, but another one is taking up the space.

This one is supposed to be a Spring baby but she has other ideas. She arrives in a tearing hurry at the back end of January. Just like Mercy, she's born at home. Miss Iris, the tenant in the front room, comes upstairs to stay with Mummy while they wait for the *hambulance*. Daddy takes Ruby and Janie downstairs but Mercy clears her lungs and screams blue murder at the thought of being separated, so Mummy says, 'is aright, mek Mercy stay wid me.'

Mummy moans and Mercy sits close and pats her head with the wet flannel. Miss Iris suggests that Mercy goes to get water for Mummy but Mercy is wise to that trick and refuses to leave Mummy's side, respectfully suggesting that Miss Iris go and get the water herself instead.

'But what a faisty pickney eh?'

In between *contraptions*, Mummy and Miss Iris talk about how, the more babies you have the quicker they are born and this one is number eight. Even though the baby is the wrong way round and months too early, they manage. Mummy just stays very calm, leans on the chest of drawers and keeps saying; 'not my will but thine O Lord. Not my will but thine.'

But even though she is hanging by her neck with her body on the outside and her head still on the inside, the not-Spring baby is kicking for all she's worth. Mummy and Miss Iris let gravity do its thing and eventually her head slides out like a lollipop, complete with a loud 'pop' and a gush of liquid. Mercy has to scamper out of the way.

Girl number eight is slick with slime and blood. A head full of shiny black curls and a mouth as big as a whale. She shrieks her way into the world, eventually opening diamond-hard eyes to glare at Mercy saying, 'what on earth are *you* doing here?' The vein in her neck bulges like a demented snake and Mercy is sure that any minute now she is going to explode. She is both frightened and awestruck, the new one has shown her a thing or two about making an entrance.

Ta-da indeed!

And then, exhausted from her bravura performance the new-one crumples, exhausted, on Mummy's belly and decides to stop breathing. She's overdone it with all the melodramatic crying. She's only been on the inside for seven months, not nearly long enough. Miss Iris starts patting her, rubbing her back and singing to her while they wait for the afterbirth.

> *We'll soon be done,*
> *With troubles and trials.*
> *When I get home.*
> *On the other side.*

Miss Iris can't sing as well as Mummy and Mercy doesn't think Jesus is a friend of this new baby's but she keeps her thoughts to herself as she has upset Miss Iris once already today.

Nee-naw, nee-naw. The *hambulance* finally arrives with big, bustling, white people in uniforms who smell of antiseptic as they march into the house. The midwife cuts the cord, delivers the placenta – that's its proper name by the way –, wraps up the new baby and says they have to take her away because she is underweight. Miss Iris helps Mummy into the *hambulance.* Mercy trots along behind, convinced that her services are still required, until the midwife says she is definitely not allowed.

What?

She is shoved back into the house.

Mercy screams and screams and screams and the cord vibrates but Mummy can't hear her. Miss Iris picks her up and hushes her for a while but when Mercy won't stop screaming, Miss Iris gets fed up and gives her back to Daddy. Daddy, like Mercy, is not renowned for his patience. He gives Mercy two good slaps and that stops the screaming dead in its tracks.

They name her Eve, or Evie for short (for long?). Mercy wonders if it's really short for evil. How long before Mummy and baby Evie come back from the hospital? Mercy doesn't know. It could be days, or weeks, but it feels like years. All she knows is that the light went out of her life the moment the *hambulance*-men shut the front door. All she can do is spend all day sitting in the cellar kitchen, gently banging her head against a door. The hollow thud of forehead on wood reverberating around her body deafens the pain. it's like New Monya all over again, except this time she is home and Mummy is in hospital and she doesn't know if her messages are getting through because the cord might be broken.

Thud, thud, thud. Daddy takes a well-considered course of action and ignores her. He puts food on the table and if she wants to eat it, 'dat ah fi 'ar business.' Janie tries to give her something to eat and tells her Mummy will be back soon but she doesn't believe stupid Janie with the big round eyes.

Eventually it's Ruby, severe serious Ruby, who comes and sits next to her. Mercy says nothing. Ruby says nothing either. Mercy turns her back on Ruby and Ruby does the same. They sit there back-to-back. Mercy can feel Ruby's bony spine

pressing into her. It's not the same as Mummy's softness but it's
something.

Mercy shuffles around so that her back is against the wall
again, and after a while Ruby swings round too. Slowly and
casually, nothing to do with Mercy, she just, you know, fancied
moving. Now they are touching at the shoulders, arms, and
knees. Mercy wouldn't go as far as saying she likes Ruby but
there is something about her silent presence that kind of helps.

*

And then, one day, abracadabra, like magic, Mummy comes
back. She's carrying Baby-Evie wrapped up in a shawl. Ruby
and Janie run over to see the new baby and touch her fingers
and toes. Mercy stays at the door. She is not on speaking terms
with Mummy.

As far as she is concerned, *I have no Mother.* She is deserted
and left for dead. From this day forward she will be all alone
in the world. A solitary soul trudging remorselessly through
life. In her mind's eye she experiences many years of living the
life of a Hermit, never speaking to another living soul until she
shuffles off this mortal coil. The injustice of Mummy's betrayal
burns her soul to a shiny, little block of anthracite.

Mummy sings to her, strokes her head and calls her 'Mercy-
Percy,' and 'Moom'. She turns her face to the wall and her back
to Mummy, but Mummy keeps on singing.

I shall not be moved, thinks Mercy resolutely. Five minutes
later she relents and deigns to allow the traitorous Mummy to
cuddle her.

It is not long before Evie reveals herself to be Evie by name,
evil by nature. Mercy wonders if it is because she is actually
a little dragon who is used to breathing fire and is struggling
with boring old air. Last time Mercy saw her, she was limp and
slimy. Now she reigns like a Queen. Her arms stick straight out
sideways from her body like Jesus on the cross. Her hair is all
fluffed like it's been in rollers. She has a dramatic widow's peak

just like Daddy's. She even has his frown with the two scowling vertical lines between her deep set eyes.

If Mercy was born indignant, Evie is born angry. Her fury at the world into which she was so unexpectedly ejected knows no bounds. Every time she wakes she cries seemingly in shock that she is on the outside. But there's no sending Evie back. She's here for good. Her skin is slightly lighter than the others and her hair less tightly coiled. Mummy says Indian people come up and talk to her in their language because Evie looks like a little Indian baby.

Daddy delights in this one who looks just like him with a temper to match. Evie's eyes are watchful and wily. The whites are so white that she looks like a cartoon with her Betty Boop cheeks. She doesn't move her eyes, just swivels her whole head from side to side like an owl. Where on earth did this one come from.

6

Dolly

Mercy is two years old today. It is the middle of December and she is heartbroken. No celebration, no birthday present, nothing. It's like everyone has forgotten, if they ever remembered in the first place. She goes to sit on the step to have a good and proper sulk. Mummy comes to find her and says nevermind she will get an extra big Christmas present and kisses her on both cheeks. Mercy tries to smile but it comes out all wobbly. She counts every one of the days and every one of the fourteen nights, wondering what she will get for her Extra Present. A new dress (not something that Janie has grown out of), a pair of shoes or a hat.

Christmas morning and Mercy is almost exploding with excitement. But she gets exactly the same Christmas present as the others: a blue cardigan from C & A that makes them all look like a matching set. Mercy is so mad she trembles with the injustice of it all. She wants to cut the silly blue cardigan to shreds. Instead she has to line up with her sisters and have a picture taken to record the exact moment of her humiliation.

She tries to be a good girl because Mummy likes her when she is good. But her brow furrows and her bottom lip pouts and wobbles and she feels her face get hot. She dare not look up in case they see how she feels. Keep it inside, she tells herself. Don't let them see. But her blood fizzes like pop and she begins to shake. She tries to pinch herself to stop the shaking but it is no use. She can't smile for the picture.

Daddy sees. 'Pickney-gyal,' he says, 'stop knit up yuh brow.' Daddy never calls her Mercy. It is always 'Pickney' or 'Dat one.' She hates Daddy. One of these days she's going to escape. She'll wind in the frayed cord and take Mummy with her; he can keep the others.

Mercy doesn't know what knitting up her brow is or how to stop it. She forces her lips apart over her teeth but that's worse. Whatever face she pulls is the wrong one. If she doesn't get it right, Daddy's big hand will come down in a slap.

Mercy makes a plan. She will remind Mummy every single day that she is supposed to get her very own birthday present. After all, Mummy did promise. She must have forgotten. And in that case the solution is easy: keep reminding her.

At first Mummy says, 'Soon-soon.'

But the days turned into weeks and still no present. Mummy gets less and less grateful for Mercy's daily reminders. Eventually she says children should be seen and not heard. When Mercy asks why, Mummy says; 'because I say so.' But that isn't a good enough reason for Mercy.

'But *why* do you say so Mummy?' she asks, thinking that adults should, at the very least, make sense.

Mummy says, 'Beca' me ah yuh madda!'There is no coming back from that one. At least no comeback that doesn't involve getting beaten and Mercy's desire not to get beaten outweighs her desire for a birthday present. For now.

When September comes around, Ruby and Janie get birthday presents. Although Mercy feels slightly sorry for Ruby because she gets a school uniform for her birthday, and Mercy is sure she would have gotten that anyway.

Mercy got to go with Mummy to the Uniform Shop. First they had to go to the *Govament Hoffice* and fill out 'one big, long, everlasting-form.' She had to say what school Ruby was going to, what size she is, when she was born and all kinds of foolishness.

The lady behind the desk reads back the form slowly and loudly to Mummy and says, 'Do you understand duckie?'

Afterwards Mummy kisses her teeth and says, 'Cho! Of course mi understand de Queen Hinglish. And she can well see dat I am not a Duck.'

The Lady gives Mummy a thin, pink *Serfi-ticket*. She has to take it to a huge warehouse off Manningham Lane. The best bit about that is taking not one but two green-and-white trolley buses all squashed up between Mummy and the window like they are one person again, watching the world go by. The warehouse is behind the Grammar School, a pointy Victorian building that looms over Manningham Lane like a strict headteacher.

Mummy is allowed to pick two shirts, one cardigan, one pinafore, two pairs of socks, and one pair of shoes. Along with that she is also allowed to get a PE kit which consists of a pair of black cotton shorts, two pairs of ankle socks, a pair of black plimsolls and a yellow PE top. Back home, Ruby tries on her uniforms and struts around like a model. Mercy wishes with all her heart that she could go to school so that she could wear the uniform and march up and down.

*

After many lifetimes of waiting, December comes around again. She has dropped as many subtle hints as she dare about Barbie Dolls, which has resulted in many kissings of teeth, a couple of shoutings, and one light slapping from Mummy.

Birthdaaay!

She wakes up and bounces out of bed like it's a trampoline. She needs to know if her year-long campaign has borne fruit. She helter-skelters down the two flights of wooden steps to the cellar living room.

After breakfast, Mummy tells her to wait, and comes back with a box. Then Mummy sings *Happy Birthday to You* to Mercy in her high clear voice. She gives it a Jamaican lilt because Mummy just can't sing bland, like Hinglish people, no matter how much she tries. Even when she sings *All Things Bright and Beautiful*, it makes you want to dance. The others join in, all except Daddy who sits on the sofa, head down, marking his Pools Coupon.

The box is wrapped in newspaper and too much sellotape which Mercy rips open like a starving child. And there she is. Dolly. It's a *Sindy* not a *Barbie* but that doesn't matter. It's still her very own doll. Mercy just stares at it. She forgets to say thank you. She forgets to smile, she forgets to say anything. She just gazes into the painted-on blue eyes with the three eyelashes at each corner. She can't bring herself to take it out of the pretty-pink cardboard box.

It is minutes before she hears anything.

'Lost in her own little world,' she hears Ruby say. And she sees that they are outside her bubble, trying to get through to her. She looks up hoping that her eyes are big enough to hold in the tears.

'Thank you.' Her voice is barely audible.

Mummy beams at her.

*

Mercy is sitting on her step, third one from the bottom, opposite the front door with Dolly on her lap. She sits there so often it has become known as The Mercy Step. The others know to walk around her when she sits there as she never hears a word anyone says. She is mesmerised by the little red plastic comb, pulling it through Dolly's long blonde hair. Soothing and sweet, Dolly and me.

Dolly has lost a lot of hair by now due to Mercy's repeated combings but it doesn't matter. Mummy has also lost a number of tea towels which Mercy has had to cut up to make dresses for Dolly. That does matter. She once cut up Daddy' Pools coupon to make a Pirate Hat for Dolly. That mattered a lot; it was a good few days before she could lower herself onto the Mercy Step again after that.

Part of Mercy knows that she is staring at a piece of pink plastic but that part is small and getting smaller every day, and if Mercy concentrates she can make it go away completely. The other part of Mercy, the important part, knows she is communing with Dolly, and Dolly is her bestest friend in the whole wide world. Dolly will never criticise her, Dolly will never shout at her, Dolly will never hit her and Dolly will never mock her. They can live together forever in a light, bright, shiny, plastic world.

7

Bwoy

Mercy is warm in the middle of the bed, between Ruby and Janie. Evie is in a little white cot pushed up against the bed. Almost eleven months have passed since the little bundle of disruption arrived. Fat and forever furious, Evie doesn't smile. Mummy says it is because she is premature, and she is still angry about it. Evie pulls herself up and shakes the bars of the cot. She wants to be taken out of baby-jail and put in bed with the rest of them.

Evie's face is heart shaped, her eyes are now huge and her widow's peak at the front of her hair is even more dramatic, just like Daddy's. Does he like her so much because she looks just like him; if he was a little girl-baby that is.

Mercy feels a strange pang in her belly when she sees Daddy feeding Evie. One time, when it was empty, Evie hit Daddy with the heavy glass bottle, right between the eyes. Mercy thought *All Hell is going to Break Loose*. But Daddy just laughed and laughed and said, 'Dis ya one have a temper, *to juice*,' even as the blood trickled down his face.

After more rattling of the bars and stamping of furious feet, Janie and Ruby give in and pull Evie over the side of the cot and into the bed with them. She flops over the top with her nappy covered bottom in the air and lands on her head, but that doesn't seem to bother her because she has finally escaped. The warm bodies wriggle and kick, they shuffle and argue over the blankets. Evie gives off that pukey-milky-baby smell, but Mercy still likes being in bed with her sisters, even if Evie does keep kicking her in the head.

Mercy sings 'And the little one said, 'roll over'. Maybe Evie will roll right out of the bed?

But where is Mummy? Where is Daddy? It's happening again. Mummy doesn't cook and clean as fast as before. She has still been going to work in the early-early morning and coming back to rub their faces with Vaseline and comb their hair with Mercy clamped between her thighs, then Mummy goes back to work. Sometimes she brings cake from the hospital. Mercy doesn't like Hospital-Cake because it tastes of disinfectant, but she eats it anyway because it's better than no cake at all.

Daddy is complaining again that Mummy, 'ah bring belly pon him.' Voices are raised, then there is shouting and Daddy hits Mummy and Mercy wants to fight him, but she is too small to fight a giant. One day, when she is big enough, she will fight him and rescue Mummy and they will become one again and make good their escape.

But now Mummy is gone and Daddy is gone. Mercy wonders if The Belly has been brought. Where did it come from? Is Mummy is sick, maybe her belly is hurting because she ate Yaakas. Could it be Marley-Gripe or Fluxy-Complaint? Mummy and Daddy are always eating things that hurt their bad-stomachs and then they hold their bellies and complain about *Hinglan*-food and spend ages in the toilet.

The night trundles on, with the warmth and the kicking and the pushing. Then somebody wets the bed. It's not Mercy but she can feel the warm liquid catching around her knickers. Probably Janie. It's usually Janie. Wet-a-bed-Janie. They have to get up and change the sheets. In the middle of all the bed-changing kerfuffle something else happens.

Blam! Two floors down, the front door is flung open then slammed. The whole house shakes. Mercy can't work out what Daddy is saying, but his scary shouting gets louder and louder.

'A Bwoy!' he says. 'She have a bwoy! She have a bwoy!'

What is a Bwoy? Must be something wonderful. Must be something marvellous. Must be something magical. Why has Mummy got one and where did she get it from?

Mercy is dying to see the Bwoy. It must be amazing because Daddy is so happy, shouting and banging into things. She doesn't want to go downstairs while he is still shouting because he might get mad that they are awake in the middle of the night and take off his belt.

Mummy will come back, like she did last time. Mercy can feel the little vibrations in the cord so she is not as desperate as before. When it's been quiet for a while, Mercy tiptoes down the two dark flights of stairs from the attic to the cellar, hoping to see the Bwoy. But it's not there and Mummy's not there either. Just Daddy snoring, like a Dragon in his chair-lair. His big grey jacket is also sleeping, draped over the back of the chair dragged down in one corner.

Last week she saw Ruby sneak the little silver flask out of his pocket and screw up her nose after she drank some of the amber liquid. She said it tasted like fire. Could Mercy be as brave as Ruby and drink fire? Of course she can. She holds her breath and creeps over. There is a slightly sweet smell buzzing around him. Her heart has drumsticks and they are banging on her ear drums, but she is brave. She dips her hand into the pocket and feels the cool, silver flask, curved to fit Daddy's hip.

She unscrews the cap, tips it back and feels it spread out on her tongue. It's all heat, Dragon's breath, but she swallows it all. After the last drip-drop has tipped onto her tongue she screws the cap back on and slowly slides the flask back into his jacket pocket. Now how to make her escape without waking the Dragon? Afraid to turn her back on him, she walks backwards, feeling behind her for each step. She's not light footed any more, the gold has addled her brain. She trips on the edge of the rug and falls flat on her tailbone.

Ow! It hurts but she does not make a sound. He shifts in his chair, grunts and rolls his shoulders. She is a fly trapped in amber. Mercy tries to breathe again but she chokes on her heart because it has climbed up into her mouth. Why won't it stay in her chest where it belongs?

He doesn't move again, apart from the snoring which sounds like it's coming up from underground. She eases herself up and this time turns sideways, one eye on the door and one on the Dragon, moving each foot ever so carefully. Leaving him in his lair, she heads upstairs to find clean clothes. But she is wobbly and has to hang onto the bannisters as each stair keeps changing shape like a carpeted cat, moving from under the spot where she puts her foot.

She finds clean clothes and sheets in Mummy's bedroom and drags them up to the attic. The three of them just about manage to change the bed. Ruby and Janie try to put Evie back in the cot while they do it, but she's not having any of it. So they have to roll her one way then the other to get the wet sheets out from under her. She kicks at them but it doesn't hurt because her legs are so soft and pudgy. They roll up the wet sheet and stuff it under the bed. Ruby changes Evie's nappy making sure she does not prick her with the nappy pin like she did before. Ruby is all of five, but she's still not very good at changing nappies. When she has finished, Evie's legs stick out sideways.

In the morning Daddy has to get them all ready to go to the child-minders. Mercy braces for trouble, but he doesn't say anything about the wee-wee sheet. He doesn't know what he's doing. He gives them three Weetabix each and insists that they don't waste Govament Food. But nobody can eat *three* whole Weetabix. He creams them up and down with Vaseline, his hands rough like a cheese grater across their faces. Mercy feels sorry for him. Without Mummy he hasn't got a clue.

But even so he's smiling, still smiling.

'She have a Bwoy. Yes man! Dis time she do it. To Juice!'

*

Ten, long, Weetabixy days later, Mummy comes home. She takes tiny, shakey steps. In her arms, wrapped in a big blue shawl is The Bwoy. Is that it? Mercy's face falls. *It's just a baby.*

She thought it was going to be magic, like a Unicorn, a Fairy or an Elf. Why did Mummy bring home another baby? There are already four of them. Not to mention the ones Back Home; the ones Mummy left behind, although Mercy is not supposed to know that. There isn't enough love to go around. The last thing they need is another bloomin' baby.

She is not sure why Daddy is so happy about the Bwoy but she knows that she is hurt. He never said anything good about having four girls (gyal-pickney-dem). Girls are sugar and spice and everything nice. Boys are slugs and snails and puppy dog tails. It's bad enough that Daddy is so happy about the Bwoy, but Mummy? Mummy is a Traitor, constantly cooing about her 'One Bwoy Pickney'. Evie scowls at him all day long. Mercy sends angry little messages along the cord but Mummy doesn't pick them up.

Mummy goes back into hospital to have her Tubes Tied. Now that they have their precious One Bwoy Pickney, they don't want any more. Mercy wonders which tubes are getting tied. When she asks, Mummy tells her not to push-up herself in Big-People Business. This time, though, Daddy has Learned His Lesson and only gives them two Weetabix each.

*

As soon as Evie learns to talk she tells Mummy that she should have left Devon in the hospital and asks, is it too late to take him back? Mummy laughs out loud, her floaty bird laugh, because she thinks Evie is joking. But Evie doesn't joke.

One day, after Baby Devon has learned to sit up, Mummy pops across the road to see Miss Mary. 'Unu mind di baby,' she says to no one in particular, 'Me soon come.'

But she doesn't come back soon. She's gone for ages. So Ruby goes to find her.

'Unu mind di Baby,' she says to no one in particular. When she doesn't come back soon, Janie goes to find them.

'Mind de Baby,' she says. Mercy gets fed up of minding the baby, so she goes to find them. 'Mind de Baby,' she says to Evie, and she goes across to Miss Mary's house. She waves at Joy. Joy gives her a little piece of Bun and cheese. Mummy and Miss Mary are drinking tea, laughing and chatting, horse dead and cow fat. But Mercy doesn't even get a chance to eat the piece of bun.

Mummy takes one look at her and asks, 'is who ah mind de baby?'

Ruby looks at Janie. Janie looks at Mercy. Mercy shrugs and says 'Evie?'

'Lord Jesus Christ!' Mummy drops her piece of bun races back to the house with the girls trailing behind her like three blind mice.

Evie is standing in front of the cot holding a fork. There are four little holes in Devon's forehead. Two are white dots against the brown skin and the other two are slowly dripping blood. His hands are held like when the cowboys say, 'put em up!' His eyes are wide open and his mouth makes the shape of a perfect little 'O'.

8

Stitch in Time

The dark stone Victorian terraced house is on a street called Hill View. There are eight big stone steps leading up from the sidewalk to the garden and another four wide stone steps leading from the garden to the door. Just climbing up all those steps is an adventure in itself and Mercy can see almost the whole of Bradford laid out like a ruffled blanket below them.

The front door has thick wood panels at the bottom and glass with bubbles in it at the top with stained glass panels on either side of that, decorated with red roses wrapped in thorns. Once upon a time the front door was painted green but the colour has now faded and flaked. There is a dull brass Yale lock halfway up the door. Mercy loves the feel of the oval brass knob which, when turned to the left, ratchets back the latch to open the door.

Each pair of houses shares a set of steps. Their next door neighbour is a Cairo-Tractor, although they hardly ever see him because soon after Mercy's family moved in, he built a zigzag fence down the stone steps from his front door to his garden. He even dug out a whole other set of steps from his garden to the street. They weren't as pretty as the original steps. They were the honey yellow of new stone unlike the dark smoke blacked ones leading to number eight. But it meant Mercy's family had the big steps all to themselves.

Whenever she sees the chiropractor, he always frowns and disappears into his house. Silly man. Once when Daddy's back was bad, he went next door and paid Good Money to the Cairo-Tractor but he came home with his back hurting worse than before. Daddy called him a *ginnal*.

Their house has two faces. The front looks downhill, sunny and bright all day long, even the cellar living room gets a few shafts of afternoon light in which you can see the dust dancing. In the summer the stone is warm and Mercy likes sitting on the steps by the front door watching the others playing in the garden and the city centre in the distance.

The back of the house is scary and dark. The steps from the cellar door up to the back yard are always slick and dark green, dripping with moss and bugs. The uneven stone slabs in the yard are slippery. When it rains, leaves block the little round iron drain at the bottom and Mercy thinks she might trip and fall into the smelly puddle. If she is going in the back door, she tries to skip across the soupy water with its oily, rainbow film.

The backyard opens out onto a narrow cobbled alley with a drain running down the middle. Sometimes she plays in the back alley with Joy. They race up and down the alley, all out of breath by the time they get back.

As she spends most of her time on her step, Mercy can almost feel each of the garden steps as they vibrate. She learns the particular rhythm of anyone coming to the house. Over time she can tell the dainty tip, tip, tip of Mummy's high heels from the more tired clop-clop of Daddy's shoes as he mounts the stairs. The lodgers each have their own signature. Miss Iris in the front room always stops every other step and plonks down her bag of groceries before rummaging for her keys.

Six o'clock means Daddy Come! Devon gets excited, so does Ruby and Janie. Evie is not quite so excitable. They pile over one another to get to the front door and meet him. Five little bundles of hope. Will today be the day when Happy Daddy comes through the door? When he reaches into his pocket and they hear the crinkle of paper; it's a bag of sweets, and they will get one each and spend many happy minutes sucking on sugar.

He might even lift one of them up, up, up into his arms. Up there the air is rarer, the world looks different. The view

from Daddy's shoulders is like looking down from the top
of a mountain. If he's really happy, he might lift all of them
at once. Devon gets to sit on his shoulders, one leg dangling
either side of the strong neck. Daddy's arms are so long he can
scoop Janie and Mercy up into one arm, Ruby and Evie in the
other. The man-mountain carrying his five children. Only for
a few seconds though, a few glorious seconds until they are all
tumbled back on the ground.

But most times, the crinkling is Daddy unwrapping a pack
of Capstan Full Strength. Flipping the lid with his thumb he
extracts one papery white tube with one huge hand, the other
rummaging in his trouser pocket for his chrome lighter, the
one with the magic flame. On those days, when they rush at
him, he shoos them away and says, 'Mek me ears eat grass,'
and they slink off crestfallen because they know better than to
tempt fate by trying to turn Angry-Daddy into Happy-Daddy.
All except Devon who sometimes goes *too far*, and then there
is bawling.

Mercy is on her step in the hallway so she gets to the front
door first, just as Daddy swings it open; the sharp point of the
brass latch slicing a clean, straight line into her forehead.

*

Mummy is screaming, holding Mercy over the old white
enamel bath. It's huge with rolled edges and claw feet which
make Mercy think of monsters.

Curtains of blood almost block Mercy's vision. But she can
see the bright red pumping out with her heartbeat and spilling
against the white bath. Mummy is holding a towel against her
head but the blood keeps coming.

She is screaming at Daddy to get the 'cyar' because they have
to take Mercy to 'hospikkle'. Daddy has the back car door open
and Mummy bundles Mercy into the car and holds her child
tight-tight in the strait-jacket of her lap all the way there.

The corridors are wide, floors mopped and polished to a gleam. Bradford Royal Infirmary, a dark stone sentinel high on the hill watching over the city. It looks like there should always be clouds and thunder behind it. The interior walls are painted green at the bottom and cream at the top. They trundle along, Mummy in a wheelchair with Mercy on her lap. Mercy is screaming but the sound has long since stopped coming out. She has been here before and the building frightens her more than her sliced head. Will she get out alive this time or will they keep her for months on end?

There are raised voices and nurses in blue and white and a doctor in a coat saying there is no time for Annie's Thetic so they are just going to have to stitch her up without. A nurse holds Mercy's arms and they need two nurses for her legs because Mercy is kicking hard. A big strong man holds her head still, while the doctor sews with a big curved needle and thread which burns as it slides through her skin.

*

It's treacle-time. She is in the corner of the room, peaceful, floating up by the ceiling. Way down below is a little girl in a yellow cotton gingham dress, the front splattered in blood. She has no shoes and only one sock on her right foot. Wonder what has happened to the other one? She's doing a waltz with the nurses. She moves her arms and legs and they keep time, never letting go. You can just see her little brown limbs under the hefty nurses, swaying this way and that. If you look closely, you can see the white of her skull slowly disappearing under the brown of her skin as the doctor pulls the edges together creating a lifelong line, halfway between her right eyebrow and her hairline.

9

The Big Fight

Daddy bought a Tee Vee. A big shiny brown box with a milky green screen. It stands commanding the living room like a Dalek. On Saturday mornings, he likes to watch the horse racing. They are not allowed to touch it but sometimes Mummy will let them watch Pinky and Perky, the singing pigs. In the evenings sometimes she lets them watch a film, Cowboys and Indians, but if there's any kissing, or anything sinful like that, she turns the Tee Vee off and sends them to bed, even if it's not actually bedtime yet.

There is a hubbub and a rumble and a murmur. People are starting to arrive at their house. They are dressed up like they are going to church. Mercy's family are the only ones with a Tee Vee and everybody is invited to come and watch it. Joy comes with her two older-younger sisters and Miss Mary. Mercy doesn't talk to Joy but she goes over and stands by her which is the next best thing. They are both the middle children in their families so they understand each other. Even those who haven't been invited come anyway and squeeze into the blue-walled cellar living room. There is no carpet, just a rug over the bare concrete floor, painted blood red, with chips missing here and there. Condensation is always running down the walls even when the fire is roaring.

There is a high-up window with bars at one end side of the room facing the open coal fire. The Tee Vee is up against the wall opposite the door. It is the first thing you see when you come into the room.

Daddy's friends start to arrive. They are loud and slap each other's backs hard. They bring rum and make jokes and rarely take off their hats, even indoors. There is lots of grinning and laughing, gold teeth and talk of back-home and JA. Maas D always wears an olive green suit with tight legs which finish above his ankles so that you can see his matching green socks and his shiny pointy shoes. Maas D is a Rude Boy.

Uncle Red always wears a black suit with a black trilby and a bright yellow shirt with a shiny tie pin for his wide tie. They call him Red because he is so light skinned, but the children have to call him 'uncle' because you can't just call Big-People by their names. Uncle Red has the smiliest face Mercy has ever seen. His eyes shine like little emeralds, his cheeks look like Louis Armstrong playing the trumpet. He has a little pencil-line moustache that tickles. Whatever is happening Uncle Red can see the funny side of it. He likes to pick Mercy up and swing her high into the air before plopping her down in pride of place on his lap.

Someone has brought a pear. It is carefully unwrapped from its newspaper dress and a penknife produced. Slivers of bright green flesh are sliced from around the huge green stone and passed round. Adults first, then children. Mercy gets a piece so thin she can almost see through it. She places the creamy green flesh on her tongue and doesn't even have time to savour the smooth texture before it is gone. Whenever anyone comes from back-home, they bring food: yam, green-banana, plantain and Rum, always Rum. The big-people talk about how they miss JA, sitting on verandahs as sun ah burn down country where they watch the world go by, with everybody waving and chatting as they pass.

It is nearly time; Big-People squeeze in wherever they can on the mustard yellow leatherette sofa or the matching armchairs. Mummy runs back and forth to the kitchen with tea and cocoa, dumplings and Bullah Cake. Most of the children sit on the floor but Mercy has her spot on Uncle Red's lap. Daddy rises like a king and turns on the Tee Vee. The tiny black and white characters spring to life. The excited American announcer talks so quickly it is hard to follow what he is saying.

The excitement in the room bounces off the walls and infects Mercy and she squirms on Uncle Red's lap. There has been talk about The Fight for days, and finally here it is. Cassius The Clay is strutting around the ring in his silky robe. He is magnificent, glistening with sweat in his shorts and white bootees. His massive shoulders shrug the robe off. He looks like a superhero with painted-on, glistening muscles. He is always on his tip-toes like a brown ballerina dancing this way and that.

The other guy can't get near him. He jabs at him with big comic gloves but nothing connects. The crowd in the room seems to merge with the people on the Tee Vee all screaming for Cassius The Clay. Nobody is supporting Sonny The Listing. Mercy surfs the excitement, punching the air like she could join the fight and help Cassius The Clay win.

Then, all of a sudden, the air is sucked out of the room. Mercy is struggling to breathe, like she has been pulled into an underwater world. The Tee Vee is still there, the people are shouting but she can't hear them. Hands moving, fists punching, mouths open, but somehow disconnected. The shine and colour has gone from the world and it becomes flat and monochrome. Something is wrong.

Uncle Red is holding her, bouncing her on his lap. But it is different now. There is something that wasn't there before, something hard. The people are still shouting at the screen but it is the opposite of Pinky and Perky now. They are slowed down so much that it is just a loud deep rumbling drawl. Mercy is looking around for Mummy but she can't see her and Daddy is shaking his fists at the screen, fighting the good fight. She dare not call out to Daddy in the middle of the Big Fight. The room is full of people, hip by shoulder and cheek by jowl, but nobody can see her.

She wants to get off Uncle Red's lap but she is underwater. Why do her arms and legs not work? Why can't she breathe? There is no air, so she can't speak. She is frozen. Uncle Red's arms are a steel cage and she is trapped with the hard thing pressing at her. She watches herself from the corner of the room looking down on a little girl in a red dress, hair plaited and scalp oiled with a red ribbon tied in a bow around the top plait. Bouncing and bouncing like a rag doll on a lap.

And then, the slowly moving water stills, the room comes back. Mercy's hearing and sight come back too. Although not quite the same as before. Cassius The Clay lands a Helluva Punch and Sonny is Listing. He falls on the floor, bug-uh-dups. And the referee is standing over him 'Ah-one-ah, Ah-two-ah, Ah-three-yah!'

Sonny is still on the floor. Mercy is fighting her own fight and slowly winning control of her limbs. The world speeds up again like a record going from 33 to 45 rpm. She slides down off the lap, and without a backward glance runs and weaves on unsteady legs through the crowd to find Mummy. She is standing near the door. Mercy leans up against her and wraps an arm around Mummy's leg, trying to reel in the cord and melt herself back into Mummy from the ground up, but Mummy unwraps her.

'Not now Mercy,' she says, 'Yuh no see Big-people talking.'

10

The Domino Effect

Saturday afternoon in July and it's so warm that they don't have to feed the coal fire in the daytime. Dust floats in the shafts of sunlight that reach down to the cellar from the window high up on the wall. Mummy is using her Singing sewing machine. It rears up like a seahorse, black with gold lettering. Mercy wonders why it is called a Singer, because it hums and it chunters, but never sings, but Mummy sings when she is sitting behind it. It's amazing the way Mummy can pedal with her foot and guide the material through the teeth with her hands and, like magic, two bits join together and it turns into a proper dress.

The humming of the Singer entices Mercy. She and Dolly head downstairs and settle at Mummy's feet. Mercy snaffles some of the spare bits of material to make a dress for Dolly. Well, they might not actually be 'spare' but hopefully Mummy won't notice.

Mercy, Janie and Ruby are going to be bridesmaids so they have to have new dresses with frills and ruffles and layers and layers of netting underneath. Mercy knows that she will look the best of all in her dress. At the last wedding, Janie spilled Guinness Punch (which she was in the middle of stealing) onto *her* dress and Mummy got mad. Mercy the majestic stayed clean all day long.

Mummy is wearing the pink gingham dress which she made herself. It has a wide scooped neckline and a white lace collar. It fits perfectly at Mummy's tiny waist and then flares out to just below the knee. Mercy helped Mummy do the gathering to pull the yards and yards of fabric tight to fit onto the *bodice*.

A silver thimble fits on Mummy's index finger and a pin cushion is attached to her wrist with elastic. Every now and then she stops, pulls the thread and bites through it with her big, white, front teeth. She reminds Mercy of Cinderella. She calls one of them over and holds up the dress to their fronts. She tuts as she adjusts the dress with pins here and there. It's important to keep very still when Mummy is adjusting the dress or Mercy might get a pin stuck in her side.

There is a loud Blam. 'Mi seh douze to raas!'

The noise is coming from the back cellar room. Daddy is in there playing Dominoes with his friends. There's Maas D, Bruk Foot Beris, Uncle Red and some others whose names Mercy doesn't know. They all came trooping down earlier wafting cigarette smoke before them, smiling and patting the heads of the children. Mercy ducked out of the way when Uncle Red tried to pat her on the head. His smiley face doesn't look so friendly these days. They brought bottles of Mackeson Stout and packs of cigarettes and they all wear proper grown up suits.

Mummy isn't paying any mind to any of them. Mummy disapproves of Dominoes because it is Gambling, and that is the work of the Devil.

'Blouse and skirt! He nah bluff after all,' from the back room.

Mummy keeps sewing but she grips the fabric tighter. She sets her mouth and Mercy can see two lines form in her forehead between her eyebrows.

'I tell him,' she says under her breath, 'not to bring any sinful gambling into this house.' She tries to keep on sewing but her lines are not straight any more. She stops, bites the thread and throws the dress onto the sofa.

Blam! 'To Blood Claat! Him win de round.'

'Wid de pickney-dem ina di house,' she says, 'listen dem ah chat bad word.' She gets up, clasps her hands in prayer and looks up.

'Puppa Jesus!' she implores. 'Yuh say yuh wouldn't give me more than I can bear. But Lord God Almighty this is too much. *He hath turned my house into a house of Sin. A den of vice and iniquity.'*

Blam! 'Gwaan Sonny! De wretch did have the six after all.' Mercy can hear metal scraping on wood which she knows is Daddy clearing the coins off the table because he has won.

Mummy is getting more and more Upset. 'Do,' she says looking up, 'Help me Jehovah. Strike him down'.

Blam! Blam! Kablam!

Mummy walks in a circle around the Singer Sewing Machine. 'And Jesus went into the temple of God,' she says, 'and cast out all those that sold and bought in the temple.' When she says 'cast out' she throws her right hand out in a big circle. 'And overthrew the tables of the moneychangers!'

Mercy and the others watch her work herself up into a Right State.

'I will not remain,' she says, 'in a house of Sin and Damnation.' With that she yanks the door open and heads to the back room. Mercy trots after her.

Mummy bursts in like a gunslinger into a saloon. The back room has a stone floor and an old iron stove built into the wall and a big stone sink under the window. It is lit by a bare bulb dangling from the low ceiling. Mummy is tiny compared to all the men, but she sweeps both her arms across the table, sending dominos, beer bottles and money clattering onto the floor. She grabs the corner of the table and yanks it upwards, flipping it upside down and stands there breathing thunder. 'In the mighty name of Jesus,' she shouts, 'I rebuke thee!'

It's like slow motion. The men's mouths hang open, they jump up and move back to the walls to get out of the way of the tiny tornado. Mummy stares at Daddy, her chest is heaving.

His eyes open wide and his cigarette drops out of his mouth. 'Ah... whe... di... Raas...' he says. It comes out deep and slow and Mercy can see each word form behind his eyes before they appear on his tongue. He stands up, his head almost touching the ceiling. He is still behind the overturned table. For a second nothing happens. There is no clock in the room but Mercy can hear one ticking down inside her head. Five, four, three, two, one–

Mummy runs.

Daddy runs after her.

Mercy runs after them.

Mummy shoots out the back door, her feet flying up the stairs from the cellar up to the back yard. Daddy takes them two at a time but he is a bit wobbly from the Mackeson Stout so he isn't as fast as Mummy. But Mummy is tiny and he is Daddy-Long-Legs. The steps up to the back yard are stone but they are covered in a layer of moss and Mercy slips, trips and bangs her knee as she tries to climb them.

Mummy has run down the cobbled back alley toward Aziz Shop. Mercy loses sight of them as they turn the corner. When she catches up with them, Mummy is hanging onto the doorway of the shop by her fingertips, the green paint peeling under her nails. Mercy is across the road from the shop.

'Lord have Mercy!' she is shouting to Mr Aziz. 'Unuh help me.'

'Get out!' says Mr Aziz. 'Get out of shop.'

Daddy has grabbed her round the waist with one arm. Her feet are off the ground like someone caught in a hurricane. He uses his other hand to peel her fingers from the shop doorway. Once he gets her out of the shop and onto the pavement, he raises his free arm high up and whips the back of his hand down across her face. Mummy's head jerks back, a puppet on a weak string, and blood spurts from her mouth and nose. It splashes all over the front of her pink gingham dress.

Mercy looks around. It's Saturday afternoon, broad daylight, there are people walking past, but no one looks at Mummy and Daddy. Mr Aziz closes the door to his shop and locks it. He turns the sign around in the window from 'Open' to very 'Closed'.

Mercy sees half a stone brick lying on the pavement. She bends down and picks it up. It is rough and the broken edges dig into the palm of her hand, but she doesn't care. When she looks up again, Daddy is holding Mummy by the front of her dress. The tips of her toes are on the ground, her back is arched and her head is lolling backwards like her bones are made of spaghetti. Mercy raises the half-brick up above her head as bits of brick-dust fall into her hair.

'You!' she shouts. 'Leave my Mummy alone!'

Daddy turns to look at her. He squints slightly in the afternoon sunshine. He is still holding Mummy by her dress, the blood has slowed to a trickle now but Mummy is still hanging like a ballerina arching in mid-air. He looks at Mummy, then back to Mercy, then laughs. He opens his fingers and Mummy crumples to the pavement. Daddy strolls slowly back towards the house. Mercy walks sideways in a big circle to keep away from him as she edges closer to Mummy. Her arm is aching because she has been squeezing the brick so hard above her head that it has cut her palm, but that doesn't matter. She tries to keep one eye on Mummy and the other on Daddy as the distance between them grows.

*

Mercy is having a conversation with Dolly on her step and the others are downstairs playing in the cellar living room. She is informing Dolly, in a stage whisper, that when she grows big and strong she is going to save Mummy and lock her in a tower so that she can never change her mind and go back. She will have to cut off her hair so that she doesn't do a Rapunzel and let it down for Daddy to climb up. Then Mercy will chop up the beanstalk and Daddy will come tumbling down and crack his head like Humpty Dumpty and they will never put him back together again.

11

Pied Piper

Monday morning. Ruby and Janie have got dressed and gone off to school. Mummy is not in the kitchen so Mercy gets herself a Weetabix, but there is no milk and she doesn't like it with just water, yuck. So she eats it dry and crunchy, like a biscuit. Then she goes to find Mummy. She eventually finds her in the bedroom. Looks like she's not going to work today. Mummy is sitting on the bed, the satin comforter bunched up around her. She is crying quietly, glass-drop tears falling onto the open Bible in her lap. Tip-tip-tip.

The curtains are closed so the room is dark and it smells frownsy. Mercy stands in the doorway watching, her heart splits itself into two. Half of it looks after Mercy, but the other half is looking after Mummy, well less than half, she just keeps a tiny piece for herself. She walks into the bedroom.

'Mummy?'

Mummy looks up at her, eyes wet and bloodshot. Her nose is swollen and her bottom lip is ripped. It is time for Mercy to fix-up and take charge, because Mummy doesn't have a drop of sense. Or if she did have any, Daddy has knocked it out of her. Why does Mummy stay when Daddy is such a monster? Daddy the Giant, has come down from the beanstalk to grind her bones to make his bread.

When she finally helped Mummy back into the house, Daddy and his Domino friends were gone. He didn't come back all day Sunday either. Mercy doesn't know where he is but as sure as night follows day, sooner or later, he is going to come back. And Mummy must not be there when he does. They can't just kiss and make up. Mercy has never actually seen them kiss or hold hands or anything like that. She wonders if they even like each other.

Mercy is going to have to take charge. Four isn't really old enough, but needs must.

'Mummy,' she says. 'We have to leave.' She says it nicely, kindly, like telling someone that the back of their dress is stuck in their knickers. It's not their fault that they don't know. But once they do, they really have to pull the dress out of their knickers or everyone will laugh at them.

'Daddy is a Bad-Man,' she says. 'We have to go.'

Does Mummy understand? Mercy has to find another way to tell her. Mummy is always praying down Hell-Fire on Daddy but it never seems to work. God isn't listening, because Daddy is never consumed in the fiery flames of Hell. He just comes back every evening in time for dinner.

Mercy can't leave all by herself because she's only four and she doesn't have any bus fare and she doesn't know where to go. But Mummy is Big-People and Big-People know everything. Mummy must know where to go. Mercy looks at Mummy. Properly, right into her eyes. Her wide eyes beam the words, *Mummy, let's pack a suitcase and just go.* Mercy thinks up a picture of the olive green suitcase, the one with the white edging. It has a dent in the top where someone sat on it and the locks are a bit rusty but it still works. She tries to beam it into Mummy's head. They could fit everything important into the green-and-white suitcase.

Mercy is the Pied Piper and Mummy is the children. She just needs to play the right tune to get Mummy to follow. She picks up both of Mummy's hands. Even though Mummy is a grown woman and Mercy is just a 'pickney', Mummy's hands feel tiny, like a bird's. Mercy is standing so they are eye-to-eye. Mercy puts her forehead on Mummy's forehead and sets off to find Mummy's heart. She has to squeeze in behind the eyeballs, slip round behind the brain, and climb down her spine. The head bone's connected to the neck bone. Then balance around her rib cage. It's slippery, careful she doesn't fall off.

She finds Mummy's heart; it's squashed, but she can mend it. She can use pieces of her own to fix it and get it working again; get it pumping sense around Mummy's body. Mummy blinks, once, twice and looks at Mercy and nods.

Her torn lip opens. 'Yes,' she says. That's it, just the one word, 'yes'.

Mercy nods. 'Good Mummy, Good. I'll get the suitcase.'

Mercy did it. She got inside Mummy and restarted her. She doesn't know how she did it. Can anyone else do it? Probably not because Mercy is a clever Superhero who can do amazing things. Saving Mummy is her job but squeezing in and back out again is hard work. The cord was still there all the time like a tightrope. She just had to learn how to keep her balance and edge her way inside. She is Raquel Welch in *Fantastic Voyage* finding her way inside to fix Mummy. She has lost a little bit of herself but it doesn't matter because Mummy is back.

Mercy wriggles under the bed and pulls out the green and white suitcase. No time to waste; quick before the spell wears off.

Mummy is all action now, throwing clothes in the suitcase. She starts singing, 'What a friend we have in Jesus.' Mercy is so proud. She has restarted Mummy's heart and they are going to leave and this time, never, ever come back.

Mummy is possessed like a whirlwind. When she's finished packing, she puts the suitcase in the wire tray at the bottom of the heavy navy-blue pram. Mummy puts Evie and Devon in the pram. Mercy is a big girl so she can walk next to Mummy. Mercy helps Mummy get the pram down the front steps, bump, bump, bump. They walk down to White Abbey Primary School. Mercy is skipping along next to Mummy, every inch of her body is singing. Today's the day, they're getting away. The Giant will get no bread tonight. He can grind his own bones.

Mummy waits outside the school gates for Janie and Ruby to come out at dinner-time. They run out in their smart uniforms going on and on about their lessons and their teachers and their little bottles of free school milk. Mercy is beyond jealous, because she's *still* not old enough to go to school.

Janie asks why they're not going home.

Mummy says, 'Don't cross-question me.'

Mercy adds, 'No! Don't cross-question Mummy.' Janie tries to kick her but Mercy skips over the big Clod-Hopper foot. They keep walking. Mercy thought they would be getting on a trolley bus or a train but they are just walking and walking. Bradford has a lot of hills and Mercy starts to get tired. Mummy sings songs to them to keep up their spirits. They love rounds.

Row row row your boat
Gently down the stream
Merrily, merrily, merrily, merrily
Life is but a dream

Mummy and Mercy sing the first line before Janie and Ruby finish the last, round and round they go. They all keep going, getting more and more tired but still row, row, rowing their boat. Mercy's feet are hurting by the time they get to Sister Thompson's house. Sister Thompson is nice. She hugs and kisses them all and pinches their cheeks and gives them Pear Drops. She says Mercy's cheeks are round like little apples and she would love to take a bite. Mercy would rather she didn't. Mercy can hear Mummy and Sister Thompson talking in the kitchen. Sister Thompson tells Mummy not to worry, because God sees all and her reward is in heaven. Mercy would much rather have a reward on earth.

With great fanfare, Sister Thompson opens up her front room. It's dusty and musty and there are plastic covers on the couches. She rearranges the furniture. They get a sofa cushion each to sleep on but it's all slidy because of the plastic. Mummy sleeps in the armchair with Baby Devon on her lap.

Later Brother Thompson comes home, he's not happy with, 'Miss Olive and all of her pickney-dem pack up ina mi house.'

Mercy can't get to sleep. She wants to tell Ruby and Janie about how this big adventure is all down to her. She was the Pied Piper that made Mummy leave. But they are grumbling that they are not comfortable and they can't sleep, so she decides that telling them now is a bad idea. Besides, they would not understand. They would think that she is making things up again. Why is she so different from the rest of them? They just accept the way things are but Mercy fights it all the time. Mercy knows that Daddy is a bad man, that her family is not *normal*. It is not supposed to be like this. When Daddy gets in a bad mood they all scatter, but Mercy always stays. Sometimes he won't hit Mummy in front of her, but sometimes it doesn't work and Mercy just gets hit as well.

The next day in the early-early morning, there is a big knock-knock-knocking on the door. It makes Mercy jump clean off the sofa, because she recognises the knock. Mr Thomspon opens the door and Mercy can hear Daddy's deep gravelly voice as the men talk their Big-People talk. Her chest freezes. Her lungs have to use a big stick to break the block of ice so they can breathe. It's hard work and her head hurts. Her asthma is playing up in the dusty, musty, room.

Ruby and Janie are glad to see Daddy. They run to him and hug him, each one wrapped around one of his Daddy-Long legs. Mercy hugs the corner of the room. They are sent into the kitchen and Daddy goes into the front room to talk to Mummy.

Mercy lets Ruby and Janie go first, and then she sneaks back to try and listen at the door. She can hear him pleading with Mummy. Surely Mummy isn't going to believe him. Mummy's voice is fluttery, his deep and sharp; a dove talking to a crow. They go backwards and forwards. Mummy is not going to be able to do this on her own. She needs help. Mercy tries to walk along the tightrope-cord and climb back into Mummy's head to tell him, 'Get thee behind me Satan'.

But the door is locked and she can't get in. No matter how she yanks at it, she's still on the outside. Why can't she do it again? It was hard yesterday, exhausting to make herself so small, but she did it then. She can't get into Mummy's head because *he* is already in there. He has a key. He has locked the door from the inside. He can walk in anytime he wants but Mercy has to climb and balance and struggle to get in. He is persuading her with his Sweet Talk. Doesn't Mummy know that all that sugar will just rot her teeth? Mercy is banging on the door in Mummy's head, shouting, *Don't listen to him, he's telling you lies. He's a Bad-man, he's going to do it again.*

They are Cowboys and Indians. But why is Daddy always the Cowboy and Mercy always the Indian? Cowboys have guns and she only has a bow and arrow. Everybody knows the Indians always lose.

She hears Mummy say, 'You know some-ting. Is Mercy whe tell me fi run weh.' She feels the bolt sliding across the door. She has lost the battle. Again. They are going back.

12

The Zoo

Mercy is sandwiched in the bed between her sisters. Evie on one side, Janie on the other. Ruby is on the far side of Janie. Mercy would prefer it if wet-a-bed-Janie was on the outside. But, after weeks of tense negotiations, they have agreed to take it in turns being on the inside, because whoever ends up on the outside never gets enough blanket and sometimes gets shoved out of the bed completely.

Mercy wakes up tired after dreams of fighting baby dragons who look a lot like her sisters. But it's all okay, because it's the August Bank Holiday and today is their first ever Family Outing. Apart from Church they never go anywhere all together and Daddy doesn't go to church with them because he is a Sinner-Man. It's the last week of the Six Weeks Holiday and they are going to Chester Zoo. Mercy *still* doesn't go to school yet but she pretends that she too is excited for six whole weeks off boring old Maths and English.

Hill View is a Madhouse, with everybody searching for clothes, dragging stuff out of the washing pile and arguing over what belongs to who. It is a miracle they all finally manage to get in the car at all. Mummy rushes back into the house because she has forgotten the sandwiches. And then again because she has left Daddy's drink. She packed the bright red Corona Cherryade Pop for them but forgot Daddy's flask of hot sweet tea, seasoned with a capful of Martell. Then Daddy goes back for his cigarettes. And then they can't get the fold-up, pushchair to fit in the boot with all the food and coats and what have you, and Daddy nearly loses his temper

'Ah whe di rahtid 'oman ah pack up di cyar wid all dis foolishness,' he mutters, cigarette bobbing at the side of his mouth. But disaster is averted and he gets the lid of the boot down in the end. The families on the Tee Vee are always happy when they go on trips, they sing songs and play games. Why can't Mercy's family be like that?

The girls sit in the back as usual with Mummy upfront and Devon on her lap and they set off at last. Daddy drives in his lazy, self-confident style, with one elbow on the open window and his other open palm turning the leather steering wheel. First he has to reverse out of the parking space. Always a dangerous time because he turns his head and looks over his left shoulder and, although he is supposed to be looking out the back window, Mercy can't shake the feeling that he is staring directly into her soul.

The Hillman Avenger is Daddy's pride and joy. Just the name conjures up John Steed and Emma Peel, fights and excitement. It is a superhero all on its own. The car is long, pale creamy green on the outside with large circular headlamps and a low-slung boot with silver chrome bumpers. Inside the plump ribbed leather seats are oxblood red. Mercy loves the Avengers on Tee Vee and whenever they are in the Hillman Avenger it feels like they are going on a Mission. She is Emma Peel and she will high-kick anyone who gets in her way. *Hiyah!*

The girls all wear little white ankle socks. Eight black patent leather shoes attached to four pairs of dangling vaseline-shined legs swing and kick one another. But *woe betide* if one of them gets carried away and kicks the back of Daddy's seat. A hand will shoot out and slap whichever child is nearest. Daddy's hands are all calloused and knobbly and his fingernails are yellow and long. If you get slapped on the side of the head by him, you know about it. Being slapped by Mummy is a treat by comparison.

Mummy and Daddy argue about the route, the pickney-dem, the food and the map which Mummy is trying to read while Devon grabs at the paper because it is blocking his view. Mummy kisses her teeth after Daddy and he laughs. The sun is shining; Daddy is in a good mood. Through the mirror, Mercy can see the gold tooth in the side of his mouth wink in the sunlight.

The girls squeal every time they see a real live cow or a sheep in a rolling green field. They had never been to the countryside before. They play Punch-a-Car, Mercy gets a lot of punches in because she is always the first to spot the VW Beetles. Then Janie spoils it by crying because she is a *bloomin' idiot* and she doesn't see the cars fast enough to get to punch anyone and her arm hurts where Mercy keeps punching her.

Chester Zoo has flamingos and Mercy is beside herself with excitement to see one. Daddy complains about how much it costs for a family ticket and Mummy feeds them all Pear Drops and coconut cake as they slowly move up the long, winding, queue.

After the turnstiles and the money and the arguing and Daddy kissing his teeth about how *dem-too-teef*, they are finally inside. A wide Boulevard appears with generous grass verges on either side leading to cages with monkeys and baboons who shriek and scream and throw poo at you if you get too close. The girls beg for sticks of Rock but Mummy says she doesn't have money for *hexpensive foolishness* and gives them more home-made coconut drops. Mercy feels swindled.

Way off in the distance is the lake with the flamingos. Mercy holds Evie's hand, who in turn holds Mummy's hand and Janie and Ruby hold on to Mummy from the other side. Daddy proudly pushes the pushchair-cum-chariot containing the One Bwoy Pickney.

Mercy pleads for them to go straight to see the flamingos first and for once her wish is granted. Fla-min-go, a beautiful word for a gorgeous bird. They are even taller than Mercy and more amazing in real life than she had ever imagined. Ballerinas, all their heads turning together like they've been practising for years. Mercy had secretly thought that they were actually white but had been painted pink by the Zoo people.

But they really are the brightest Barbie pink in the world. She fishes Dolly out of her pocket to show her the spectacle and receives a slap from Mummy for having brought that 'chupid piece a plastic' to the Zoo. But it's worth it to see the feathers, long bony legs, black hooked beaks and the frankly ridiculous necks which seem to sway and curve in every direction all at once.

And then Mummy screams.

'Lord God! Ah weh di baby deh?'

The pram is empty. Daddy looks around both helpless and guilty. Mummy starts berating him about how he is walking around, puffed-up like a peacock, pushing an empty pram. He forgot to strap Devon in. Everybody knows you've got to strap him in. They spend the next frantic few minutes trying to find the One Bwoy Pickney, with Mummy getting more and more frightened and Daddy looking around desperately.

Trust the One Son to ruin the day, thinks Mercy. If they never find him, they can go home with just the four of them. Then Mercy can sit up-front on Mummy's lap. She doesn't even feel bad about hoping they don't find him because he is a boy and boys are *chupid*. Anyway, if they don't find him Mummy will never forgive Daddy and then she will leave him for good. That would be amazing, killing two boy-birds with one pram-shaped stone.

Eventually, though, they see him. He is with a curly blond white lady, sitting on her knee, happily eating an ice cream. She feels his hair while pretending to pat it. Mummy falls on her like a lioness and yanks her baby off the imposter's lap.

'Dis a fmi pickney,' she glares at the woman. Ruby and Janie glare too. Devon giggles, he doesn't know what all the fuss is about. Daddy doesn't speak but nods his thanks to the white lady. And that's it. The day is ruined.

They troop back to the car in disgrace. Mercy chats with Ruby, Janie and Evie about the animals they have seen, the flamingos and the cheeky monkeys, and Daddy can't even be

bothered to slap them. Mummy clutches her One Son on her
lap cooing to him all the way home about how Mummy loves
him and (under her breath) that Daddy is a 'bloomin' idiyat'.

And that is their last ever Family Outing.

13

The Barbeque

It's winter but it's warm because the fire is roaring. The black coals glow red, then white as the orange flames crackle and dance like demons above them. The five of them are down in the cellar. Ruby is nearly six, she's the eldest so she's in charge. When the flames start to die down she picks up the iron poker and stirs them back to life. The poker is long with a round tip and made of iron. It's like a sword from those swashbuckling films. Every so often the fire coughs and spits out a little bit of red hot coal out onto the beige, tiled grate. They are supposed to use the fire-guard but the fire is so much prettier without it.

Ruby tells them all to sit quietly and be good because she is in charge. But they're not doing as they're told. They are *gillatening*, making a whole heap a noise, running up and down the stairs. Ruby is getting angry. Mercy doesn't take any notice of Ruby. She would prefer to be on her step but it's cold in the hallway so she's in the corner having her usual long chat with Dolly. She does both voices, Dolly's and hers. Dolly agrees with her on everything.

Devon is in the huge pram at the side of the fire, with its big wheels at the back, small ones at the front with shiny spokes and hubcaps and white-walled tyres. Janie is playing with him, dangling a rattle just out of his reach and he gurgles and stretches his little fingers every time she brings it close.

They won't keep quiet and they won't keep still and Ruby is getting *vex*. She stomps backwards and forwards in front of the fireplace, blowing hard. She's in charge and they are not doing as they are told. She's had enough.

She takes the poker and shoves it into the flames. She keeps twirling and poking until the end of the poker turns a bright glowing red. She tells them to line up, first Janie then Mercy then Evie. Mercy knows that you have to obey your elders, and Ruby is the eldest after all.

'Hold out your hand,' Ruby says. Janie's bottom lip is wobbling as she holds out her right hand. Ruby anoints her with the poker on the palm; there is a hiss and steam and the smell of burning. Janie screams and runs away. *Big Baby*, thinks Mercy. Ruby steps in front of Mercy the Brave. She holds out her right arm. Ruby taps her on the forearm just below the elbow; Arise Sir Mercy. The skin hisses and crackles like a brown sausage, popping open to reveal the pink underneath.

Mercy wails.

Ruby takes a step to her left and stands in front of two-year-old Evie.

'Hold out your hand.'

'No!'

Evie runs away down to the end of the cellar corridor and out the back door into the cold. She won't come back inside.

Ruby takes another step to the left. She lifts up Devon's vest, holds down his kicking legs and presses the poker onto his round brown belly. At first there is no sound from Devon. A long silence. Then slowly his mouth opens wide in the shape of a kidney bean, his tongue vibrates like a fork and he screams and screams and screams.

*

There are footsteps, the front door slams, *balaam*. Mummy and Daddy are back. They're coming down the cellar steps; Mummy tip, tip tip, followed by Daddy, clop, clop clop, They're carrying bags and muttering to each other.

Janie runs to the door and holds out her arm to Mummy.

'What! Wha'aapn?' Mummy drops her shopping.

'Ruby-burn-me-wid-de-poker.' Tears spill down Janie's face. The others lapse into and out of patois when they talk but Mercy never does. She always speaks properly, actually.

Probably from all that time in the hospital listening to the Doctors and Nurses, soaking up the Queen's English.

'Lord Jesus Christ,' Mummy drops to her knees.

'She burned me too,' says Mercy, holding out her arm. Mercy doesn't cry but there is now a pink area, the size and shape of a small leaf, where the brown skin is missing and the flesh underneath is bubbling pink and yellow.

'Ruby why? Why Ruby why?' Mummy is screaming. 'Why you burn yuh sister-dem?'

Ruby hangs her head and says nothing.

Mercy knows why. They were bad, they were fresh and rude and feisty. Bad children have to be beaten. Spare the (hot) rod and spoil the child.

'A wheh Evie deh?' Daddy is looking around for his favourite bad-gyal.

He finds her outside in the backyard crying and carries her back into the house. He asks if she is hurt and she shakes her head. She has some sense. She ran away, she was not burned.

He comes into the cellar room with Evie high on his shoulders. He looks at Mercy and Janie and laughs. 'Weh mek unuh stand there like blasted idiot and mek Ruby burn unuh?'

Mummy is over by the pram examining Devon. There is a huge weeping blister on his belly.

She's crying, between sobs saying, 'Why, why, you burn me One Bwoy Pickney?'

Ruby says nothing.

14

Mercy has been waiting to go to school since forever. A sponge dried out in a desert she is hungry for knowledge. School is the rain she needs to grow. For two whole years she has been watching forlornly as Ruby, then Janie, trot off every day in their school uniforms looking all smart and neat with their hair plaited, their T-bar shoes and little ankle socks. She was sure she would die of longing before it was her turn. She was worried about leaving Mummy, that the cord might finally snap. But the pull of school was too strong.

Joy is the same age as Mercy but two months older, so this makes her a wise and respected elder. They talk about what they will learn when they go to school. Well Mercy does most of the talking. Mercy cannot understand why Joy is not as eager as her to go to school. Joy's house is a happy house so she does not need to escape so much.

Joy likes Dolly too and helps design fabulous clothes which they sew sitting together on Miss Mary's settee. Once, on *Blue Peter*, Mercy learned how to make a three piece suite for Dolly. She and Joy collected egg boxes and sticky-back plastic (Mercy wonders why they don't just say 'sellotape'), and spent hours making perfect miniature furniture and then arranging Dolly artfully upon it.

Mercy has so many questions, but there is only so much she can ask Mummy. There's no point in asking Daddy anything unless it's about horse racing or dominoes, and even then he will just say, 'unuh mek me ears eat grass' if he's in a good mood, and slap them if he's not.

There is so much Mercy wants to know. Why is air invisible? Why can you feel it but not see it? Why do you never see the sun and the moon at the same time? Why does water fall down not up? Why did Mummy stop having babies after her tubes were tied, and are they the same as the tubes on the washing machine? Why won't Mummy leave Daddy for good instead of going back, *every bloomin' time*. Although she knows better than to ask that last question out loud.

Eventually after some half-hearted answers, Mummy says, 'Suppose your nose was a door post, what would you do about that?'

But my nose isn't a door post, thinks Mercy. She wishes Mummy would make more sense. She's always complaining that some people 'noh have a drop a sense,' but sometimes Mercy thinks Mummy has very few drops. Now, after years of hanging around at home or at the childminder it's finally time for Mercy to go to White Abbey Primary.

She's going to be in the Infants. She does not like the word 'infant', because she's a big girl but Infants school is still school and that's better than no school at all.

When the day finally comes, Mercy bounds out of bed like it's Christmas morning. Actually, this is better than Christmas morning. On Christmas Day they eat lots of food, but they have to share one orange between five of them and it's not easy to cut an orange into five equal pieces. (If the One-Bwoy-Pickney wasn't around it would be so much easier.) By the end of the day there is always an argument and Daddy gets mad about something and plates get smashed and Mummy ends up crying and begging him to settle himself down, but he never does.

But today she gets to learn things, and unlike Christmas presents, there is no limit on what she can learn. She is a bit worried about leaving Mummy behind because everyone knows she is Mummy's Little Shadow but Mummy can't be in two places at once. If Mummy doesn't go to work, the sick-people-dem will starve.

Today, Mummy creams her face with an extra layer of Vaseline. She sits on the floor and Mummy clamps her between her knees and twists her hair in six big plaits. It hurts when Mummy drags the comb through it but today Mercy is too excited to complain. The plait at the top of her head is tied with a little red ribbon. She wears a white blouse, a dark grey Pinafore, a navy blue cardigan, white ankle socks and Startrite shoes. They are all Janie's cast-offs (and before that Ruby's) but Mercy doesn't care.

She's a film star going to a premiere, Rita Heyworth walking the Hollywood red carpet, strutting her way to make her debut with old hands Ruby and Janie. Mummy gives her a letter to take with her. She reads it out to Mercy first. It says: 'To whom it may concern. This is Mercy Hanson, she is five years old, please accept her in Reception. Yours sincerely, Ornette Hanson.'

Mercy hangs on to the letter for dear life. If she loses it, they might send her back home and she would die of despair. They go down Toller Lane, with Mercy in the middle, seeing as how it's her first day. When they get to school Mercy isn't sure where to go but Ruby and Janie take her to the Secretary's Office and they hand over the note.

'Where's your mum?' asks the scary white lady with her grey hair tied back in a bun and half-moon glasses balanced on her nose.

'She's gone to work, Miss,' says Ruby.

She shakes her head and says, 'honestly, you people.' She writes something in a big book and sends them to the Hall.

Mercy has heard all about the hall from Ruby and Janie but now she gets to see the hallowed space for herself. It has shiny wooden floorboards that look like they've been polished every day since the beginning of time. The high ceilings are held up by huge pieces of curved wood that must have come from massive, curved trees. There are classrooms all around the hall, each with a door leading onto it. The lower half of the walls is painted wood but the upper half is all panes of glass so anyone in the hall can see into all the classrooms. It smells of polish, bleach and learning.

Ruby and Janie take her up to the front of the hall and tell the teacher that she's new and she is told to sit in the front row. Mercy sits cross legged next to a brown girl who says her name is Shameem and asks if Mercy will be her friend, Mercy smiles and nods. Some of the Mummies are still in the hall. They obviously don't know that five is more than old enough to go to school by yourself. One Mummy is crying. She does not want to let go of her daughter. But the teachers shoo her out and tut to each other saying, 'there's always one.'

A lady walks onto the stage and says she's the Headmistress. She welcomes them to White Abbey Church of England Primary School and tells them that when their name is called they must go with the teacher. Mercy is relieved that Black Children are allowed into the White Abbey.

A blonde woman with big glasses and lots of hair comes to the front and says, 'I am Mrs Kaplinsky, Reception Teacher.' She sounds a bit funny, like she is not really from Bradford. When Mercy's name is read out she stands up and joins a crocodile line and they walk into a classroom.

There are thirty little wooden desks in the classroom. Each one has a built-in chair, a lift up lid and a little ink well. Mrs Kaplinsky says, 'You vill sit at ze same desk every day. You vill all hank your coats on a coat peg in ze hall.'

When they go back into the classroom, Gina, the little girl whose silly Mummy was crying, starts to cry too and says she wants to go home. Miss Kaplinsky is not having any of her foolishness and tells her to be quiet. But Gina has no intention of being quiet. She wants her mummy. Mrs Kaplinsky walks over to her desk, grabs her by her ear and drags her to the front of the room. She tells her to hold out her hand. She takes a ruler out of her desk drawer and slaps the girl on the hand with it. It's not a hard slap, not really, nothing like Daddy's slaps but the girl's hand goes pink. She looks shocked and suddenly stops crying. Mercy doesn't think Gina's Mummy or Daddy ever slap her at home.

Mrs Kaplinsky looks around the classroom. 'Any-vone else?' They all sit neatly with their shoulders back and their arms crossed doing exactly as they are told. Mercy is sure that Mrs Kaplinsky can hit a lot harder than that.

She holds up a big blue book and says it's called a 'register'. It has everybody's name in it. 'Ven I call out your name you zay "here Miss Kaplinsky."' After Mercy Hanson Mrs Kaplinsky calls, '*Jameem* Hussain.' Shameem looks uncertain.

Mercy puts her hand up like Ruby and Janie told her to.

Mrs Kaplinsky says, 'vaat is it?'

'It's *Shameem* not Jameem.'

'Zat is vot I said.'

Mercy asks, 'Why do you talk funny, Miss?'

Mrs Kaplinsky's eyebrows shoot up to the top of her head and she splutters.

'Vot did you say?'

Gina chimes in, 'you do talk funny, Miss.' Shameem looks at her shoes.

Mercy wonders if Gina hasn't been caned enough for one day, but she is glad for the back-up.

Mrs Kaplinsky's mouth screws up into a tight little 'o'. Then she stops and takes a deep breath.

'I,' she says proudly, 'am from Poland. I came to England after ze Var. Now, zere vill be no more qvestions about my accent.'

Mercy is worried that she won't understand Mrs Kaplinsky and then she might get hit with the ruler so she listens very, very carefully.

Mrs Kaplinsky says her job is to teach them reading and writing (*viting*) and arithmetic (*arissmetik*), and if they do a good job, in the afternoons they can draw and paint and she will read them a story. They go through all the letters of the alphabet as Mrs Kaplinsky points them out on the board. They do capital letters and lowercase. Mercy is happy because she already knows the difference between capital and lower-case. Despite Mrs Kaplinsky, school is going to be fun.

They are each given their very own exercise book to write their letters in. There is a page which already has the letters printed in pale blue and Mercy has to trace over the lines. Mercy loves the curling tails of the g's and y's and is glad there is a 'y' in her name.

She smudges the words a little bit because she's writing with her left hand. Mrs Kaplinsky comes up behind her.

'Vat are you doink?'

'I'm writing,' says Mercy, who is confused because she is doing exactly what she was told to do.

'Hold out your hand,' says Mrs Kaplinsky. Mercy holds out her left hand and Kaplinsky slaps it hard with the ruler. It's a much harder slap than Gina got. Her eyes fill with tears but Mercy doesn't make a sound. She just looks up at Mrs Kaplinsky, waiting for the explanation. She knows that the real reason is her questioning of the accent. But she also knows that Mrs Kaplinsky won't say that. She has to come up with another reason to hit Mercy. Big-People don't like being shown up, especially by children. Mercy should know that by now.

'Ziz is wrong. You vill not write viz your left hand. Not in my clazzroom.' Mercy is devastated. She has been practising letters at home with Ruby and Janie and she can do them really well, but only with her left hand. If she has to start again with her right hand she will be rubbish. She will be behind everyone else instead of way out in front.

When Mrs Kaplinsky is not looking, Mercy switches the pencil to her left hand and quickly copies out the letters. Then she puts it back in her right hand, smiles to herself (and Gina), and pretends to go over them all again.

When Mercy gets home she can't wait to tell Mummy all about school, sitting in the hall, the strange food for school dinners, the noisy playground, the drawing she did and tricking Miss Kaplinsky, the ruler, and, and, and...

But Mummy isn't listening. She just nods and says, 'mmm good,' to everything Mercy says as she makes dinner. Mercy's heart breaks but she uses some of the thinning cord to tie it back together. Why is Mummy always too busy to listen to her? And why, when she does listen, does it feel like she doesn't really hear?

15

Holy Ground

Last year Mercy went to The Ear Nose and Throat Hospital, Mummy calls it The Hee-en-tee. It was more of a little clinic than an actual hospital. Mercy was glad because what with all the stabbing and the pinching and the stitching, she really doesn't like hospitals. The Doctor-Lady told Mummy that she would probably grow out of her asthma (*hasma*). Which was good news as Mercy was well and truly fed up having to wheeze and choke for breath, like when she had New Monya and she thought she was going to die. She lived, but only by paying a very heavy price, closing off part of herself. She is the only one with Asthma and the others mimic her wheezing sometimes.

On the way home they passed a particularly nice looking stone building on Carlisle Road. Perfectly symmetrical with two huge splayed bay windows on either side of an arched door. Mercy knew it wasn't a church because it didn't have a big pointy steeple but it was still pretty special. It had recently been sand-blasted and the honey-yellow of the Yorkshire stone glowed in the sunshine.

'What is that building, Mummy?' asked Mercy, stopping and pointing at it.

'Mmm? Oh Carlisle Road Library.'

'What's a library, Mummy?

'A place wheh dem keep books.'

'What do you mean, 'keep books'?' Mercy was intrigued to know that there were more books in the world than just the Bible and that they were all actually kept somewhere.

'Yuh can borrow books to read dem.'

'Borrow? You can...*borrow* books?' A current of excitement so strong ran through Mercy that she was sure Mummy could feel it through her fingers.

'Do you have to pay to borrow them?' Mercy's mind was already whirling. This was momentous news. You could read the books, find out all the knowledge and store it in your head. Once it was in your head, nobody could take it back out again. The only question was where a four-year-old was going to find the money.

'How much does it cost to borrow a book, Mummy?'

'It noh cost nothin', but if you take them back late you hafi pay a fine.'

'What's a fine?'

'If you do something bad they charge you a little extra money.'

Mercy stopped, staring at the ancient solid oak doors that led into the library. They were propped open and inside was another set of doors with glass in the top half but she wasn't tall enough to see through them. Mummy walked on. After a few steps she noticed that Mercy was no longer with her and turned back.

'Can we go inside and borrow some books, Mummy? I'll remind you when it's time to take them back and then we won't have to pay a fine.'

'Mercy come on! Mi noh have time fi yuh foolishness. You leff Govament book-dem ina Govament library and stop form-fool.'

Mercy took one last lovelorn glance at the glass doors, waving goodbye to the many books behind them and the acres of knowledge which they contained.

*

Mercy loves school almost more than Dolly (who is definitely not allowed to go). From that very first day she stopped being Mummy's shadow and swivelled her gaze towards knowledge. Who knew that Mercy could be happy to leave Mummy every morning and go to school! The cord was still there, still linking her to Mummy but slack now, not frightening and tight like it used to be. She was no longer suspended by a rope which might be cut at any moment. Most days when she got home Mummy was there; tired and not listening but she was there. Perhaps Gina's mum wasn't so silly after all. It would be nice to have a Mummy who missed you when you went to school. Mercy knows that Mummy loves her but it's not enough. It's like she's getting a teaspoon of it when she really needs a bucket. She is slowly starving. Books help to feed her up. It's not the same as cuddles from Mummy, but Mercy has to make do.

Today Mrs Kaplinski is taking them on a trip to the Library and tells them if they are very good they will be allowed to bring one book each back to school with them. Mercy vibrates with excitement. Finally she is going to get to walk through the hallowed doors. Into an actual library, to see the precious books.

She worries desperately that somebody will do something wrong and Mrs Kaplinsky will punish them all by cancelling the trip, as there's nothing she likes more than finding-fault and punishing the wrongdoer. But for once everybody behaves and after morning break they queue up two by two like the animals from Noah's ark. Mercy isn't sure whose hand she wants to hold but feels Gina's fingers slip between hers, solving the dilemma before it has really presented itself.

Although it is barely a ten minute walk from school to the library it feels like another country. Before they are allowed into the library Mrs Kaplinsky hisses at them to be on their best behaviour. Either side of the spacious lobby are two rooms; on the right is the Adults library, on the left Children's. They nod obediently as the Librarian opens the glass door and ushers them in. The aroma of old paper and ink is as delicious to Mercy as Mummy's Sunday dinners.

She forgets to keep walking, just stands there staring at the books. From floor to ceiling, every shelf is crammed with them, all shapes and sizes holding the promise of eternal knowledge. Her bottom lip slowly drops open, her eyes grow wide and she can feel the universe expanding around her.

'Keep moving slow coach.' Shameem bumps into her from behind and she is jolted out of her reverie and into the cavernous room itself. They have been learning scripture verses for church and Exodus One verse three floats into her mind:

> 'Put off thy shoes from off thy feet,
> for the place whereon thou standest is holy ground'.

After a lifetime of waiting, Mercy Hanson is inside a library. They sit on the carpet in a semi-circle whilst a lady who is called a Librarian (although Mercy thinks of her as the Mother-of-Books) explains what a library is and how it works. If their parents sign a form they can become junior members of the library and come and take books out, read them at home and bring them back. Mercy's face falls. She already knows Mummy is never going to sign to let her bring books home from *'Govament library'* because Ruby brought a library book home once and Devon scribbled in it. Mummy had to pay for a new book. She complained for weeks about that.

Apart from the Bible, there are no books at home, so Mercy reads the back of the Weetabix box; it contains niacin, iron and riboflavin. Ooh *ribo-flavin* what a word! She reads the washing powder box. She even reads the little sticky label that comes on the Saltfish packet so she knows that it's not just any old fish, it's salted North Atlantic Cod.

They are allowed to read one book in the Library. Mercy struggles with the bounty before her, eventually choosing *The Ladybird Book of Greek Myths*. She renames herself Mercy the Mythmaker. She doesn't just read about Odysseus and his adventures, she becomes him. She is standing on the prow of the ship, with a sword and sandals with straps and big strong muscles. She can feel the wind of the Aegean ruffling her hair as she builds the Trojan Horse to rescue Helen of Troy (Dolly). Ajax is strong but stupid, like Daddy, but Odysseus can always outwit him. Never has she wanted to stay inside a building more. The half brick in her stomach disappears, her house disappears, Mummy, Daddy, all of them gone in a puff of pages. Mrs Kaplinksky has to call her three times to get her out of the book and she waves her imaginary sword at Gina all the way back.

Back at school, all Mercy can think of is story time and which of their borrowed books Mrs Kaplinsky will read to them. They sit in a circle on the floor at her feet, her accent, for once, perfect for the subject matter, as she transports them to the forest of Hansel and Gretel.

Mrs Kaplinski always sits with her right leg crossed over her left and when she gets to interesting bits of the story her right white stiletto bobs up and down. After Hansel and Gretel she agrees to Mercy's desperate, arm out of the socket, request to read Odysseus, but she reads it way too fast. There isn't enough time for Mercy to strap on her sandals and gird her loins. Mercy knows what loins are, but she's not too sure about the girding.

'Can you read it slower please, Mrs Kaplinsky.' Leaning forward eagerly, Mercy puts her hand up but she speaks before being given permission. She feels her head jerk backwards as Mrs Kaplinsky's right foot shoots forward, kicking her slap-bang in the middle of her forehead. Her bottom jaw drops open, not so much in pain but in shock.

'You kicked me!'

'I did not!' says Mrs Kaplinsky, looking slightly shocked herself.

Mercy is used to people twisting the facts and denying reality, usually her sisters claiming that they haven't eaten the last custard cream, but this is the first time someone has told her to her face that something she has just experienced has not actually happened. Mrs Kaplinsky often hits them with the ruler or drags them to the front by their ears, but even Daddy never ever kicks them. Kicking children in the head is definitely not allowed. Mercy jumps up, runs out of the classroom into the hall, out of the hall into the playground, and out of the playground onto White Abbey Road. She does not stop running until she gets home.

Mummy is in the middle of cooking before going back to the hospital for her second shift. Mercy blurts it all out in between tears, pointing to the still-swelling bump on her forehead. She is thankful for the physical evidence because otherwise she might start believing Mr Kaplinsky that it never happened.

'In Jesus Holy Name!' says Mummy as she listens in horror. She turns off the stove, grabs her coat in one hand, Mercy in the other, and they march back to school, even quicker than that time she stomped down to the butchers on Preston Street because he'd sold the children a Sick-Chicken instead of a nice, fat one.

'Not today, Satan!' she mutters as she walks with her quick little steps. The Reception Lady tries to ask Mummy where she is going but Mummy ignores her and marches onwards, her heels making the clip-clip noise on the polished wooden floors.

'Which one ah fi yuh classroom?'

Mercy points to the blue door with the little row of cloak hooks outside. Mummy barges in with Mercy trailing behind her. Mrs Kaplinsky's eyebrows shoot up to her hairline, and her mouth makes a little 'o' before reverting to its usual, firm, lipless line.

'How dares you?' thunders Mummy.

'Vat are you tokking about?'

'How dares yuh kick fi mi pickney?' Mummy is too angry to keep up the Speaky Spokey.

'I did not...'

'Mercy does not lie.' Not *strictly* true, thinks Mercy but now is not the time for that admission.

'Look pon di bruise pon her forrid where you did kick her!' Mummy pokes the bruise for emphasis.

'Ow!' says Mercy.

'Shet yuh mout!' Mummy glares at her.

'I did not...' stammers Mrs Kaplinsky. The children lean forward, eyes wide, mouths agog, aware that they are watching something even better than Story Time.

'Is me,' says Mummy, slapping the palm of her hand on her chest, 'give birth to dis yah pickney gyal, and if anybody gwine beat her, is me. You have no right. No right, fi lift up your foot seh you gwine kick fimi pickney.'

'I, er, I,' Mrs Kaplinsky tries to interject but Mummy is in full, magnificent flow.

'Mek me tell yuh something,' she points her index finger right in Mrs Kaplinsky's face. 'If you eveh, evah, tek up yuhself, put you han' or yuh blasted foot,' Mummy stamps for emphasis, 'pon fimi pickney again. As God is my witness,' Mummy raises her right hand to indicate that even now, God is watching, 'Dem will hafi put me ah prison fi whe mi gwine duh to yuh.'

As Mummy roars, Mrs Kaplinski's mouth falls open and stays open. It is like the Big Fight. But this time Mummy is Cassius The Clay and Mrs Kaplinsky is Sonny The Listing and Mummy is flooring her with a one-two, a left hook and a right jab and working up to the knockout punch.

Mercy imagines the referee standing over a prone Mrs Kaplinski saying, 'A-one-ah, a-two-ah, a-three-ah.' She is out for the count.

16

Daddy Dancing

Mercy can't wait to tell the others how Mummy traced off Mrs Kaplinsky. She gives them a blow by blow account and Mummy laughs when Mercy does her accent. Mercy walks around the cellar living room stamping, with her right hand in the air saying, 'as God is my Witness!' until Mummy threatens to beat her for taking the Lord's name in vain.

The next Saturday evening, they are packed off to bed and told sternly to stay there, with a box on the ear just to be on the safe side. Licks-in-case is absolutely not fair. Mercy hates it when they get hit before they have actually done anything wrong. If you have already been beaten you might as well misbehave but she can't think of what to do. She is almost too busy being resentful to hear it, but the music intrudes on her mood anyway. Joy and her two sisters come over with Miss Mary who is helping Mummy set everything up.

Blue Beat wafts up the stairs along with the faint clink of bottles and hearty Jamaican greetings. A Big-People's Party is going on in the cellar to which they are definitely not invited. The faraway buff-buff of music coming through the walls and the floors and bewitches them.

Ruby gets out of bed first, tiptoeing to the door like a cartoon baddie. The floorboards creak beneath the threadbare blue and red imitation Persian rug. Ruby is in charge as usual, but she stops with her ear to the door and just listens, unwilling to go further.

Janie gets up next and tiptoes behind Ruby stepping almost exactly in her footsteps. She concentrates so carefully that she bumps into Ruby who elbows her. Mercy gets out of bed and stands with her hand on her hips watching them. They can't decide who is going to be the first to sneak downstairs. Going it alone almost certainly means getting beaten if they get caught, even though they already got licks-in-case.

There is lots of:

'You first.'

'No *you* first, I went first last time.'

Eventually Devon can take the suspense no more. He walks tall, pushes past and steps out with his four sisters behind him. He thinks he is their Fearless Leader; they think he is a Useful Idiot. Mercy raises her eyebrows at Joy to ask if she wants to come too, but Joy shakes her head. She and her sisters stay in the bed, they're not getting themselves into trouble in someone else's house.

Halfway down the stairs, Mercy yanks Devon back by the cape of his Batman pyjamas and takes his place in the front. They descended in a line; Five Go Exploring. The door at the top of the cellar stairs is half open so they don't need to worry about its noisy hinges. Besides, tonight the music is loud enough to drown out a herd of elephants and they are slightly quieter than elephants.

As they descend the music gets louder. Excited though they are, Mercy feels like she is descending into the pit of hell. Is this what Fire and Brimstone sounds like? Mummy is always reading Bible passages out to them about Hell and Damnation and where the wicked go to perish. The sun turns to darkness and the moon turns to blood. Stories from the Book of Revelation give Mercy nightmares but Mummy seems to like them.

The strong sweet smell of Rum Punch wafts up the cellar stairs. The five of them are almost drunk on it before they get down to the bottom of the stairs. The door to the cellar living room is open and the Big-People inside are swaying to the music. The light bulb in the cellar living room has been swapped for a red one and gives a rosy glow to everyone in the room. There are around twenty-five people, most holding a glass of Punch strong enough to fell a sturdy cart-horse.

Rum is medicine for everything. Sore throat? Mummy rubs Bay Rum on your chest mixed with Vicks VapoRub. Headache? Bay Rum dabbed on your forehead. Belly ache? Ganja soaked Bay Rum rubbed on the belly. Belly Come Down? Sip Rum and water. Mummy doesn't drink except for medicinal purposes. Daddy snorts at Mummy's medicinal rum and says that she is a secret *Bumper*. At Christmas he makes a Proper Rum Punch with sorrel and nutmeg and a host of other secret ingredients. He also makes Guiness Punch which is actually Mercy's favourite because it has condensed milk and it's creamy. When Mummy and Daddy aren't looking they drink whole shot-glasses of the Guiness Punch and pretend to *turn bumper*, staggering around holding their heads. Mercy holds her glass with her little finger raised trying to be all posh and sophisticated like Mummy.

The women have round curvy bodies; their bottom halves seemed to move independently of their tops. They sparkle at their ears and wrists. Well-oiled shiny hair is piled high in top-knots with the odd ringlet descending in front of the ears. The men either have on tight suits with trousers that stop above their ankles revealing bright socks and shiny pointy shoes or loose baggy ones like Daddy with oversized long double-breasted jackets. Everybody is dressed to Fowl Foot.

But when she looks closely, Mercy sees that the people in the room aren't so much dancing as shuffling in a circle. They are watching something, someone in the middle. What or who is so interesting? It's hard to see, so they have to squat down. Eventually between the high heels and the stockings and the fishtail dress, they see him.

Daddy is dancing. He wears his suit and his Trilby and an orange shirt with a brown striped tie. *My Boy Lollipop* is playing as he shimmies his shoulders from side to side and bends his knees. His six foot six frame slowly leans backwards further and further until his entire body is perfectly balanced horizontally on the tips of his toes. Even at that unlikely angle his shoulders still shimmy and he continues to defy gravity. His cigarette never moves from the corner of his mouth, its glowing red tip mesmerising Mercy like a snake. Finally gravity intervenes and Daddy puts his right hand back and touches the floor. The crowd erupts in cheering. The five of them have never seen Daddy dance before.

'G'wan Sonny!' Someone shouts approvingly and people clap. But Daddy isn't done yet. He removes his hand from the ground while still on his tiptoes and still bent backwards at the knees, body almost parallel to the ground. The back of his jacket sweeps the red concrete floor as he comes up. He never loses the beat and his shoulders never stop their shimming. Slowly he regains the vertical, a lop-sided grin on his face with the lit cigarette still in the corner of his mouth.

He dances forward towards Mummy and takes her hand. She reluctantly allows herself to be pulled into the centre of the room. She is wearing the mermaid fishtail dress so her steps are tiny and dainty. They look like the most amazingly mismatched pair. Fred Astaire has become a giant and Ginger Rogers has fallen through the looking glass and become tiny. But Mercy has never seen anything so beautiful.

Mercy sat on the floor beside Mummy when she was making the fishtail dress. The material is blue with rainbow colours fading in and out of it but it also shimmers like the sea. There is a zip at the back of the waist behind a big bow and off the shoulder sleeves. Mercy knows that Mummy could be a proper, proper film star in the fishtail dress. When Mummy wasn't looking Mercy cut off a bit of material from the frilly hem of the dress. She made a perfect replica fishtail dress for Dolly; well it didn't have a zip because she couldn't find a tiny zip but it slopes off Dolly's shoulders just like Mummy's and Mercy hopes Mummy won't notice the tiny bit of missing material from the back of the dress.

Mummy isn't a flamboyant dancer like Daddy, but she knows how to wiggle one knee in front of the other as her hips sashay from side to side and the glitter and the glint from the rainbow fishtail dress sparkle around the room. She is on the dance floor for barely a minute but she makes her mark. Everybody cheers for the host and hostess with the mostess. Other people start filling the floor, shaking a leg and cutting up a rug.

Miss Mary spots them, laughs and points. 'Coo Sonny pickney-dem ah watch dem Daddy dance.' Daddy spins around, furrows his brow and swings his laser gaze in their direction and they scatter.

Mercy gets to bed first. Janie, Ruby and Evie jump in together and they all wedge in under the covers, with Joy and her sisters there are seven of them in the bed. Mercy hopes that Daddy will remember that they got licks-in-case so there will be no need to beat them again in the morning.

17

Pant-O

Christmas is coming. They've been singing carols and there is a Nativity in the Hall. Ruby hopes to be the Virgin Mary but the black children only get to be the sheep. But, much more importantly, two weeks before Christmas is Mercy's sixth birthday. Will she get a present this year? She has been reminding Mummy every day, but she has to be careful not to overdo it.

Everyone at school is talking about the Pant-O. Mercy doesn't know what a Pant-O is. Could it be a different kind of trousers? But why would everybody be so excited to go and see a pair of pants? Bell bottoms from C & A, the ones with sequins around the hem, might be worth a trip though.

Ruby is given a note to take home for Mummy to sign so that the three of them can go to the Pant-O. But Ruby is a bloomin' idiot and loses the note. On Saturday morning Mercy finds it in the lining of Ruby's coat, it fell through a hole in the pocket. It takes her ages to get it out. It's all scrunched up and the ink has gone a bit smudged and blue. Mercy reminds Ruby to ask Mummy to sign it. Ruby doesn't seem very grateful that Mercy found the note and doesn't even say thanks. Bloomin' idiot.

Mummy is sitting on the yellow sofa when they get downstairs. She is singing to Devon who sits on her lap like he owns it. Daddy is smiling at him too. His gold tooth winks when he smiles, it's not scary at all. Mercy still doesn't like Devon. It was bad enough when Evie was born but now Devon has arrived Mummy hardly has any time for Mercy anymore. Just as well Mercy is going to school now. Last week she was chosen to read out loud in Assembly.

They stand in a little line with Ruby at the front, Janie in the middle, Mercy at the back, just like Three Kings of Orient, hopefully presenting gold, frankincense and myrrh to Mary and Joseph and the Baby Devon. Daddy takes the piece of paper, squints at it, kisses his teeth and passes it to Mummy. Whenever there is anything to read Daddy always gives it to Mummy.

She reads it and then screws up her face. 'Tee-ata!' she says, 'Tee-ata! Mi nah sen mi pickney-dem go ah noh bloomin' Tee-ata. Is the work ah the Debble.' She screws up the note and throws it in the bin. The hopeful look slides off Ruby's face, and Janie starts to cry. It wasn't gold, frankincense and myrrh after all. The Three Kings will have to go back to The Orient with their offerings rejected.

Mercy tries to shush Janie, but she is too far gone. She got over-excited about going to see the Pant-O. Mercy knows that this will not end well.

'Pickney, shet yuh mout,' Daddy says, and Janie tries but she can't stop. She is doing that nasty snot-crying and tears are streaming down her face like someone left the tap on. Mercy slowly backs away from Janie because she can tell from Daddy's face what's coming next. He's going to give Janie something to cry for and she doesn't want to get dragged in. Sometimes she is not sure Daddy can even tell the difference between the girls. When he doesn't know who did it, he beats them all, which really is not fair.

He grabs Janie so fast it's like magic; one minute she's standing up, the next she's over his knee being flattened like a pancake by his palm. It reminds Mercy of Tom and Jerry when the black lady, the one without a face, slaps Jerry with her broom. It doesn't make any sense to tell Janie that he's going to give her something to cry for, because by the end she's crying more than ever. Daddy doesn't have a drop of sense.

Later on in their bedroom, to try and cheer up Janie, Mercy pulls the crumpled note out of her pocket which she retrieved from the bin. (It's not *stealing* if you take it out of the bin.)

'We could copy Mummy's name,' she says, running her finger along the dotted line.

Janie's eyes grow wide.

'Nooo!' says Janie.

'We'll be in big-trouble if we copy her signature,' says Ruby. *Signature*, thinks Mercy, she'll remember that magic word.

'But the Pant-O is in school hours,' wheedles Mercy. 'If we don't tell them...'

It's up to Ruby to decide, but Mercy makes sure to whisper to her and Janie at every opportunity over the weekend that no one ever needs to know.

Mummy has a lovely curling signature, like waves on water. But it's in joined-up-writing and none of them know how to do that yet. But Mercy can draw and a signature is just a special kind of drawing, isn't it?

The hardest thing is finding enough paper to practise on. She finds an Air Mail letter in Mummy's handbag. Mercy knows that airmail letters are expensive so she can't use that. Eventually they decide to tear off the top of a box of Weetabix. After lots and lots of practice Mercy thinks she's got it. There is only one chance to write it on the note from school; if she gets it wrong, the plot will be foiled and it will be a disaster.

Mercy is very careful, copying Mummy's signature onto the dotted line with absolute perfection. She's the hero of the hour; a proper artist. No one will ever know.

On Monday morning the three of them set off for school, Ruby at one side, Janie at the other and Mercy in the middle holding both their hands. They don't often let her walk in the middle, much less hold her hand, so she's happy. Ruby is in charge of the note and they take it to the Secretary's Office.

They queue up with Ruby at the front, Janie in the middle and Mercy at the back. The School Secretary is very scary, with her glasses in the shape of half a circle and a chain attaching them to her face. There are two dimples either side of her nose where the glasses live. Her clothes are the wrong size and Mercy is sure the button at the front of her blouse is going to fly open one of these days. She likes to shout at children who don't bring their dinner-money on time.

'For the Pant-O,' says Ruby, holding out the piece of paper with a slightly shaky hand.

The Secretary takes the note and looks at the signature. The three of them hold their breath. The looking seems to take so long that Mercy thinks she might faint. Can she tell? What will she do? Are they in trouble? She squints slightly and peers over her glasses at Ruby. 'Did your mum sign this?' Janie takes a breath like she's going to confess. Ruby kicks her, because everybody knows that Janie is a blabber-mouth.

Ruby nods her best innocent nod. Janie and Mercy nod too, even more innocently. There is a long silence while the Secretary stares at them but they say nothing, and she says nothing. Eventually, she puts the note in a big envelope full of other notes and says, 'Go on then, off to class with you.' Mercy has to remember not to skip down the corridor, because that will make it too obvious.

They're going to the Pant-O!

Their teacher tells them that they can wear their own clothes instead of school uniform because it's a special trip but Mercy knows that if they wear their own clothes Mummy will know that something is up.

The Pant-O is on Friday afternoon, the last day of term. It's also Mercy's birthday and she is so excited that she doesn't know what to do with herself. This year she's not bothered that she hasn't got a present. The Pant-O will be her present. Mummy sings Happy Birthday to her over breakfast and ties her hair with a new blue ribbon, kisses her on both cheeks. Mercy pretends that the excitement is all about being six but really it's about her first ever trip to the Tee-ata.

After dinner-time a long, gleaming blue-and-white bus pulls up outside school. It's only got one story instead of two and it's called a 'coach', which rhymes with 'roach'. It takes them to town and pulls up outside an enormous wedding cake of a building, which Mrs Kaplinsky says is called the Alhambra Theatre. Ruby, Janie and Mercy hold hands and cling onto each other because the building is terrifying inside. There are blood red carpets everywhere and scrolls and whirls and curls painted in gold and heavy velvet curtains. It looks to Mercy like Hellfire and Damnation. Have they just walked into the Book of Revelation? Did the moon turn to blood and drip all over the Tee-ata? The squishy seats are so high that their feet do not touch the ground. It's not just children from White Abbey Primary, it looks like every child from every school in Bradford is in the building, all screaming and shouting.

It's the biggest building Mercy has ever seen. The ceiling is so high that their house could fit inside three times over. There are enormous brass lights dangling from the ceiling, which Mrs Kaplinsky says are chandeliers. Mercy worries that, what with all the shouting, they may fall and crush them to death and then they'll really be in trouble.

Then something goes wrong with the lights and everything slowly goes dark and Mercy wishes she had never copied Mummy's signature. No one has told them what is going to happen. Did the Tee-ata not pay their light bill, is that why the electricity has run out? They are going to need a whole heap of sixpences for the meter. Janie whimpers and Ruby kicks her and hisses, 'shet yuh mout.'

The blood-red velvet curtains at the front slowly open, they are drawn sideways and upwards, at the bottom huge gold tassels ripple in the low light. For a moment Mercy is convinced that Daddy is going to step out from behind the curtains with his belt at the ready. They are going to get caught.

But it's not Daddy, it's some kind of creature with huge yellow hair and a big bosom and wide skirts in bright colours, and enough lipstick to start a shop. The creature says, 'Hallo my little darlings'. It looks like a woman but sounds like a man. And it says, 'What a gay day,' and some of the teachers and some of the children laugh. It's only then that Mercy realises that she has been holding her breath, so she lets it out and laughs too.

The Pant-O is like the Tee-Vee come to life. It's like living inside an actual colour Tee-Vee with characters you can talk to. And when the lady-who-is-not-lady says, 'Oh no it it's not,' they get to scream, 'Oh yes it is,' and no one tells them off for shouting. And the Prince is actually a girl. When the Baddie with the sword creeps up on the Goodie they all shout, 'he's behind you!' but the Goodie turns around way too slowly. Mercy is sure they are doing it on purpose so that they have to keep screaming, 'Behind you!' at the very top of their lungs.

And there is a genie with a huge turban, waistcoat and baggy trousers and a magic carpet. The carpet actually flies around the stage with its tassels trailing behind it. How do they do that? It's real magic. Mercy wishes with all her heart that she was on it. Flying away from Mummy and Daddy and the shouting and the hitting and the never knowing when everything is going to kick off. She never knew there was so much fun to be had anywhere on earth. And she is laughing so much she has to cross her legs so that she doesn't wee herself, but Janie doesn't cross hers fast enough. Ruby and Janie are falling all over themselves pointing and screaming and for the next two hours it's not just the best Birthday, it's the very best day of Mercy's whole, entire, life.

When the curtain comes down at the end, some of the children start crying because they want the show to go on. Mercy doesn't cry but she knows how they feel. She takes one last long lingering look at the theatre. This space that was so terrifying two hours ago is now a warm red and gold womb that she never wants to leave. She tries to fold the memories neatly and pack them in the suitcase of her head so she can take them out and look at them again later.

They pile back onto the coach, with teachers counting them on two by two. It's a short ride back to school but it feels like they went to the Moon and back. They walk back home skipping and laughing and shouting, 'Behind You!' But when they turn into their street Ruby stops and pinches them both on the arm. It hurts.

Mercy starts to cry. 'Ow! Why did you do that?'

'Don't say anything about the Pant-O,' says Ruby, suddenly all serious. 'If you tell, we'll get beat'n.'

'I won't tell,' says Janie, rubbing her arm.

'You didn't have to pinch us,' says Mercy.

'Yes I did,' says Ruby, 'I'm the eldest.' What she means is that she is the one who will get blamed if something goes wrong. So she's punishing them in advance, licks-in-case. Mercy frowns; sometimes she thinks Ruby is worse than Daddy.

'Of course I'm not going to tell,' says Mercy. But she wishes she could tell Mummy what a wonderful time they had and that although it did look a bit like Hell at first, the theatre really isn't the work of the Devil, it's where the Angels go to play.

None of them tell. They get clean away with it; the perfect crime.

*

When Mummy takes in their dinner money at the beginning of the next term, the witch in the glasses on the chain says, 'I do hope your girls enjoyed the Panto, Mrs Hanson.' And she hands Mummy the permission slip, the one with Mercy's almost perfect copy of her signature, and she does that white-people smile, the one that doesn't reach the eyes.

And Mummy purses her lips, glares at Mercy and says, 'When we reach back a yard, I gwine strip off de black skin leff di white.'

18

Medusa

Mercy walks past the Library on Carlisle Road every day on her way to and from school. Every time she passes it she looks up at the honey coloured stone building with its symmetry and silence and thinks of the many books and the knowledge hiding inside. She wishes she lived in a library. She wishes she could go inside and borrow books, but that's not allowed and after the Panto palaver she doesn't think she will get away with copying Mummy's signature again.

Today she stands completely still and watches as the doors open and people go in empty handed and come out carrying precious Library books. Mercy's heart hurts for all the knowledge in the books that she will never have. She has read all the books in the little school library and she is getting bored. She has read all the fabulous words and needs new ones. She wants to cry but she can't just stand outside a library crying for books. She stands there so long just imagining how happy she and Dolly would be to sit in the children's library and read books, that she starts to shiver.

The Mother-of-Books comes outside. 'You alright lovie?' She wears a green and white checked mini-skirt and a white shirt and flat shoes. Her glossy brown hair is tied back in a bun and she has glasses-on-a-string like the School Secretary, but they are tortoiseshell and not so scary. She reminds Mercy of that skinny, blonde model on the TV, the one with the huge eyes.

Mercy nods her head.

'Are you cold?'

Mercy hadn't noticed that she was getting cold because she had left her body behind and her mind had wandered into the library where it was warm and smelled of old paper, dust, ink and polish. Mercy doesn't know what to say that won't get her in trouble, so she just stares at the Mother-of-Books and blinks her big eyes.

'Do you want to come inside?'

More than anything, but is it allowed? Mummy didn't sign the form for her to join the Library.

'Can I?' She asks so quietly that the Mother-of-Books has to lean closer to hear her.

'Course you can. The Library is free for all.'

What? Why did no one tell her she could just walk inside a library? Mercy feels so angry at Mummy and Daddy and the teachers at her school. Someone must have known but no one told her. Why do Big-People keep so many secrets from children, or tell them part of the truth but not all of it? And then when you ask questions they tell you not to 'cross-question' them. She's so angry she wants to kick someone.

'Are you sure?' Mercy doesn't want to get her hopes up if there is a catch. Has the Library lady forgotten some important information like, maybe Black children are not allowed in. In all the time Mercy has been standing outside the Library she has only seen white people go inside. Mercy has seen Civil Rights marches on the Tee-Vee, and in America Black children can't go to swimming pools and stuff and a little girl called Ruby Bridges wasn't allowed to go into a school and the army had to take her in, and Ruby Bridges had her hair in big plaits just like Mercy. Then there was the time Daddy came home all bruised and bloody because some white men got hold of him on his way home from work. They said he was taking their jobs. But Daddy said none of the white men would ever do his job. Mummy put Dettol on his bruises and he winced. Mercy thought he was going to cry. Is that why he's so angry all the time?

'You can read the books in the library free of charge but you'll need a library card to take one out.'

Mercy frowns at her, then thinks of Daddy always saying, 'stop knit up yuh brow.'

Mercy says nothing, her brain is working overtime to see if this is a trick.

'Suit yourself then,' the lady turns and walks up the steps into the library. Mercy gingerly follows her. It might be a trap but she has to take a chance. She feels like she is walking on stage at the Tee-ata and that audience is shouting 'behind you!' but she dare not turn around. The Library lady holds the heavy oak door with the bevelled glass open for Mercy and she gets to step inside and be swallowed up like Jonah and the Whale except she wants to stay inside the belly of the whale. In the hallway she looks at the left hand door to the Children's Library, the name is painted in curly gold lettering above the door. She wills her hand to push the polished brass handles to go inside. But it's still too good to be true. She looks up at the lady.

'You can stay as long as you like lovie.'

So Mercy takes a deep breath of library air, imagines Dolly is here with her for courage, and maybe Joy too because Joy likes reading as well, and pushes the big heavy door and steps inside. It's completely different from the day she came here with school. There is no one in the room, just Mercy and the books. The windows are high up so she can only see the sky. The clouds are smiling at her as they bob along. There are boxes of books on legs like a coffee table but with books inside it. There are padded child sized stools all around it they are bright orange with brown piping and very comfy to sit on. She takes a deep breath and pulls out one of the books, a big picture book about Greek Mythology. She waits with it on her lap for a moment, just in case. But nothing happens so she opens it, like the curtains opening at the Alhambra Tee-ata. She is sucked in like a genie into a lamp. She is Medusa the Gorgon and her hair is snakes. Anyone who looks at her will be turned to stone.

Could she get Daddy to look at her? She is Jason and the Argonauts going on adventures to find the Golden Fleece. *She* wouldn't be seduced by the Sirens, like Daddy seduces Mummy all the time. She would stand her ground. She doesn't look up for the longest time. She doesn't have to look behind her to worry about the others fighting or Daddy losing his temper or Mummy calling her to do jobs. She can just sit and read and it feels like a carnival for her mind. It's almost as much fun as the tee-ata but different, calmer and more immersive. With the tee-ata they had no choice about what they were seeing. But with books Mercy can see whatever she likes; she can paint the pictures herself to go with the words, and she loves painting with her mind.

Mercy is so lost in Ancient Greece that she almost jumps out of her skin when the Library Lady taps her on the shoulder.

'I did call you a few times, but you didn't hear me,' she says by way of apology for startling Mercy. The Library Lady's eyes look so big with her black eye make-up that Mercy wonders how they fit into her small head.

'Five-thirty lovie, closing time.' She sees Mercy's face droop, 'but you can come back tomorrow. We're open every day except Wednesday afternoons and Sundays.'

Mercy nods and closes the door to Medusa and Jason. She almost hears them beg her not to leave them as the pages of the book trap them inside. Then she tries her hardest to climb back into Bradford. She feels her hair, no snakes. She pulls on her gabardine coat (no longer a toga) and ever so slowly walks out of the library. The air smells different outside. The clouds are gone and it's getting dark. The sky is *indigo*; she learned that colour just last week, it's a fancy shade of purple, but with a personality all of its own. It reminds her of Adednego who was thrown into the fiery pit with his mates Shadrach and Meshach, but they did not burn.

She hurries home and gets there just in time for dinner, tiptoeing inside bracing herself for trouble. But nobody notices

that she is late and she tells no one (except Dolly) where she
has been. She keeps her head down and eats her dinner with
just the odd Medusa stare at Daddy, but he stubbornly refuses
to turn to stone.

19

Joy Ride

February is cold and wet and no matter how often she recites the memories of the Pant-O to Dolly, they begin to fade. She is left with 'Oh yes it is' to which Dolly silently replies 'Oh no it isn't', the-lady-who-is-not-a-lady, and the flying carpet. She often takes Dolly and they leave The Mercy Step and fly around Arabia. Sometimes she lets Mummy come with them but most of the time it's just her and Dolly.

Dolly and me. Tee hee hee.

Now that Mercy has Carlisle Road Library she hurries there every single day after school. Ruby and Janie laugh at her but she doesn't care. She can sit in peace and lots of quiet and never has to look up until she finishes a book or the mini-skirted, big-eyed lady tells her that it is closing time. Then she leaves as slowly as she can and dawdles her way back home. Mummy doesn't mind Mercy going to the library and no one else notices that she isn't there.

Ruby and Janie play with each other and Evie and Devon play with each other, well they fight mostly but every so often Evie will let Devon join in with one of her schemes, mainly so there is someone to blame if they get in trouble. Mercy is left on her own. If she didn't have such a vivid imagination, it wouldn't be much fun being the middle child; Mercy in the Middle. But then, she can always sit on her step with Dolly and go on adventures, so that's something.

When they all watch Star Trek, the others call her Spock because she is so serious and logical. But they'd be serious and logical too if they got hit for having the wrong expression on their faces. She has to work out what she is doing wrong so that she can correct it. She has to study Daddy like he's an exam so that she can work out what he is going to do next.

Sometimes she goes over to see Joy who is also very serious, slim with long limbs and able to run way faster than Mercy. When they race to the end of the back alley and no matter how fast Mercy runs, she can never outrun Joy. Joy's mummy, Miss Mary is a big woman who gives Mercy big hugs, squashing her face into an ample bosom. She smells of talcum powder and when she walks her skirt rides up revealing fat, strong, thighs. Mercy is almost mesmerised by the rolling movement of her hips as she walks. But Miss Mary is 'Big-People' and Mercy never speaks to her except to say thank you when she is given food.

Miss Mary keeps the Pardner Money and Mercy sometimes gets sent over to take the money when Mummy is busy. Miss Mary's house is filled with more furniture than Mercy thought humanly possible. There are doilies, antimacassars and plastic covers over everything, even the carpet. And there is a picture of a wimpy looking, blonde Jesus on the wall. Mercy thinks that even Dolly looks tougher than him. Did he *really* cast the Money Changers out of the Temple?

Miss Mary doesn't have a husband, but she has three daughters. Miss Mary and her family come to church but they are not regular like Mummy. Miss Mary wears lipstick and Cutex which Mummy says is sinful. Mercy doesn't think that's fair because Mummy is very beautiful and has a tiny waist, and even without lipstick she looks like a Film Star. When Mercy saw *Gone with the Wind*, Scarlett O Hara reminded her of Mummy. She had the same flashing eyes and perfect hair and wasp waist. Miss Mary looked more like the Mammy. Mercy waltzed around the house with Dolly for days afterwards saying, 'Frankly my dear I don't give a damn,' until Mummy slapped her for using bad words.

This evening it's raining hard outside. There is a fat, full, moon. They're in the cellar eating dinner. Mercy is eyeing

Devon and Evie's plates to check if they have been given more food than her. Daddy is telling stories about back-home, long and involved about horse dead and cow fat. They are hanging on his every word because Daddy's stories always have a funny ending. Mercy doesn't always understand the endings but Mummy and Daddy usually laugh uproariously, so Mercy joins in too. They all do. They are laughing, not at the story, but because when Daddy is happy they are happy, and for a little while at least Mercy can relax.

Then it happens. Thud. The whole house shakes with a noise which they can feel as well as hear. It comes from outside, in the back alley.

'Massa God!' says Mummy. 'Ah wha' dat?'

Daddy rushes out the back door, Mummy follows him and Mercy, grabbing a piece of chicken from Devon's plate while he is distracted by the melee, follows them.

They are standing in a circle in the back alley. Rain is coming down steadily. The droplets are briefly illuminated by the orange street lamps as they head towards the ground. The cobblestones are shiny and slick, varnished with rainwater. What are they all looking at? Mercy swallows the last piece of chicken and edges closer.

There in the alleyway just outside their backyard lies Joy. Her eyes are closed and the rain drips down her eyelashes. There is a bubble of blood at the corner of her mouth which is slowly getting bigger. Why is she blowing bubbles? A white man is kneeling over her. He says he is a doctor; he was on the bus and saw the car hit Joy. It was speeding up Whetley Hill and took the bend too fast. It hit Joy so hard she flew into the back alley, and landed outside their house; a hit and run.

As the rain comes down more blood bubbles out of Joy. In the orange light everything looks the same colour, Joy's skin, the blood and the cobblestones, it's all an orangey brown. Joy looks as serious as ever. Apart from the bubbles, there is not a mark on her. The rain on her flawless face looks like water on a peach. Mercy watches from behind the circle of adults, squatting down between their legs, wanting but not daring to reach out and touch her friend.

The next bus comes up Whetley Hill and Miss Mary gets off. She is coming home from work. Mummy runs to meet her, hugs her tight and whispers in her ear. Miss Mary yelps then covers her mouth. Mummy half drags, half carries Miss Mary to the alley. Miss Mary wails like a wolf howling at the moon.

Mercy has never heard a human being make a sound like that. Miss Mary drops to her knees and cradles Joy's head. The white doctor-man tries to tell her to leave Joy, that they have to keep her still, but she bats him away like a fly and holds and rocks Joy, all the while making a sound like the earth splitting from the middle outwards.

Mercy feels like it is too rude to stay and watch Big-People crying like that, but when she tries to get up she finds she can't move. So she stays crouched down in the back alley. It doesn't make any sense.

Miss Mary's skirt has ridden all the way up and her girdle is on show. She is still howling like she is emptying everything inside her onto the ground with her child as the ambulance finally arrives. She fights with the drivers to stop them taking her Joy. Deep down, without anyone telling her, Mercy knows that Joy is dead. But she shakes her head trying not to believe it, wishing she could go back to the Panto and the magic carpet and fly back to a time before Joy crossed the road. She understands why Miss Mary is fighting to keep her daughter. If Joy stays where she is, time might stop and then rewind a bit, Joy will wake up again and her serious face will pronounce on important matters. Daddy has to help lift Miss Mary and Mummy uses her skirt to dry the snot from Miss Mary's face and say, 'Hush Miss Mary, hush. She wid Jesus now.'

They help her into the ambulance. The driver and the other man look at each other and shake their heads as they place Joy onto the stretcher, her limbs loose and her clothes dripping wet.

Has Joy gone to heaven? Mercy looks up but she only sees clouds, if Joy is up there could she send a message? Mummy is sure there is a heaven and even surer that there is a hell but Mercy is not sure at all. The library books talk about Elysium and Hades which are a bit like heaven and hell, which one is right?

Miss Mary seems to deflate in the days afterwards. What was once bouncy firm flesh becomes dead weight as she drags herself along. She takes to her bed. It turns out that Joy did have a Daddy but he is married to someone else and Mummy and Daddy whisper about how he should 'fix-up and come and bury him *outside* pickney'. Mummy persuades Daddy to go and talk to him. It turns out that everyone knew the man was Joy's Daddy (even his wife) and Daddy manages to persuade him to do the right thing.

Mummy has to go over and help wash and dress Miss Mary for the funeral. She comes to the Baptist Church on Carlisle Road all docile and weak like a sick baby, with a flat look in her eyes. It takes three of them to hold her up. As her legs give way, Mercy sees a puddle of liquid form at her feet.

Now there is a hole in Mercy's world where Joy used to be. But it's no use telling Mummy. She will only tell Mercy not to push herself up in big-people's business. She wishes she could get Mummy to go inside *her* and see what it is like for Mercy to have her friend die just like that. But Mummy doesn't think like that. Mercy has to look after Mummy, not the other way around. She feels a special kind of lonely sitting on The Mercy Step with Dolly these days. Dolly doesn't understand about people dying because Dolly is a *chupid* piece of plastic.

20

The Jockey Club

A few weeks after Joy's funeral, it seems like everybody except Mercy has forgotten her. Life just goes on as before, just that much sadder for Mercy. She has dreams about orange rain and Joy trying to talk to her but just blowing blood bubbles. Ruby kicks her for thrashing about in her sleep. Mummy goes to work twice a day, Daddy shouts and rages if dinner is not ready on the table when he gets home, and instead of rushing him for sweets they scatter like mice in case he takes it out on them. Mercy wonders if the men got him on the way home from work again and if they did, is she glad?

Being six is better than being five because Mercy knows her way around Mrs Kaplinsky now. Being good at school is easy because there is so much to learn and no matter how crotchety Mrs Kaplinsky gets, she is never as bad as Daddy, and she's not allowed to hit Mercy anymore, yay!

Mercy has learned to write with her right hand. It didn't take long, and sometimes she does mirror writing with both hands at the same time. But she still likes to draw with her left. She is firm friends with Gina now whose mother has finally stopped crying when she brings her to school. Mercy has to look after Mummy and *she* doesn't cry very often, so she can't imagine what it's like for Gina having to look after a mother who cries every single day.

*

Saturday morning sees Daddy watching the horse racing. Nobody watches horse racing like Daddy. He doesn't just watch, he is there at the racetrack, peering over the fences, checking the fetlocks, inhaling the scent of the grass and soaking up the air of anticipation. When the gates open, it's like he's on an actual horse, especially if he's betting on one.

If Mummy's religion is Church, then Daddy's is horse racing. He likes to get himself nice and comfy before the start. He sits sprawled out on the sofa, with a few bottles of Mackeson Stout and a pack of Capstan Full Strength, all within arm's reach.

Daddy is the only person Mercy has ever seen smoke and drink at the same time. He scoots the cigarette to one corner of his mouth and pokes the bottle in the other corner. Mercy watches him, thinking that he might choke, but he never does. The cigarette just bobs up and down like his Adams apple as the stout glugs from its upturned brown bottle down his gullet. Daddy can finish a bottle practically in one go. His swallows are so big Mummy calls them 'gwaps', after the sound they make. After he finishes one, it's onto the next with the 'psst' of the bottle opener and the bubbly smell of malt as the lid tumbles to the floor.

If she can, Mercy retrieves the bottle tops because they make excellent furniture for Dolly's house. But it's tricky, because if they make too much noise when he is getting ready to watch the horse racing he shouts at them and says, 'Pickney-dem! Unuh mek mi ears eat grass!' Which Mercy thinks is funny because everyone knows that ears can't eat, and if they could they probably wouldn't want grass. Mercy can't think of anything more boring than horse-racing. It just means they have to keep quiet all afternoon while the horses run around the track again and again and the commentator talks like they're dying to go to the loo.

Daddy's race starts and he leans forward with his elbows on his knees like he's about to clamber inside the telly. The gates, which have been keeping the horses and jockeys in their individual little prisons, fly open. They set off, but there's always one who doesn't want to come out, like it's shy. The rest of them start to thunder around the track, flicking up clods of earth with their hundreds of hooves.

The commentator talks about the horses like they are his old friends, and they probably are. 'And with three furlongs to go, it's *NiceAndTasty*, in the lead followed by *MakeMyDay* and then *GoodShipLollipop* closing in.'

Daddy yells, 'Come *on NiceAndTasty*! Ride him jockey. Ride him!' And he mimes holding the reins, sometimes getting halfway up out of his seat and leaning even further forward. Daddy is way too big to be a jockey but no one is going to tell him that.

'And as they go around the bend, *NiceandTasty* goes wide on the corner, *GoodShipLollipop* sneaks throughout the gap and they head down the far side. *MakeMyDay* is making ground and overtaking *NiceandTasty*. *MakeMyDay* is opening up a commanding lead.'

Daddy is holding the reins and bouncing like a cowboy chasing after indians, his jacket is flapping behind him. 'Dats it! Come on, come on, use de whip jockey. Beat him!'

'And they're closing on the final furlong, they're neck and neck, it's going to be a photo finish.'

'Come on my man! Ride, ah seh ride him!' Daddy is yelling at the telly but it's not going to make any difference to a rider who can't see him and a horse who can't hear him. Sometimes his hat falls off his head because he's riding so fast and hard. Sometimes Devon gets carried away and joins in, shouting, 'Come on *NiceandTasty*, come on, catch up.'

Even though she knows it's silly, Mercy sometimes gets excited too. She wants *NiceandTasty* to win the race, not because she likes horse racing, but because it will make Daddy happy for a while. Daddy's horse rarely wins, but until they get to the finish line there's still hope.

'And it's a barnstormer of a finish with the *GoodShipLollipop* taking it by a nose over *MakeMyDay* with *NiceAndTasty* fading on the final furlong.'

Daddy kicks his hat, tears up his betting slip and says 'Cho! Raas Claat. Nevah should a waste mi money pon dat deh ole nag, They want fi melt down dat blasted 'orse for glue.' Mummy comes in from the kitchen and says, 'In Jesus holy name Sonny! Stop use bad-word in front of the Pickney-dem.'

But just once in a Blue Moon, Daddy's horse wins and he jumps around like an idiot and picks up whoever happens to be near him, usually Devon, and throws him up in the air and catches him and says, 'Whe mi did tell yuh. I did know seh my man would come good. Yuh see how him ride de horse. What a race. Yes man, *to juice*, what a race.' And Devon will join him in re-enacting the final furlong. Devon is actually really good at the commentary like a parrot repeating every word from the commentator.

Daddy takes Devon with him when he goes down to the bookies to collect his winnings. When they eventually come back, Daddy brings a little white paper bag of sweets for them all. Although Mercy prefers it when Daddy wins, she would rather he didn't watch horse racing at all because watching Daddy cycle through every single one of his enormous emotions makes her too nervous.

This afternoon after the horse-racing, Mummy reminds Daddy that he said he would take her out for a driving lesson. Normally they would go and leave Ruby in charge, but after that time with the poker, Mummy says they will all have to come. Mummy changes into her trousers for driving. Mercy has never seen her wearing trousers, they are slim and black and have straps that go under the soles of her feet and they make Mummy look all sophisticated, like Emma Peel from The Avengers.

Normally when they go out Devon sits on Mummy's knee and the four girls squash up in the back, there is usually lots of kicking, shoving and pinching. This time since Mummy will be driving, Devon will have to sit in the back, because One-Bwoy-Pickney or not, Daddy will not be seen in the passenger seat of his own car, 'wid pickney deh pon mi lap.' So the five of them are squashed up in the back and no one wants Devon on their laps, with his bony boy-bottom but Ruby is the eldest so she has to have him. Mercy is in the middle with Evie, and Janie is on the outside looking out for Bumper-Cars.

Mummy can actually drive, but Daddy doesn't know that. She says 'is just dat, mi noh have di cerfi-ticket.' Sometimes when it's really cold or raining hard she will drive them to school. The ride is all jerky and bumpy but they get there. When she drops them off she says, 'no badda tell unuh fadah.'

Later, Mercy asks Mummy how to drive and Mummy tells her all about the ABC's; accelerator, brake, clutch and the gearstick and the gears. Mercy sets up chairs and boxes and persuades Devon and Evie to come for a drive with her. Devon doesn't have many uses but he is very good at car sounds, especially the screeching when they go around a corner and the hiss of the brakes. He can even do the perfect 'psst' of bus doors opening.

Today, Daddy cusses while he adjusts the seat to bring it forward because he is six foot six and Mummy is five foot nothing. Even with the seat pushed all the way forwards Mummy's feet barely reach the pedals. She has to have a cushion to see out of the windscreen. Finally she is strapped in and ready to go. She puts the gear stick in neutral and waggles it about a bit to make sure.

'Put di gearstick in neutral,' says Daddy.

'Yuh no see I put it in neutral *ahready*,' says Mummy, waggling it around some more.

'Alright,' huffs Daddy, 'now check yuh mirror.'

'I check it *ahready*.'

'Well check it again ooman.'

Mercy wonders if they will ever actually set off.

'Hindicate,' says Daddy.

Mummy quietly kisses her teeth and flicks the indicator switch.

She slowly releases the clutch and she presses down on the accelerator and the car jerks into life. The five of them all clap spontaneously in the back and the car judders to a halt.

'Now look at dat,' says Daddy, 'yuh stall it.' Then, without turning around he reaches back with one of his long arms and slaps whoever is within reach. Evie ducks, Mercy is in the middle so she gets it.

'Pickney-dem, Shet up!' he says. Evie grins because Mercy got hit.

Mummy starts again and the car lurches along the cobbles of Hill View towards Hollings Road.

'Mek a left,' says Daddy.

Mummy indicates right.

'Blasted ooman,' says Daddy, 'ah seh, left to rahtid.' He holds up his left hand and waves it off to the left.

'Stop cuss Sonny,' says Mummy, ' I cyan tink straight.' She indicates left and they turn. Hollins Road is a very steep hill.

'Covah yuh brake,' says Daddy gripping his seat.

Mummy brakes and they all fall forward.

'I never say fi *brake*,' says Daddy, 'I say fi *covah* yuh brake.'

'Well I tink seh you want me fi brake,' Mummy shouts.

They all shuffle back into place in the back. The Hillman Avenger does have seatbelts but it's for three people and not much use for five, so Mercy braces her feet against the back of the front seat just in case they stop suddenly again.

'Pickney! Tek out yuh blasted foot outta mi back,' grumbles Daddy. Mercy ducks to the left just in case Daddy's arm flies out again, but it doesn't. Evie doesn't expect Mercy's sudden movement so their heads knock together making a sound like two coconut shells.

'Ow!' Evie shouts, 'Mercy buck me ina me head.'

'I never,' says Mercy, painfully aware that she is back within striking distance. 'It was an accident.'

'If unuh mek mi tek off mi belt,' says Daddy, 'Ah will tan unuh behind.' Evie smirks.

Mercy clenches her teeth and her fists. There is nowhere to escape the long arm of the law, and therefore no way of hitting Evie without retribution.

Mummy is making her way down Hollings Road. Mercy is driving with her, hands on an imaginary steering wheel, feet tap dancing between accelerator, clutch and break. She thinks about climbing in through the back of Mummy's head to help her drive, but she has never done it when Daddy or the others are there. She does not know what would happen if she tries, and something tells her that it would not be a good idea if they knew that she could get inside Mummy.

She does her best from the back seat. Mummy is going very slowly and there are cars forming a queue behind her. They get to the bottom and she does a lovely right turn onto Thornton Road. Mercy is so proud of her. When I'm a grown up, she thinks, I'll never let Daddy in *my* car. Things go smoothly until they get onto Preston Street which is both narrow and steep. A lorry heads towards them in the middle of the road and Daddy shouts, 'keep left ooman, keep left.'

Mummy pulls the steering wheel to the left but she overdoes it and the car slides into a ditch at the side of the road. It all happens very slowly at about ten miles an hour. They all scream and slide into each other and Mercy uses the cover to thump Evie for telling on her. It's a very satisfying thump.

Now Daddy is yelling. 'Blasted raas-claat ooman. Yuh go crash mi car!'

Mummy is screaming. 'I did well see dat truck but yuh,' she points at Daddy. 'Yuh fighten me wid all ah yuh shoutin'.'

Daddy raises a hand like he's going to hit Mummy but the truck driver comes over and he lowers it.

'You lot alright?' asks the truck driver. He's ruddy like a cooked prawn, bald and wears a white T-shirt and has tattoos down his forearms.

Mummy straightens up and says, 'Yes thank you, we are just fine,' in her best Speaky-Spokey. So the truck driver goes back to his truck and Daddy starts shouting again. Mummy just ignores him, takes her handbag, gets out of the car and walks off towards home. Mercy climbs out and follows her before anyone can say anything. All the others stay with Daddy and the car, lopsided and lying in a ditch.

21

When I Grow up

Why does everything with Daddy have to be an angry rant? If Mummy can already drive, why doesn't she just go and get her cerfi-ticket herself? Better still, why doesn't she pack them all up in the car and drive away for good? Mercy wishes she could understand why Mummy puts up with Daddy. Is this what married people do? Argue and fight and pray to God to strike the other one dead? Well Daddy doesn't do any praying, that's Mummy's department.

The cellar living room is warm and stuffy because the fire is burning but the doors are closed. She came straight home from school because the library is closed on a Wednesday afternoon. Daddy is at work and the others are running about somewhere in the big rattly old house. It's just Mummy and Mercy. Well it would be if Sister Norman wasn't there too. But if she tries hard Mercy can ignore her and pretend it's just the two of them.

Mummy is on a split-shift again which means she goes to work in the morning to cook breakfast for the sick people-dem at the hospital. Then she comes home to cook and clean. Then she goes back to the hospital to cook dinner for the sick people-dem. The soup is bubbling on the stove so Mummy is having a little sit down and a chat with Sister Norman, who has come over to borrow her Pentecostal Hymnal. Mummy tells her all about how the *cyar* turn over in a ditch and Mummy and di *pickney-dem* barely managed to escape with dem life. Mercy smiles to herself because she knows Mummy is exaggerating but she also knows she is not allowed to push up herself in Big-People conversation.

But then in a way Mummy is right. Daddy and his miserable self could have killed them all. It's one thing to shout at

Mummy when she is cooking (never fast enough for Daddy) or cleaning (getting in front of the TV), but to shout at her when she is driving? Well, Mummy is right. It's a miracle they all got out alive, imagine if they had hit the truck, they would all have been flattened. Mummy complains heartily to Sister Norman about Daddy and Mercy wonders if the reason she stays with him is to give herself something to complain about.

Mummy puts her feet up on the three legged wooden stool because they are all swollen from walking to the hospital and back twice a day. Mercy gets the little silver and ivory pen knife out and starts to pick Mummy's corns. She's very careful but every now and then Mummy goes, 'Ouch! Mercy, mind mi toe.'

Mercy can tell that Sister Norman wants her to go away and play with the others and leave the Big-people to chat. But she has no intention of going, even if they would play with her. So Sister Norman changes tack and pretends to be interested in Mercy.

'Soh Mercy, weh you want do when you grow up?' Sister Norman smiles at Mercy and it's a bit scary because she has false teeth and they look too white and even and perfect.

That, thinks Mercy, is a very good question, and it deserves some serious consideration. She puts down the penknife, places her hand on her chin and has a proper think. She could be a teacher like Mrs Kaplinsky. Well, not exactly like Mrs Kaplinsky because Mrs Kaplinsky is mean. But then some of the children in her class are very stupid and take a long time to learn things and that's why Mrs Kaplinsky hits them. Mercy doesn't think she would have the patience to explain things a hundred times. So, not a teacher.

What about a Dinner Lady, because, like Mummy, they get to take home the leftover food at the end of day. But the children are always shouting in the dining hall and dropping food everywhere and Dinner Ladies (why aren't there any Dinner Men?) have to empty the pigswill which is absolutely revolting.

Lollipop Lady? They can stop traffic which is like a superpower. But then they are outside in all weathers and Mercy doesn't like it when it's too cold. It makes her chest hurt.

'Awright, Mercy,' says Sister Norman. 'I tink yuh was such a clever Pickney. Yuh noh even know wheh you want do when you grow up?'

'Don't rush me,' says Mercy, 'I'm thinking.'

'But what is dis?' says Sister Norman, all huffy. 'Di pickney faisty eh?"

Mummy hides her smile. Mercy has no idea why Sister Norman expects her to make such an important decision on the spot. After all she will be grown up for a long time so she has to consider all her options. She begins pulling at the circular flap of dead skin she has lifted with the penknife from Mummy's little toe. It's thick, pale yellow and slightly stretchy.

She thinks about Neil Armstrong and his 'one giant step for mankind'. But they aren't any girl astronauts and there certainly aren't any brown ones. And what if the spaceship broke down, like Daddy's car, in the middle of outer space, and they had no air? She wouldn't be able to breathe and she would die. After months and months in hospital with New Monya, Mercy has had enough of not being able to breathe for a lifetime. So no, not an astronaut.

Mercy remembers the long haired people on TV waving their scarves and dancing. She has finally made a decision.

Sister Norman and Mummy have started talking about church. On Sunday, Pastor Foster preached about women wearing the garments of men taking on roles which were not theirs.

'God has given us all the place in this world and we should occupy it with grace and humility.' He said at the end of his everlasting sermon. He really seemed to be enjoying himself and all the men said loud 'Amen's'.

Mummy came home fuming. She was still angry about it now.

'I cyan believe how him goh preach pon me!' she says pouting her lips. 'I did only wear di trousers for driving. Somebody must ha' see me and go chat mi business to him.'

'God sees all,' says Sister Norman, shaking her head sadly.

Mummy kisses her teeth loudly. 'I don't know where it seh in the bible that women cyan't wear trousers.' Mummy is getting herself all worked up now.

'Well,' says Sister Norman, quick as a flash, 'women shall not wear that which pertaineth unto a man, neither shall a man put on a woman's garment: for all that do so are abomination unto the Lord thy God. Deuteronomy 22:5.' She seems very pleased with herself that she can quote scripture. Mercy thinks about the man dressed as a woman in the Pant-O and wonders if he knew that he was an abomination. And if he did, did he care? *Oh yes he did. Oh no he didn't.*

'Well,' says Mummy, 'but dat verse mean seh women shouldn't wear *men's* trousers. It noh mean we can't wear fi wi ownah trousers.'

'Who are we,' intoned Sister Norman clasping her hands like she is about to start praying, 'to question the will of God.'

Mummy clamps her mouth shut and says nothing for a while, and Mercy remembers that Sister Norman lives at the top of Preston Street, near where the car went into the ditch.

'Aha,' said Mummy triumphantly, 'render your heart and not your garment. *Joel 22.* God sees what is in your heart. I only wear di trousers fi modesty when I was driving.'

Mercy is getting annoyed now because Sister Norman asked her a question and doesn't seem interested in the answer. She goes up to Sister Norman and tugs on the sleeve of her coat.

'Sister Norman,' she says, 'I'm ready to tell you my answer.'

'But Mercy,' says Sister Norman 'Pickney-dem mustn't push-up dem-self in Big-People conversation.'

'But,' says Mercy, 'I know what I want to be.'

'What a trial,' says Sister Norman, 'dis child of yours is someting' else.' She looks at Mercy and smiles her scary smile.

'Awight Mercy, is what you want to be?'

Mercy stands up straight, shoulders back like she's in assembly, looks Sister Norman dead in the eye and says, 'when I grow up I want to be a Hippie.'

'Yuh what?' splutters Sister Norman.

'A Hippie, I want to be a Hippie,' says Mercy a bit louder just in case Sister Norman didn't hear her properly. 'Because they have Free Love and I want some and I haven't got any money to pay for it.'

Sister Norman tips her head back. She leans so far back that Mercy thinks the top of her head might fall off. The laugh comes from deep in her belly and makes it jiggle. She laughs so much that tears start streaming out of her eyes and rolling around her plump cheeks.

Mercy does not know why what she said is funny, or why Sister Norman is laughing so much. She feels hot and flustered and a bit embarrassed because she knows that Sister Norman is laughing *at* her not *with* her.

'Dis pickney,' she says wiping her eyes with the heel of her palm, 'Lord she gi me joke.'

Mummy smiles but doesn't laugh and Mercy is grateful for this because if Mummy laughs at her as well it will be too much.

'You cyan't be a Hippie Mercy,' says Sister Norman, her cheeks still jiggling.

'Why not?' asks Mercy indignantly.

'Dem people is hun-godly. Dem is disgusting and, and … promiscuous.'

'What's promiscuous?' asks Mercy.

'Yuh too young fi know 'bout dat. But is not di kind of free love yuh looking for.'

'Well,' says Mercy, standing her ground, 'Pastor Foster says God is love and God doesn't charge money for his love so that's free love isn't it?'

Sister Norman's bottom jaw snaps shut with a clack of her shiny teeth.

Mummy presses her lips together the way she does when she is trying not to laugh.

Sister Norman draws up her shoulders and says, 'Pickney. No badda tek up yourself come cross-question Big-People.'

'But you asked me what I wanted to be Sister Norman.'

Sister Norman's eyes narrow and she gives Mercy a hard stare.

She turns to Mummy. 'Dis ya pickney too renk and faisty.'

Mummy says nothing. Mercy takes a small step back. She can see where this is going and she does not like the look of it.

'Dis Pickney want beat'n,' says Sister Norman looking expectantly at Mummy.

Mummy shifts uncomfortably in her chair, but says nothing.

'Spare the Rod and spoil the child. Proverbs 13.24,' says Sister Norman.

Mummy frowns and Mercy wonders if she is going to get beaten just because Sister Norman says so. She wishes Mummy would stand up to people, to tell them 'no' to their face instead of going along with whatever they tell her to do and then complaining afterwards how they 'made' her do it.

'Mercy,' says Mummy. 'Yuh cyan't talk to Sistah Norman like yuh and she is companion. Yuh must say yuh sorry to Sister Norman.'

Mercy burns with indignation. How can she be faisty if all did was give an honest answer to a question? Why does she have to say sorry? She wants to say: 'I will not'. She wants to pick up the pen knife and stab Sister Norman in feet which look like shiny, brown, balloons expanding out of her shoes. She looks up. Sister Norman has her arms folded and is looking at her like she is a little Demon. Mummy has a stern look on her face but Mercy knows that it is all for show.

She stares daggers at her tormentor and says, 'I am very sorry, Sister Norman. I did not mean to be *renk* and faisty. I'm not going to be a Hippie when I grow up. I will just go to church, read the bible and fast and pray every, single, day.'

Mercy has the fingers on her right hand crossed behind her back.

Sister Norman is not satisfied. She looks like she can't tell whether Mercy is still being faisty or not. She wants Mercy to get beaten. If Mummy wasn't here she would beat Mercy herself. But there seems to be some sort of rule that you can't beat other people's children in front of them.

'Hmmph,' says Sister Norman, getting up to leave. 'She would ah nevah faisty like dis if her faddah was here.'

Mercy is going to have to stay out of Sister Norman's way. She doesn't think Mummy will be much help this time; her victory over Mrs Kaplinsky was a one-off.

22

Praise the Lord

Sister Norman doesn't have to wait too long for her revenge. Church is supposed to start at ten am on a Sunday but ten o'clock has never seen them enter the building. It is usually gone eleven by the time they rush in, all flustered from their journey. The Pentecostal Church is on the first floor of a big old building in town, The Hallfield Function Rooms. It has big stone pillars at each side of the big red door.

On Sundays it's just their church upstairs and, once a month, the Dog Show downstairs. This means they have to weave their way through all the various breeds of dogs before they get to the stairs. Although Mercy does not really like dogs, she was mesmerised the first time she saw an Afghan Hound. It looked like Dolly come to life, all straight, golden hair; long pointy nose and haughty expression and its owner was exactly the same.

The upstairs room has old wooden chairs arranged along a central aisle and a lectern at the front. Mercy's family are not the only latecomers; almost everybody is late, because they don't want to get there on time and wait for all the latecomers. So Church starts later and later every week. Morning church is supposed to start at ten am and finish at two pm and evening church starts at six pm and goes on until ten; it's a long day.

The first hour is always Pastor Foster desperately lecturing everyone about the need for punctuality. 'Heaven won't wait,' he says, waving his finger at them. But he is talking to a mainly empty room. So he has to say it all again when everyone arrives, but there are *always* more latecomers. Mercy wonders why he bothers.

Church is a bit like a school assembly, because they sing hymns and have announcements. But school assemblies are short. Church starts with choruses; anyone can start a chorus and it's usually a short happy song, like:

Soon and very soon
I am going to see the King
Hallelujah Hallelujah
I'm going to see the King

Mercy likes the choruses because they get to stand up, sing as loud as they want and clap. Not just any old ordinary clapping but double and triple clapping, on and off the beat. Mummy always brings her tambourine and if she is in a good mood she lets Mercy play it. Although Mercy can't do all the syncopated tambourine playing that Mummy does, not yet anyway. Janie can, but she has to be good at something.

After that there is a prayer to welcome everyone, latecomers and all, and then the service is properly open. Someone from the congregation is asked to read a Bible Chapter or two. Mercy thinks it is a mistake to let people pick their own chapter because some people choose really boring stuff like all the ones where Abraham begat Jacob; Jacob begat Esau, and Esau begat Derek. Well there isn't actually a Derek but there might be for all Mercy knows because the begatting goes on so long that she gets bored and stops listening. Once Pastor Williams visited from Birmingham and he chose to read some of the rude bits from Songs of Solomon:

Thy hair is like a flock of goats going down from Gilead.

There was some tutting about that after the service but Mummy said that he is a man of God and if it's in the Bible it's okay to read it in church. But Mercy noticed that no one read from Songs of Solomon after that.

Children are placed on the front rows, within slapping distance of a parent or proxy. When someone gets hit it's exciting, as long it's not Mercy. There is a definite trick to winding up your siblings whilst remaining the innocent party. Devon is the easiest one to do. During prayer time Janie tells him that he has a carrot face. If Devon wasn't originally self-conscious about his long pointy chin he certainly is by now.

Over time there is no need to actually *say* 'carrot face', Janie just mimes the stroking of a long beard and, if timed correctly, Devon will explode and have to be hauled kicking and screaming outside to be given a good hiding. Everyone can hear the thwacks and yelps before he is dragged back in red-eyed and penitent.

Every week the children have to memorise a verse from the Bible and come up to the front and recite it out loud. Pastor Foster declares that it is cheating to do John 11 verse 35, because *'Jesus Wept'* is just two words and that does not take a lot of memorising. On the first Sunday of the month anyone who has learned the names of all the books of the Old or New Testament can come up to the front and recite them all. But you have to know your stuff because if you get one wrong everyone laughs and the shame is awful.

'You too fool-fool!'

'You miss out Timothy!'

'Lamentations!'

'Deuteronomy!'

'Pickney is a bloomin' dunce.'

Mercy can do them all, Old and New, and she even remembers the doubles like Samuel, Kings and Chronicles. The prize is your own little Bible which is a bit daft as you must have had a Bible to be able to learn all the books in the first place.

Then they have a Testimony Service where anyone can stand up and say what God has done for them that week. People often talk about getting money when they really need it. One man, who was obviously not a regular, stood up and shouted about how grateful he was to God because he had no money to pay his light bill and then he won five pounds on the Pools.

He even waved the actual five pound note shouting 'Glory to God in the highest.' He was a little unsteady on his feet as he sat down. There was a murmur of disapproval from the congregation because Pools is gambling, and gambling is a sin. No wonder Daddy doesn't come to Church. Afterwards Mummy said, 'dat man ah Bumper,' and Mercy thought that he did smell of Martell brandy.

Then there is the Offering. If children have been particularly good they will be allowed to take around the offering plate, stopping at each aisle to send the plate to the end for everyone to put in their money and then move it to the next aisle. Some people put their money in a special blue envelope which is called Tithes. Mercy is not quite sure what that is but she knows it's a lot of money and the people who put in Tithes do it very proudly, puffing out their chests and coughing to make sure that everyone sees.

Pastor Foster preaches in a deep, sad voice. Half of the sermons seem to be about the way women dress. One week he preached about the evils of slingback shoes, and how ungodly it was for a woman to reveal her heels. It was because Eve tempted Adam, he reminds them, that humanity was Cast Out of the Garden of Eden.

The week after Sister Norman got a new pair of glasses which reminded Mercy of Catwoman, with lots of rhinestones on the edges; there was a long sermon on jewellery and Adornment. The following week Sister Norman was back in her old glasses frowning furiously for the whole service. There were sermons on the sinfulness of sleeveless dresses, short skirts, make-up or devil-paint. And that was well before the cardinal sin of women wearing trousers was broached. Mummy threatened to find a different church to go to after that one.

This Sunday Pastor Foster is going on about the Sheep and the Shepherd. Except he's not a very good Shepherd because he keeps losing his sheep and spending ages trying to find one of them. It makes Mercy think of Little Bo Peep. After that they sing *'There were ninety and nine,'* which has got to be the slowest, saddest song in the whole of the Pentecostal Hymnal.

During the Ninety-and-nine, Mercy feels sleepy but she tries to fight it. She feels herself falling but catches herself, then she nods off again. This time she doesn't catch herself in time and only wakes up when she is past the point of no return. She and her chair clatter loudly to the floor and everyone looks at her. Sister Norman pounces and pulls her upright, pinching her on the tender inside of her upper arm for good measure.

'Be sure your sin will find you out,' she hisses as tears spring to Mercy's eyes. 'Have respect for the house of God,' she says plopping Mercy back on her chair. Mercy stays wide awake for the rest of the service.

23

Ariel washes whiter

'What's his name?' asks the policeman.

Mummy is screaming at Daddy, 'Sonny! Sonny!' she shouts. 'In the name of Jesus Christ Sonny. Stop it!' She drags at his blue and white striped pyjamas but it's no good. She is so much smaller than him so she can't shift him. He is slumped forward on his knees and there isn't much space in the small kitchen.

It's early Saturday morning and Mercy is shivering in her nighty at the top of the cellar steps. Janie and Devon are there too. There was so much banging and shouting last night and Mercy couldn't get to sleep. When she finally did she dreamed of rag dolls and flying bricks. Now Janie and Devon are crying. Devon has a really silly cry, he just opens his mouth and one long deep 'aahhh' comes out, until he runs out of breath and then he starts it all again. Janie is all wobbly like she is going to fall down the steps.

Mercy just watches them all like it's a strange film. Then she realises that the policeman is talking to her. He has tried asking Mummy, but Mummy isn't taking any notice of him. He squats down on his knees and looks Mercy in the eye. She had never seen a policeman up close before. His face is bright pink with little broken veins on his cheeks and his eyes are grey. The strap from his helmet cuts into his chin. He's obviously not very good at shaving as he has some toilet paper stuck to a little cut under his chin.

'What's your name lovie?' he asks.

'M-m-Mercy,' she is annoyed about the stuttering because she always speaks in a loud clear voice. She is not frightened, after all she is seven years old. She does not want the policeman to think that she is all hysterical.

She tries again. 'My name is Mercy.'

'Okay, Mercy. The ambulance will be here soon to take your Dad to the hospital. What's his name?'

'Erm,' Mercy doesn't know what to say as she doesn't actually know Daddy's name. Mummy calls him Son or Sonny and his friends call him Long-Son because he is so tall but she thinks those are only nicknames.

'Son?' she says as that sounds more formal than Sonny.

The policeman frowns. 'Is that his proper name?' he looks past her to Janie but she is just standing there with her mouth hanging open. Neither use nor ornament as the Headteacher says.

Mummy is still pulling at Daddy.

'Have you turned it off?' says the policeman.

'Wha?' Mummy stares at the policeman but her eyes do not focus.

'Turn it off at the mains. Where's the mains?' The policeman is getting a little exasperated.

Mummy looks up at him, trying to work out what he is going on about. Her eyes are wild. Mercy had never seen her looking like that before. The tie-head that she went to bed with is all skew-wiff and wisps of hair stick out at all angles. The belt of her red cotton dressing gown has come loose. She is wearing her nighty underneath but the scoop neck is hanging open and Mercy is worried that the policeman will be able to see her titties.

The smell is awful, pungent and slightly rancid. The back door is wide open so it is going away, but only very slowly.

'Mercy,' says the policeman. He squats down again. 'Do you know where the gas meter is?'

Of course Mercy knows where the gas meter is because she sometimes has to feed sixpences into it. She nods, and leads him to the back cellar room where Daddy used to play dominoes with his friends, (although they never played in there again after Mummy got mad and cast them all out). Mercy doesn't go in that room much as it is dark and damp and dirty. It has a large stone sink under the window and the remains of an ancient black range along the back wall. The chalky white paint flakes off wherever you touch it and the mouldy dust tickles her nose and makes her *hashma* worse.

The bulb is blown so Mercy holds the door open so the policeman can see where to switch the gas off. The light glints off the meter key twist. Mercy loves hearing the sixpence clatter into the chamber as she turns the metal knob. It almost makes going into the back cellar bearable.

He switches on a large black torch from his belt and quickly finds the meter. Above it is a huge red plastic covered lever pointing upwards. He yanks at it until he manages to pull it down into a horizontal position.

'Thank you lovie,' he says. 'Now your dad's name is Sonny?'

'No,' says Mercy, 'it's Son.'

'Son?' asks the policeman, 'are you sure that's his name?'

'They call him 'Sonny' sometimes,' offers Mercy, beginning to feel a bit silly. She has only ever heard Mummy call him 'Son'. Until now she didn't think there was anything unusual in not knowing her father's name.

There is a commotion back at the stairs; the ambulance-men have arrived.

In their black uniforms they look almost the same as the policeman but their caps are flat instead of pointed and they have different stuff dangling from their belts. The two of them carry a stretcher down the stairs. Mummy is still crying but she is a bit calmer now and has, thankfully, re-tied the belt on her dressing gown.

'I cyan move him!' she says to the ambulance men, still tugging helplessly at his pyjama top.

'Don't you worry yourself about that love, we're here now. We'll get him out,' says one of the ambulance men. The one with a bristle-brush moustache.

'How long has he been here?' asks the other one.

'I don't know,' says Mummy. She has switched to Speaky-Spokey. 'I wake up about half a hour ago and I smell gas. So I come down to check, see if I leave the cooker on, and I find him.'

'Was he like this when you found him love?'

'Yes!' says Mummy, suddenly getting very angry. Mercy thinks she is going to kick Daddy up the bum as he kneels there on the floor with his head in the gas oven. His feet are gnarled and the skin around his heels is white and flakey because he never creams them. His pyjama bottoms have ridden up his legs revealing little curly hairs growing out of the ashy grey skin that covers his hard calf muscles. His toenails are dark yellow and look like he hasn't cut them for ages.

'What's his name,' asks the Ambulance man.

'Irael,' says Mummy.

'Is-rael?' asks the Ambulance man.

'No,' says Mummy, '*Irael*, his name is Irael.'

Mercy looks at Janie. She has the same surprised look on her face as Mercy. *Irael*? Daddy has a name and his name is *Irael*? No one has ever told them his real name. They both burst out laughing. Irael, what kind of name was that? The policeman looks at them and the laughter dies on their lips. Mercy is worried that they might get arrested for laughing at a serious moment. Mrs Kaplinsky would certainly hit you with a ruler for that, so what will the police do?

Daddy is groaning now as the Ambulance men pull his head and shoulders out of the oven. The sound that comes from deep in his belly has been sitting there for centuries. This is not the Daddy Mercy is used to; she is not sure if she prefers him helpless or angry.

'Ariel!' says the ambulance man. 'Come on Ariel, we'll get you to hospital, get you all sorted out mate.'

They get him on his feet but the fly of his pyjama pants falls open and Mercy sees his thingy. She quickly turns away. Mummy pulls the drawstring tight and the Ambulance men get a hold of him one under each arm and half-walk, half-drag him up the stairs. The policeman catches up the rear, just in case he falls backwards.

Devon and Janie hold hands as they watch this strange group of men make their way out the front door and down the garden steps. Mercy stands off to the side, an image pops into her head of the Disciples taking Jesus down off the cross.

'That's it, Ariel', says the policeman, as they help him into the ambulance, 'there's a good lad.'

As Mercy shuts the front door, she catches a glimpse of the Cairo-Tractor staring horrified over the garden fence. They go downstairs to find Mummy kneeling on the floor in the cellar living room praying.

'Lord God Almighty,' she says. 'You who know all things. Lord of Lord and King of Kings. I'm begging yuh. Spare him life.' Most of the time Mummy is praying for God to strike him down and now that he's down she's praying for God to save him. Mercy wishes she would make up her mind.

After that, every time Mercy sees a box of Ariel washing powder, she thinks of Daddy with his head in the gas oven.

*

Mummy takes one of them with her each day when she goes to visit Daddy, starting with Devon (of course). They come home all excited about seeing him but Mercy is just glad he's not in the house. On the last day before he comes home it's Mercy's turn. She doesn't want to go. She's still very nervous walking down the corridors of Bradford Royal Infirmary and she has to remind herself (and Dolly who has secretly tagged along) that *she's* not sick so they can't keep her and prick her, poke her or stitch her anymore.

It's a shock to see him sitting up in the bed with greying stubble and a thingy in his arm looking not just skinny as usual but totally emaciated, like his skin is trying to divorce his bones. He smiles when he sees her, like he's pleased or something and she wonders if this is actually Daddy or an imposter wearing his ill-fitting skin.

Mummy has her Bible and Daddy lets her pray for him resting her hand on his head and anointing him with Olive oil which drips down his forehead. She gets carried away and prays so loudly that the nurses come and ask her to keep it down. While she's praying, (quietly now) Daddy catches Mercy's eye and winks at her. It hits her as hard as a slap. This friendly Daddy is such a shock to her system that she slowly backs away, gets Dolly out of her pocket and sits at the foot of the bed playing with her, while keeping one ear on their conversation.

Mummy tells Daddy that she's not going to leave him because what God has bound together in holy matrimony let no man put asunder. It doesn't sound very comforting that she's only staying with him because God has forced her to. Mercy wonders if that's why he put his head in the gas oven; because he thought Mummy was finally going to leave him. Try as she might, Mercy doesn't think she will ever understand Big-People. If he doesn't want her to leave him he should just stop hitting her.

24

The Girl who could fly

The truce is short-lived. A few weeks out of hospital and Daddy is back to his old self. If anything he's worse than before. He has to reassert his authority because they all saw him weak as a kitten propped up on pillows. Mercy climbs up the creaky wooden stairs from the cellar living room to the ground floor, careful not to *mek-noise* as she passes the tenants' rooms.

Once in the cold blue bathroom Mercy pulls out the red plastic box from under the sink. If she stands on her tiptoes she can just see into the mirror. It has eight sides and bevelled edges creating lots of broken Mercy reflections around the edge. It is faded in the corners and a couple of spots in the middle so it looks like the olden-days. A sad little olden-day girl stares back at her; plaits pointing this way and that with a scar on her forehead. The ears are small and the eyes are a bit too big for her head. Her eyelashes curl back on themselves forming almost perfect circles.

Mercy examines the face closely, because it belongs to someone else; the faint wispy eyebrows with the wide gap between them; the nose which is a little bit turned up at the bottom; the round lips which when closed, form an almost perfect circle. And then there are the apple cheeks which Mummy's friends seem to find irresistible, public property to be kissed, squeezed, patted, pinched and occasionally bitten.

She practises a smile. The corners of her mouth pulling up and backwards revealing small white even teeth. It doesn't look right; the eyes don't look right. She lets her face rest and tries again. The apple cheeks form as she opens her mouth. They look like someone has stuffed two little golf balls into her face.

This time the smile is a little better but it still hasn't reached the eyes.

Mercy knows she has to get it right. There is a right way to smile and a wrong way. She thinks of Dolly and of making clothes for her. This makes her happy. When Daddy comes home she wants to smile for him. She turns a three-quarter profile to the mirror. If she can sneak a look at herself before she knows she is being watched she can catch the right smile before it turns into the wrong one.

The real problem is the eyes. It's only a proper smile if the eyes are happy. Mummy sometimes talks about white-people smiles; how they only smile at you with their mouths, nobody thought to tell their eyes to join in the party.

Two floors down she hears the front door slam. Balaam! Daddy come!

He will go straight down to the cellar living room. There might just be sweets. She races down the three flights of stairs but she's the last one down to the cellar. They are clamouring at him asking for sweets. But he's in a Bad Mood. Dinner is late. Mummy is tired and busy. She only got in from work half an hour before Daddy.

'Ah weh mi dinner deh?' he booms.

'Soon come Sonny,' she says, pushing pans about on the stove.

But Daddy is angry now. Dinner should, 'deh pon table,' when he gets home.

Doesn't he know Mummy just got home herself, Mercy frowns.

'Pickney!' says Daddy, turning on her. 'Stop knit up yuh brow.'

The more she tries to stop the worse it gets. Her brain tells her face what to do. Be happy Mercy, be happy. But she cannot manage it. She can feel her shoulders climbing up towards her ears, the muscles in her neck taut and expectant. The half-brick that lives in her stomach is getting bigger again.

*

Now I'm flying. I lift off so fast that my shoes stay on the ground. Scruffy brown leather T-bar sandals with a brass buckle and dirty cream crepe soles. The right shoe stays put but the left one falls over onto its side. I ascend, like an Angel, the air sucked out of my lungs.

The colours in the room sing bright and shimmer like a heat wave. Gravity has released me from its heavy grip and time has gone haywire. I don't need a magic carpet anymore. I can fly by myself, moving both fast and slow, yet part of me completely stationery, and all at the same time. It is impossible but it is happening. My big, little brain is working hard but it can't keep up. I don't know when my feet left the floor. Tingling toes, lengthening limbs, belly drop.

Deep space. Limbs slowly flailing. I will be the first Mercy on the Moon? Go Mercy go. Collision, impact imminent, irresistible force meets immovable object. The immovable object is the wall of the cellar living room, blue painted cement with little sandy holes where the damp has bubbled through.

I am the irresistible force. As my back crumples into the wall, breath deserts my lungs. Every molecule of air runs out through my wide open mouth in one big woosh. Paint and sandy cement rolling onto my green woollen jumper and swapping places with wisps of wool left clinging to the wall.

Gravity is back, reasserting its authority, dragging me down, earthbound. Arms out like a crucifix I am slipping down the wall towards the corner where it meets the floor. Concrete grey, worn shiny by feet.

I unzip my skin. The zip is made of bone and cartilage, like the toughest of fingernails interlaced down my front. There is a faint thrum and purr as the teeth of my zip disengage from each other and open me up to the outside air. I pull back the skin and climb out of flesh and bones left crumpled on the floor. I climb on air, solid like steps, up to the corner of the room, top right-hand side.

Will I stay up here where it's quiet or will I ever go back? I look down at what used to be my body. The vomit slowly rolling down the side of my face and pooling on the floor. I can see across to the charging bull in the trilby hat on the other side of the room. Nostrils breathing heavy cartoon air, horns growing out of the sides of its head filling the space. Up here I am safe. In my corner, in another world, another dimension.

I don't know how long I'm up there as time slides backwards and forwards over and under itself. Like an autumn leaf on a breeze, I slide and float back down into the body on the ground. The unzipped carcass seems cold. But I dip my ghostly foot into the belly like a hand into wet tripe. Then I slide my foot into the trouser leg. Toes re-inhabiting the skin. Arm wriggles into flesh, my fingers fitting like a glove underneath the nails.

I shuffle into the torso, a slightly too tight dress. Flexing my newly inhabited fingers I rezip from the belly button up past the solar plexus to the collarbone. Mercy is back.

Lungs are out of action. Every ounce of air has been pushed from them. I wait as my skull wraps around my rattled brain like a bone bonnet. Connections remake, neurons refire, synapses are crossed and the message finally reaches my flattened lungs.

Breathe.

I am reborn into a world of pain. My lungs start up like ancient bellows creaking open to haul air back into my body. Blood travels up and down taking oxygen around to the fingers, toes and everything in between, spilling a little from the gash at the back of my head. My taste buds spring to life and register acid vomit in my mouth and I cough and spit. I lift my head to see Daddy turning on his leather heels and walking out of the room.

25

Black Jack

Mercy spent the rest of the day in bed with Mummy rubbing her back, feeding her soup and complaining that God is going to strike Daddy down for his wickedness. Mercy didn't hold out much hope because Mummy had been asking God to strike him down for years and he's still standing. But soon there is another emergency and Mercys flying is all forgotten.

'Clothes. We need clothes!' Daddy was frantic, rushing around their bedroom grabbing clothes from each girl's drawer. Mercy was horrified as he grabbed her brand new C&A crimplene dress. Most of her clothes are hand-me-downs from Ruby or Janie, but this dress was new. A navy smock with sky blue sleeves and red criss cross stitching across the chest.

Why? she wants to ask. What's going on now? But she knows better than to cross-question Big-People. Downstairs, Mummy is flapping and Daddy is shoving the clothes he grabbed into a big black bag. Mercy hopes he's not going to throw them away!

It's only then that Mummy mentions the ship that catch-a-fire in the middle of the *Hatlantic* Ocean. What ship? Why did Big-People never tell them anything? After they are sent to bed, they speculate wildly on *wha' gwaan*. Janie says she heard Daddy tell Mummy that his brother's wife was coming to England with their children. Mercy never even knew that Uncle Dubbs had a wife, never mind children.

Mercy tries to ask Mummy why Daddy has taken all their best clothes but Mummy says, 'No badda push-up yourself ina Big-People business.'

Sometimes, Mercy hates Big-People.

On Sunday, after morning Church, Mummy cooks double the amount of rice and peas and chicken as usual. A knock at the front door and Daddy lopes upstairs, taking them two at a time. There is shrieking and laughing and the next minute a whole heap of people troop down the stairs to the cellar living room.

First through the door is Uncle Dubbs who, like Daddy, looks like he's been carved out of mahogany. There isn't an ounce of fat anywhere on him. His cheeks are hollow, with cheekbones almost pushing through the skin but his eyes are bright like burning coals. When he smiles he too reveals a gold tooth in the corner of his mouth. He even has the same vein on the side of his forehead that snakes its way up and under his Trilby hat.

'Unuh!' Daddy announces. 'Come say hello to unuh cousin-dem.' They all shuffle forward in a bunch with Ruby at the front. 'Hello' they chant as one.

From behind Uncle Dubbs steps Aunty Mabel, a short round woman with eyes that at first look happy but when you look closer they appear very sad. She speaks in a voice so high that it is disorienting to hear the voice of a little girl come out her mouth. Her dress is blue with white lace on top but it is way too small for her and stretches tightly around the belly, which, after a few minutes she stops trying to suck in.

And then there are the cousins, six of them. Mercy tries to take them all in but she stops dead at Lennie, a girl exactly the same height as Mercy. Lennie's dress is a navy smock with sky blue sleeves and red criss-cross stitching across the chest. Mercy's eyes widen, her chest tightens and her fists clench. She has to make an almighty effort to stop herself from dragging her best dress off Lennie's back.

Over dinner Aunt Mabel tells the story in her high-pitched girly-voice about the ship catching fire in the middle of the *Hatlantic*, and the four days it spent slowly sinking before a rescue ship finally arrived and took them to Gibraltar, then another ship took them to Hinglan. Her voice catches in her throat when she recounts how little Freddy tried to jump from the burning ship to the rescue boat. He nearly fell in but one of the sailors managed to catch him by his jacket.

'If him did hit the water...' she stops and sniffs. Freddie is sitting beside her, he looks to be around four years old. He giggles.

Mabel slaps him hard across the top of his head. 'You could ah dead!'

Freddie rubs his head but doesn't cry. He must have a very tough skull.

The cousins look funny, they're all skinny like their dad but they all have hamster cheeks and huge eyes like their mum, like the genes were just thrown into a bowl but not mixed up very well.

'We loss *hevery*-ting,' says Aunty Mabel. 'We reach Hinglan with just the clothes wheh de pon we back,' She starts crying again. Uncle Dubbs pats her shoulder and says; 'Hush noh Mabel.' But she is not going to be hushed.

'Yuh,' she says, cutting her eye at her husband, 'yuh wasn't there! Is me one ha fi travel wid all di pickney-dem.' Uncle Dubbs came to England the year before Daddy but it took him longer to save up and send for Mabel because she wouldn't come without all her children.

'We ha fi rely pon di kindness of strangers even fi the clothes wheh deh pon we back,' Aunty Mabel sniffs. Mercy looks more closely at her dress, it looks a lot like one of Mummy's, but Mummy has a tiny waist and Aunty Mabel definitely does not.

'Sonny and Liv is family,' pleads Uncle Dubbs, trying to calm her down. 'Dem is not stranger.'

Mercy still wants to fight Lennie to get her dress back but now she feels bad about it. She tells herself that she should be a Good Samaritan. But deep down she would much prefer to be a Bad Samaritan.

After that the cousins come round most Sundays. Cousin Bobby and his brothers and sisters talk funny. They say 'flim' instead of 'film' and 'axe' instead of 'ask'. The others laugh them to scorn, begging them to talk and then howling at the backwards-sounding things they say. Mercy just stands and watches, remembering all the kerfuffle when they first arrived.

Mummy grumbles about how she has to Feed the Five Thousand and couldn't Mabel cook one Sunday?

'Liv,' pleads Daddy, 'yuh know seh the whole family live in ah just two room. Is where she fi find place fi cook?'

Despite being as skinny as Daddy, Mummy says Uncle Dubbs can eat like a farmer-horse. Even so Mummy always serves the men first. Then she brings in plates for Aunt Mabel and the boys, then the girl cousins, and finally Mercy and her sisters; but by now it's mainly, neck bones and chicken-back. In between complimenting Mummy on the food; Daddy and Uncle Dubbs, pat their bellies, burp loudly and wipe their mouths with the backs of their hands.

The children are sent off to play after dinner and told not to bother Big-People. They scatter running up and down the three flights of stairs from the cellar to the attic and find places to play hide and seek.

*

Mercy is hiding with cousin Bobby under the big bed up in the attic. No one has found them yet.

'Want a Pear Drop?' asks Bobby.

'Yess!' whispers Mercy. Silly question.

She giggles as she sucks on the yellow and pink pear shaped sweet. It takes a while to suck off the sugar coating and get to the tang and zip of the sherbet underneath. She always tells herself that she will suck it until it finishes but she always ends up crunching it when it gets tiny, for that last hit of sugar.

'Want some more?' asks Bobby in a stage whisper.

Mercy nods in the dark.

'I'll wi give you more if …' He trails off.

'What?'

'Noh badda tell nobody.'

'I won't,' says Mercy conspiratorially.

'Mek me put me han' ina yuh baggy.'

'What? That's nasty!'

There is silence. Why does he want to do that? Big-people do silly things, but Bobby is not a grown-up yet, even though his voice goes up and down all the time and he doesn't seem to be able to control it.

'You want di Pear Drops or not?' he asks. His breathing has changed, there is something husky in his voice.

Mercy thinks for a moment. She wants more Pear Drops.

'Alright,' she says.

'Roll over pon yuh back.'

She rolls, the springs of the black iron bed are inches from her nose and she struggles not to sneeze from the dust. It also smells a little bit of pee from all the times Janie has wet the bed. His fingers feel slippery like a fish between her legs. He breathes hard like he has just run a long race.

Mercy tries to ignore him and concentrates on sucking on her sweet sherbetty Pear Drop. Anyway, it doesn't really matter because Mercy is not under the bed any more. She is on a magic carpet floating around the skies of Arabia, just her and Dolly as the night air whooshes past her ears.

*

Mercy stands firm in the middle of the floor up in the attic bedroom. Her round little fists pressing into her non-existent hips. A deal is a deal.

'Sweets first,' she says.

'I will gi' you dem tomorrow,' he says.

'No,' says Mercy, resolute.

'Come noh, Mercy,' he begs. He looks like he is going to cry.

'I want the Pear Drops. You said more Pear Drops.' Mercy is all of seven and she knows that if you promise something you have to do it. Cousin Bobby might be twice her age, but he isn't going to get one over on her.

'Look here soh Mercy!' he says, holding out his hand. 'Black Jacks is better dan Pear Drops.' He smiles a too-wide smile with his too-big teeth. In his palm are four thin oblong sweets with an image of a smiling golliwog on each wrapper. Mercy likes Black Jacks and Fruit Salads but Pear Drops are the best of all. She shakes her head slowly, her bottom lip pushes out.

'Pear Drops,' she says quietly but stubbornly.

Bobby scowls. Then, quick as a flash, he flicks at her bottom lip.

'Ketch up yuh lip!' he sneers, as he stuffs the sweets in his pocket and turns on his heels. As his gangly legs trip down the steep attic steps he drops two of the Black Jacks. Mercy waits for a split second to see if he notices before grabbing them and stuffing them into her pocket.

Cousin Bobby might be twice her age but, like all boys, he's still an idiot, she smiles to herself. She and Dolly are going to have a lovely time. Black Jacks are chewy and sweet and they taste of liquorice and sugar. They make your teeth stick together and leave a telltale black streak on your tongue, but it's worth it.

*

There is commotion in the family, but for once it's not their branch of the family who are in trouble. It's Uncle Dubbs; well not exactly Uncle Dubbs, but his children. Blabbermouth Janie is the one who hears the news first and relays it to Mercy like it's the Apocrypha.

'Aww...' she says long and deep, drawing it out.

'What?' asks Mercy.

'Aww... this is reeeally bad.'

'What, what is it?' Mercy wants to pinch her and not just a pinch but a *wrinch*, which is one of Sister Norman's especially painful pinch-and-twists. But if she does that Janie won't tell her.

Ruby joins in, 'Stop dragging it out you Bongo-head.'

Janie cuts her eye after Ruby, and takes a deep breath: 'Cousin Bobby's been expelled!'

''No!' says Ruby. 'What for?'

'Well,' says Janie, flapping her hands like the news is just too hot to touch. 'He were caught int' cloakroom touching little girls.'

'Touching?' asks Ruby. 'Touching, where?' But Mercy knows where.

'The school could't hush it up,' says Janie, it's all tumbling out of her now, 'because two of 'em told their parents.' Mercy wonders bitterly if he gave them Pear Drops or Black Jacks?

'Is he going to go to prison?' asks Ruby.

'I dunno.' If Bobby is arrested will Mercy have to go to court and say *I swear by Almighty God?* She doesn't think *she* did anything wrong, but then he didn't force her, she agreed, and she got the Pear Drops, more than once. Will she go to jail? Her head is fried with trying to work out when Dixon of Dock Green will turn up at the front door.

'Mummy says he can't ever come to our house ever again,' says Janie, *'beca' mi ha too much gyal-pickney,'* she imitates Mummy perfectly.

Mercy is mortified, partially because she thought it was just their secret and now she finds out he's been doling out Pear Drops to half of Bradford. She decides that it's best not to tell anyone except Dolly. Uncle Dubbs and his family don't come round for Sunday dinner again after that.

26

Sink or Swim

It's Thursday so it's swimming lessons. Mummy complains whenever they go swimming, on account of the fact they come back all dry and ashy because they don't get enough time to oil their skin afterwards.

'Mek sure unuh cream unuh skin and come back look like somebody pickney,' she grumbles as they roll up their swimming costumes and towels.

Every week for almost a year now Mercy has been going swimming. They walk in a crocodile, two by two up to Drummond Road baths. Mercy is usually really good at learning stuff so she is perplexed that, despite all the lessons, she hasn't mastered swimming.

She walks along the bottom doing furious front-crawl arms. Every now and then she lifts her feet off the bottom, but sinks like a stone, so she goes back to her swim-walking and the teacher doesn't seem to notice. Mercy actually considers the fact that her inability to swim remains undetected to be quite the feat.

On Thursday evenings Mummy argues with imaginary teachers as she tries to comb out hair which has shrunk to almost nothing when wet and become a tangled mess when allowed to dry like that. The only way she can get a comb through it is by wetting it again and slowly teasing it out. She cusses about white people not knowing the first thing about black hair and skin, while dragging the comb through Mercy's hair with significantly more force than necessary.

When Mummy 'forgets' to send their swimming kit, a stern note is sent home saying that physical exercise is essential and could she make sure they have the proper kit next week. On top of the ashy skin and trashy hair, Mercy often catches cold because she is not given enough time to dry her hair at the end of swimming lessons. Coming out from the warm fuggy pool into the cold air is a recipe for a cold at best and an asthma attack at worst.

Today is the swimming test. Mercy is sure she can pretend just like she has done all the other times. But it turns out that the test is not going to be at Drummond Road Baths, but at the Big Victorian Swimming Baths in town, just behind the Alhambra Theatre. A coach comes to pick them up from school and as they pass the Alhambra Mercy thinks of the Pant-O and the magic carpet. *Oh no she doesn't! Oh yes she does!*

The building has the name etched into the black stone in scrolling olden-days writing. The smell of chlorine slaps Mercy in the face as they troop into the building. Like Drummond Road, it is one of those pools with the individual changing cubicles opening out directly onto the pool itself. The noise of squealing and over excited children bounces off the white and green tiled walls.

Changing for swimming is always a pain in the neck, or to be more accurate a pain in the bum, as Mercy's swimming costume, a hand me down from Janie, is too small for her and rides up between her cheeks. Next year it will probably be handed on to Evie if it isn't too tatty by then. Although in Mercy's house there is no such thing as 'too tatty'.

They have to line up along the Deep End. Mercy starts to get slightly worried. She thought the test would just involve doing a width across the shallow end like they do at Drummond Road and that she could half-thrash, half-doggy-paddle her way across.

She can't walk along the bottom at the Deep End. Bevin James is behind her in the queue. It's not that she likes Bevin or anything, boys are not something to be liked; but he is the only one in the class who can draw as well as Mercy.

She doesn't want to get shamed by him finding out that she can't swim. So Mercy comes up with the foolproof plan of watching the people in front of her very carefully. She is sure she can pick up this swimming malarkey from observing them. As each child jumps in, they resurface, kick their legs out behind them like a little frog and breaststroke their way to the other end. Mercy manages to convince herself that seeing is doing, and that by the time she gets to the front of the queue she will, definitely, be able to swim.

The part of her that lives in her fantasy world on the Mercy Step with Dolly has convinced her that it really can't be that difficult; as the queue in front gets shorter and shorter a little voice in her head urges caution but Magic Mercy waves it away. She sets her jaw and somehow manages to convince herself that if she wishes wide and deep and hard enough, then when she hits the water, the ability to swim will infuse her. What would Mummy say? *Oh ye of little Faith.*

Gina jumps in. She is skinny and swims like a fish. Shameem is more dumpy but she too can swim, like a buoyant blowfish. The examiner nods at Mercy and blows his little whistle. Mercy jumps and as she jumps she screws her eyes shut and she wishes. I can swim, she tells herself. I *can* swim. She can see herself wriggling through the water, the wetness sliding off her as she frog-kicks her legs and parts the waves with her hands. She can do it, look at her go. Mercy Hanson can swim like Flipper the Dolphin complete with squeaks and clicks, leaping in and out of the water like a silver bullet. No one ever swam so far so fast. They are all clapping and cheering as she emerges at the other end and takes a glistening bow. *Thank you, I love you, thank you all.*

But all the wishing in the world doesn't work. In real life she swims like a large brick. She hits the bottom and, using her feet, manages to push herself back up to the surface of the water which breaks over her like chemical foam.

For the forever that she was in her mind, she was perfect. Why did reality have to come crashing in like a tidal wave? She tries to move her arms and legs like the kids in front of her. Frog kick legs, breaststroke arms. But she has forgotten when to kick and when to move her arms. She is completely upright in the water instead of lying face down. She goes precisely nowhere before sinking below the water again.

Just before her head dips under she sees Bevin James staring at her in a mixture of bewilderment and second-hand embarrassment. She wills herself to try again. After all, Mercy is clever, Mercy can learn quickly and Mercy is good at everything. But reality continues to poke her in the eye and clog up her nostrils. Even with all her magical powers, learning to swim in between jumping off the end of the pool and hitting the water is beyond even Magic Mercy.

Although this is something of a major embarrassment, she will not make it worse. She will not scream or draw attention to herself. Well not any more than she already has. And given the fact that she has not moved anywhere, despite all of her thrashing, and given the other fact that the whole queue is watching, she has already drawn a lot of attention; and not the adoring kind. She is starting to get tired and also beginning to get more than slightly worried.

She shoots a panicked glance at the second instructor at the side of the pool. He has an implement which looks like a very long fishing pole with a netball hoop at the end. She watches in horror as he swings it around into the middle of the pool and over her head. She is genuinely undecided as to whether it would be better to drown and therefore not see everybody's faces as her limp body is dragged from the water, or to allow herself to be rescued alive and live through an eternity of shame.

She is not given a choice in the matter. The second instructor expertly loops the fishing rod contraption over her thrashing head and arms and twists it so that it tightens around her and she is dragged kicking, (but not screaming) to the edge of the pool. She has been thrashing so much she barely has the strength to lift herself out.

The Instructor has to squat down and haul her out. He tries to get his hands under her armpits but misses and instead pulls at the straps of her costume which causes the crotch to wedge itself firmly between her cheeks, revealing her naked, brown, bottom to the world in all its globular glory.

She might as well have died in the pool because she is dying of shame now anyway. The girl who walks along the side of the pool back to the changing cubicle, carefully ignoring the eyes of Bevin James, is not Mercy Hanson but her grim ghost.

27

Artistic Licence

Mercy trudges home from the Swimming Test feeling sorry for herself, too tired even to go to the library. She liked being six, she's not so sure about seven. Not only did she not pass, but this is her first ever failure in life. Strong words were had by the Examiners to her teachers about putting a child in for the test who any fool could see couldn't swim. Up until then it hadn't occurred to Mercy that it might not be her fault.

She thought she just wasn't the athletic type. She reads books, that's her thing. From now on she will stay in her lane. She's still worried the police might come and arrest her for cousin Bobby and the Pear Drops. What if they interrogate him like the Nazis in those war films in a small room with a swinging light bulb, and he cracks under pressure and gives up his accomplices?

Mercy is sitting on the floor of the cellar living room in her favourite corner opposite the door because it's too cold in the hallway to be on her step. There is something comforting about feeling a wall either side of her and a floor beneath. She only has to keep watch across ninety degrees, so no one can sneak up on her from behind and scare the living daylights out of her. The others make fun of her because she is so jumpy.

She wishes she didn't scare quite so easily, but it's hard to relax when Daddy might explode at any minute Ruby and Janie are playing with each other and Evie and Devon are fighting, but it's play fighting. Evie would miss Devon if she didn't have him to be her enemy. Mercy is on her own; she wonders why the rest of them are so different from her. Is it because they didn't get New Monya and spend almost a year away? They don't know that they live in a madhouse.

She has a little blue lined Oyez notebook in her hand and Dolly in her lap. She is drawing, starting with the mustard yellow leatherette sofa with its dark brown bobbly cushions, the red painted concrete floor and the blue-red Persian rug. Light comes from the letterbox shaped window high upon the wall behind her. The coal fire throws out a crispy, dry heat.

On the other side of the wall she can hear Mummy in the tiny kitchen and smell the Saturday Soup. She knows there will be oxtail, black-eyed peas and yam and green banana and the funny little dumplings Mummy makes that are the shape of stretched out leaves. Sometimes Mummy will let her roll the dumplings and drop them into the pot with a bubble and a plop.

The door opens and Daddy strides in. He's not wearing his hat and his hair curls to its sharp widow's peak on his long, shiny forehead. He heads over to the sofa and the others scatter as he sits himself down. He's so tall that his legs and arms are all acute angles. He fishes in his jacket pocket and brings out his Pools Coupon. Mercy knows that for the next hour or so he will be marking the pools, so she will be able to watch him unobserved. She finds him endlessly fascinating, like watching a sleeping bear. His eyebrows are luxurious like twisted ropes and they can move such a long way from shading his eyes to halfway up to his hairline, creating deep lines in his forehead.

Eyes are deep set and the whites are slightly yellow. His nose manages to be both hooked and flared at the same time; an eagle on the wing, always scanning for prey. Even in the summer he wears a vest, which he calls a *marina*, under his shirt a blue, bobbly jumper and his jacket on top, which gives him a square, wide-shouldered look.

He runs his hand down the list of teams each one identified by a picture as well as words and marks little x's in the boxes making a random pattern on the graph-like paper. Mercy looks back to her notebook and starts to draw what she sees; from the widow's peak, to the frown of concentration, to the ever present cigarette at the right hand corner of his mouth; its fiery tip, a little devil hovering two inches in front of his face. Mercy watches the cigarette burn and wonders how Daddy knows when to tap it on the heavy glass ashtray just before it falls.

She draws the square shoulders and the sofa and the ashtray but mostly she concentrates on his face and especially the slope of his cheekbones which look carved from a block of solid black granite. She takes her time because she wants to get it right, like maybe it will show her what makes him tick. And if she can understand him, she will know what's coming next.

She is so caught up in her drawing that she doesn't see him slowly put down his pools, stand up and walk over to her. It's only when he is looming six feet above her blocking out the light that she looks up. She's so startled that she drops her pen and book.

'Whe you ah study pickney?' he says. His voice lands on her head from a great height.

She picks up the book from the floor and just about manages to keep her hand steady as she hands it to him. The others hold their breath and watch, Evie even stopping mid-kick. He squints at the drawing of himself, widow's peak, brow, cheekbones and all. He takes a deep draw on his cigarette and the tip glows bright red. Mercy is worried that the hot ash will fall and burn her, but it stays attached.

'It favour me to juice!' He laughs out loud, a booming laugh that echoes around Mercy's head and she does not know what to make of his favour.

Mummy pops her head around the door to see what's going on and Daddy shows her the drawing. Mummy smiles and it's like the light from a lighthouse swooping around to bathe Mercy in safety.

'What a clever girl eh!' She gently takes the notebook from Daddy. She looks at the portrait from all angles and then hands it back. Mercy feels ashamed that she has been caught watching him. Seeking his approval feels weak, and what's worse, he has given it to her.

'Ah no fimi side a family dat come from.' He says but he is laughing. Usually when her parents say that they are talking about some negative trait in their children that has not been inherited from them. But this time he's talking about her ability to draw. Mercy wonders if it has occurred to him that it hasn't come from either side of the family. She learned to draw by sitting silently, watching and recording what she sees, and wants to see, on paper. Her Oyez notebook is full of little drawings, of houses with happy families and gardens with roses and tulips.

He heads back to the sofa to continue with the pools, it takes barely two of his long strides to cross the room. It seems to take a lot of concentration for Daddy to decide who is going to win, lose or draw. Devon sidles up, places an elbow on his thigh and leans against him. Mercy wonders what it would be like to casually walk up to and lean on her father. Even if she wanted to, her body would not let her do it. She would shake too much and that would probably set him off. Best to keep watching from a corner with two walls and a floor for safety and Dolly as her silent talisman.

Daddy scratches his head, Mercy is fascinated by the long arm as it reaches up, the curling fingers and the scrape of blunt nails as they rake across his scalp.

'Pickney,' he says 'unuh' come pick grey hair.' He's looking at her. He hasn't used her name, he never does. But he is definitely looking at her with what looks like the beginnings of a smile. She wonders if he really means it and if he does if she should obey. Is it a trap, a trick to pull her within slapping distance?

But what if it isn't? Mercy doesn't understand what she's feeling. Part of her would never voluntarily go anywhere near him but another part longs to be accepted into his circle even if it is the outer circle of hell. She carefully puts down Dolly, the Oyez and the Biro, jumps up and hurries over like she hadn't given it a second's thought. She is an actor playing a part, but a part on which her life depends. She's so far outside her body that she is almost in a trance by the time she reaches him; a puppeteer trying to make her little wooden puppet move like a real, live, girl.

He lowers his huge head. At the front of his hairline just to the right of the widow's peak there are some tiny curling grey hairs, growing out of his scalp like weeds in a tidy garden. Only someone with small and very dexterous fingers can grasp each one and pluck them out.

Mercy is struggling, she can see the elusive hairs clearly, but like someone who has just downed a shot of Wray and Nephew, the sensory overload of being so close to him is almost too much for her. She examines the dark deep shininess of his skin. She could, if she were so inclined, count every pore. The thicker hairs of his moustache encroach on his top lip. The slightly sour man-smell of him along with the mustiness of his clothes tickles her nostrils. It is not unpleasant, just intoxicating, overwhelming. As far as she can remember, she has never spent this much time close to her father; well, not whilst the atmosphere was calm enough for her to really observe him.

She sets about the task of grasping a tiny curly hair between thumb and forefinger. It takes quite a bit of doing to get the hang of holding onto the hair tight enough to be able to pull it from his scalp with a satisfying yank as his scalp goes taut, forming a little tent.

Devon is all thumbs, no good at picking grey hairs so he just sits at Daddy's feet but Evie joins her at the other side and each time they pull a hair they lay it carefully on Daddy's trouser leg so he can inspect it. Without speaking to each other, Evie and Mercy compete to see who can pull the most grey hairs. Little wispy piles build up on each of Daddy's thighs.

He takes long, slow, breaths which Mercy realises with a start, are sighs of contentment. Mercy gets carried away and accidentally pulls out a black one. They don't come out as easily as the grey ones and Daddy says, 'Cho!'

Mercy freezes for a moment, with the offending hair caught between finger and thumb. Evie triumphantly smirks at Mercy. *She* hasn't pulled out any black ones. Daddy goes back to his slow steady breathing and Mercy lets the black hair fall to the floor and quickly finds a grey one to replace it with. He nods. They carry on, but much more carefully now, as slowly but surely Daddy begins to snore.

28

Hinglan

When Mummy is in a good mood, after she has been reading the Bible and singing *Nearer my God to Thee*, Mercy can sometimes persuade her to tell the story of how she came to Hinglan.

Then, they sit cross legged at her feet and she begins. It's so much better than Jackanory. Mummy's stories are best in the winter when it's cold outside and she transports them across the *Hatlantic* Ocean back home to sunny JA. Mercy knows the story inside out and back to front, but that doesn't matter. In fact, it makes it better. It's all about Mummy's sing-song voice. No one puts more emotion into telling a story than Mummy. Hearing her get caught up in telling the tale is like floating off on a real magic carpet.

So here we go.

'Sonny come to Hinglan first and him bredda, get him a job ina Foundry. Then him save up and send fimi.'

'Him nevah have money for a plane ticket so mi hafi to come by boat. De *Belgrade* wasn't a small boat, it wasn't a big boat, it was a helluva (she pronounces it Helleba) boat, big as ten houses, all pile on top of dem one another.' Mercy can see Belgrade making its steaming, stately progress across the high seas.

'Me leff Anita and Francine wid mi cousin-dem, but dey couldn't manage four pickney. Mona was two but Sonia just bruk outta shell, not even a year old. I never did want to leave her. But Sonny seh it would only be five years. We would make big-money in Hinglan, goh back-home, buy a piece of land, build-up house and make a better life for we family.'

Mercy knows what it was like for baby Sonia to lose her
mother because Mercy can remember, deep in her bones, what
it was like when she was in hospital for months on end, all
alone and desperate. Sometimes it feels like a bit of her was left
in the hospital. Mummy says she was never quite the same after
that. Maybe Mummy forgot how to mother her and the two of
them have been trying to work it out ever since, trying to reel
in the cord and reconnect. Now it's more like an electric wire
that has lost some of its plastic coating and the signal doesn't
always get through.

Has baby Sonia forgotten Mummy? Did she get left alone
for months on end? Can a cord stretch across the Atlantic?
Even though she has never met her, Mercy feels close to Baby
Sonia. They would have a lot to talk about.

Mercy has to remember to stop daydreaming.

Now, back to The Story.

One day when she was going to the market Mummy met
Miss Higgins, who was a complete stranger, and they got
chatting. 'She tek one look pon Sonia and seh 'My, my, what a
pretty baby,'

'I tell her seh I looking for somebody to take Sonia because
I going to Hinglan, and

Miss Higgins seh, 'give her to me noh.'

But Mummy said she could only have Sonia if she took
Mona as well. And so, just like that, Miss Higgins took them
both. Mercy has to be very quiet at this part of the story because
if she sighs too loudly, or says anything sad, Mummy might
start crying and not tell the rest of the tale.

The only stories Mercy has in the house are the ones in the
Bible and Mummy's stories. The Bible is way too full of fire and
brimstone and people smiting each other with the jawbone of
an ass. Mercy much prefers Mummy's stories.

The ship was due to leave Kingston at six in the morning
and Mummy had no way of getting there from Miss Higgins'

house. She had to set off when it was still dark and walk almost all night.

'I hug Mona tight and kiss baby Sonia one last time. It was all mi could do fi stop myself from burst out a bawl.'

She could only bring one suitcase with her so she had to sell or give away all the rest of her belongings. It took three whole weeks to sail from Jamaica to England. The ship made one stop in the middle at Tenerife.

'Whole heap of young people, getting up to all sorts of sinfulness pon dat ship. One couple even get married. The Captain did the ceremony. There was dancing every evening but me is a God-fearing woman so me noh go dance. Mi and some of the other Christian women set up a likkle Church and we sing and pray come evening-time.'

One man even died on the boat and they had to keep his body in the freezer until they got to Tenerife. Mummy saw them take it off covered in a white sheet. She tells them about the dolphins that swam beside the boat for miles and miles. She never tired of watching them flashing silver in and out of the water. Did Mummy wish she was a dolphin and could swim to Hinglan?

'I share a cabin way down in the bowels of the ship with a lady called Miss Judy who is a Christian so we get on just fine.'

Miss Judy was going to Kensal Green in London but they kept in touch and eventually Mummy got to go to London and visit Miss Judy. She still didn't get to Buckingham Palace though because London is a big place and Buckingham Palace is a very long way from Kensal Green.

'Mi stomach couldn't digest the food on board the ship because it was spaghetti. The crew-dem was Italian and dey nevah understand me when I axe for milk. Soh me hafi point and say 'La Milka'. After that, every day me go down ah di kitchen and de same sailor laugh and give me a glass of 'La Milka'.

After three long weeks, the Belgrade finally docked at Southampton. Mummy actually shivers when she talks about how cold Hinglan was. It was December 1959 and she was only wearing a linen jacket. She nearly froze to death. When she says that bit, she crosses her hands over her chest and goes stiff as a board, like she's lying in a coffin.

She was angry that Daddy hadn't told her how cold England was, especially as she was coming without a coat in December. There were white people in Southampton holding up signs saying, 'Welcome to England,' and asking them if they needed any help. Mummy needed to get to Waterloo Station and they showed her the right train and helped her buy a ticket. When she got to London she had to make her way across the huge city to Kings Cross to get a train up to Bradford.

'I get on a Tube Train.'

'What's a tube train Mummy?' Mercy knows but she likes hearing Mummy describe it.

'Is a special kind of train in London. It run in some breed of dark, screaming, tunnel underground. Is like di Bowels of Hell.'

Mercy shivers every time Mummy talks about the Tube-trains. She imagines Satan himself with his scaly red skin, horns and black cloak, clipping their tickets and if they've got the wrong one, they have to stay in the Bowels of Hell for all eternity.

Mummy was disappointed that she never got to see Buckingham Palace, or meet the Queen. Mummy loved the Queen because they're the same age, they both had four children and they were both married to tall dashing men. Mercy thinks Mummy is mistaken about that; Daddy is definitely not dashing, but she knows better than to interrupt. Mummy thought the Queen would thank them all personally for coming to the aid of the Mother Country after the devastation of the war, but it seems like she never got around to it.

London was huge and smokey and dark, even in the middle of the day. There were no leaves on the trees.

'Dem all favour skellington!' Mummy twists her hands into the shape of a skeleton-tree when she says this bit.

'Mi tink seh dem all dead or disease.' Mummy didn't know that trees which lose their leaves in winter are *deciduous*. Mercy rather likes the word, it rolls around nicely on the tongue.

Mummy was shocked to see poor white people in London. She thought England was going to be like the movies where everyone was rich and the women wore suits nipped at the waist and spoke like the Queen and the men wore bowler hats and carried rolled up umbrellas. Or if they were a bit poorer at least they were happy and they had lots of buttons sewed onto their hats and jackets and jumped in the air, clicked their heels and sang 'half a sixpence.'

Mummy saw a beggar on the street outside Kings Cross Station. She gave him a sixpence, but he told her he didn't, 'want *your* bloody money' and threw it in the gutter. Every time she tells the story she gets more angry at the beggar. 'Instead a di blasted man gi me back mi money. Him fling it wheh.' Mercy gets angry too. One of these days she is going to go to London and find the beggar, give him a good telling off and get back Mummy's sixpence.

Daddy met her at Forster Square Train station in Bradford. 'I nevah tell him 'bout di beggar and mi sixpence, or him would get vex pon me.' He took her to the little room in the house that he had rented. Mummy was outraged at the ramshackle state of the house and the fact that they had to share a kitchen with four other families.

'Him shoulda find better place fi put mi!' Mummy's eyes still get fiery with fury when she thinks back to the rented room.

'But you see dem did have Colour-Bar in Hinglan most people wouldn't rent room to we. One time yuh Daddy, Maas Dubbs and Mass D tek up demself seh dem a go pub. Di Hinglish run Dem!'

She couldn't believe that all the houses were joined together and didn't have any land around them to grow food.

'And de smoke. Lord have Mercy! All the smoke come out of the chimneys make them look like factory. The first three weeks I was just coughing from all di smoke till my system get used to it.'

Mercy thinks of the adverts for Esso Blue with the song *Smoke gets in your eyes*. Mummy always buys Esso Blue for the paraffin heater in the bedroom.

Mummy's first job was piece-work at a coat factory in Little Germany. That meant you get paid for each piece you sew. Mummy was a good seamstress back in JA so she sewed fast.

'De other Hinglish ladies tell me fi slow down because it mek dem look bad.'

Because England was so cold Mummy thought the government would pay for heating. But they didn't. So the wages that seemed like big-big money in Jamaica didn't go very far in Hinglan. After they paid for rent and heating, bought her a decent winter coat and sent money back to mind the children in JA, they had nothing left.

'Not a red cent.'

No matter how much she saved. Mummy could never save enough to send for the other children. And on top of that, more and more pickney-dem came. Mercy is affronted to be referred to as one of the 'more and more.' She would have been perfectly happy if Mummy had just had her and none of the others. Mercy doesn't know exactly how babies are made, but she is sure Mummy and Daddy should have worked it out by now. She knows that Mummy got her tubes tied after she had Devon and that stopped the babies.

Sometimes, when Mummy tells the story of coming to Hinglan, she gets her hanky out and wipes her nose. Mercy wonders what it must be like to make a big decision like that and not be able to change it. 'Not a day goes by', says Mummy, 'dat I wish I never left mi pickney-dem.'

Sometimes, at the end of the story she gets out the picture of her holding baby Sonia on her hip, Mona leaning onto her leg and Francine and Anita at the other side.

'Cost a whole heap a money for a photographer. I never have money fi hire de studio, so we have de picture take outside.'

Mummy looks so young and fresh in the pictures. Even though it's in black and white, Mummy's skin looks golden and her slim ankles are shiny. But her face is very sad. The vegetation behind them is so lush. Mercy wonders why they couldn't have stayed and just grown their own food.

Eventually the world outside intrudes. The dinner is cooked, or Mummy has to go to work, or it's past bedtime; and try as they might, they can't persuade her to tell them any more stories. When Mercy goes to bed she dreams of Jamaica, big green breadfruit, juicy mango and guinep; foods she has never seen in real life. She dreams of Miss Higgins and Baby Sonia and Mona and she wonders if she will ever get to meet them or go to Jamaica. And if she does, will it feel like 'back home', will she ever want to leave paradise and come back to cold, dreary, Hinglan? She still wants to be a Hippie but she hasn't shared this particular ambition with anyone else since Sister Norman laughed her to scorn. There must be more to the world than a basement in Bradford and one day Mercy is going to explore it all.

29

Jumping Middens

Stomp, stomp, stomp; pause: thud. Stomp, stomp stomp, pause; thud. Again and again. The rhythm of the footsteps is soothing. It's like dancing, just the footsteps and her heartbeat. By the end of the row her heartbeat has grown so big that it is taking up all of her body, banging on her rib cage like the man at the start of those Rank films who bangs the gong, the sound is everything and everywhere. There is no room for anything else. Just footsteps, flying and heartbeat.

During the pause Mercy is airborne, the wind in her face, the cloud covered sunlight in her eyes. For nearly a whole second before her right foot lands, she is free as a bird. Sure footed, the ball of her foot makes confident contact with the large sloping roof of the midden. She feels the shock of the impact travel up her leg and jiggle her insides. Her breath keeps time with her footsteps, a big inhale when she leaps and the 'oof' as the air escapes her lungs as she lands.

Janie is behind her, and Tracy is behind Janie. Mercy is eight, Janie is nine, but her friend Tracy Barraclough is all of ten and clearly thinks it is beneath her dignity to be playing with an eight-year-old.

Stomp, stomp, stomp, pause thud. One after the other they jump the middens on Hollings Road. It is a steep hill so jumping middens on the way down is easy, gravity just pulls them along. The hardest bit is getting up on the first midden. They have to stay out of sight, make sure that they are not caught as they clamber onto the rough soot-black, York Stone of the first outside privy. Then they haul themselves up onto the roof.

Mercy never ceases to be amazed that each roof is made out of one huge slab of stone. How did they manage to lift it all the

way up here way back in the olden-days before they had cranes?
The outside toilets are semi-detached, one at the bottom of
each back yard. Each one butts up against its neighbour with
a gap of around five feet before the next pair start. Most of
the houses have inside toilets now, but not all of them. And
even if they do have inside toilets many of the inhabitants of
Hollings Road still use the outside one. Mainly the men, when
they want some peace and bloody quiet.

If they are lucky, or unlucky depending on how you look
at it, they might land on an occupied midden. An angry white
man will come out and swear at them while shaking his fist
and tell them to 'Ger on out of it'. Once an old man came out
with his trousers round his ankles; his willy shaking like a slug
wearing a white fright wig, as he threatened, 'I'll bray you little
buggers if I ever get me hands on yer.'

Tracy hooted like a drain and said he must have been doing
a number two and he probably had poo running down his legs.
Tracy is Janie's friend. Mercy is a bit frightened of Tracy. She
is loud and 'common' with hair that always looks a bit stringy.
It doesn't really have a colour, it's sort of mousy green. She said
she was a flaxen-haired maiden and Mercy laughed out loud.

'At least it's not like that brillo-pad like you've got on top
of your 'ed,' Tracy shot back. Janie laughed and Mercy shut up
after that. One time she rubbed Mercy's cheek with her index
finger and said, 'it dunt come off does it,' and Janie laughed like
a drain.

Oh, and that time; Tracey didn't actually say 'poo', she said
'shit'.

When the old men come out and shout at them, Mercy and
Janie just keep running and jumping, getting as far and as fast
as they can. But Tracy stops a couple of middens down and tells
them to, 'get knotted!'

Most of the time though, there is no one in and they can
race down the middens, stomp, stomp stomp. Jump, leap
through the air like a superhero before landing, thud, on the

next one. You don't look down when you're jumping middens. Always forwards, always on to the next, slightly sloping, slab of York Stone.

But eventually the terrace comes to an end and they have to turn around, catch their breath and go back up the hill. Most of the time they climb down off the middens onto the pavement and trudge back up the hill. But this time Tracy is on top of the world.

'I'm the King of the Castle, you're the dirty rascals,' she says, staring triumphantly at Mercy, 'Let's run back up' she says.

Mercy doesn't really want to run back up, but she will show that Tracy Barraclough. Tracy never calls her by her name, she just says 'Oi you!' or, 'Thingy,' which Mercy knows is deliberately insulting. Mercy climbs up the outside toilet from which they have just descended and takes a step back, it takes a while to get back into the rhythm of jumping middens. Then she sets off. Step, Step, step, pause; Thud. Janie next. Phew she did it, landed clean. The last few middens are really hard because their legs are tired and they are going uphill, not that Mercy will admit it though. She's going to show that Tracy. Mercy manages every single one. Janie trips on the last but one and scrapes her shin on the edge of the midden. Tracy calls her a big cry-baby and Mercy wonders why Janie is even friends with the terrible Tracy Barraclough.

Tracy sets off running and jumping. Then she gets too carried away. Step step step, slip pause; crash. The sound of her head hitting the cobblestones six feet below is like a mouldy cabbage dropped onto concrete. Not exactly a 'splat' but very close. The heft and the weight behind it makes Mercy's insides curdle.

After Joy this is the second one she has seen. It isn't as bad as Joy because she doesn't really like Tracy much. No one needs to tell her Tracy is dead. Her head is a funny shape and a dark pool slowly spreads from it like the syrup from a fallen ice cream.

She is screaming. Who is screaming? Not Tracy, Tracy isn't moving. Is this scream inside Mercy's head, again? It's the kind of wail that comes from the belly and works itself up though the guts and tumbles out the mouth like verbal vomit. But it's not Mercy, it's Janie, screaming and wetting herself at the same time.

Mercy opens her mouth, but all that comes out is a quiet, surprised 'Oh'.

30

Sisterhood

There is such a commotion after Tracy brains herself off the midden. A policeman comes to the house to talk to Janie and Mercy. After he leaves Mummy wails that they are going to be sent to a children's jail called a Remand-home. Daddy beats them, not with his hands this time but with his belt. Mercy is amazed at the belt-buckle shaped welts that come up on her legs afterwards, they look almost painted on.

They are not allowed to play out for the rest of the summer. There is an Inquest, (Mummy calls it *ah hinquess*). Mercy says it quietly to herself. Now that's a nice word, a pale pink snake trying to steal everyone's secrets. Tracy's death is ruled as *misadventure*, which means that it's nobody's fault. The man who makes the decision is a special kind of judge, called a Coroner. For a moment Mercy thinks he has something to do with Corona Pop, but then she looked it up at the library. But even though they have been ruled innocent by an actual judge, Daddy never says sorry for beating them.

A few weeks after the Inquest, they are all sitting around the dinner table. Mercy is eyeing up Janie's chicken and trying to work out how she might acquire some of it, when Mummy tells them all to be quiet because they want to discuss something. Mercy pricks up her ears. Discussion? Mummy and Daddy have never, ever, *discussed* anything with them. They are told what to do and that's that. Any answering back and the belt might come out. Mercy wonders what is so important that it needs a discussion. Is somebody dying? If so she hopes it's Daddy.

When everyone is finally quiet, Mummy tells them that Mona, their big sister from JA, will be coming to live with

them. Mercy knows all about Mona and the others from
Mummy's stories. Mummy always said she was going to 'send
for' them but it never happened. Every month they send money
back home, and every year a barrel is packed and shipped to JA.

It's fun helping Mummy pack the barrel with all sorts of
clothes and shoes. One year Jamaica ran out of soap. Mummy
said the Americans were starving Jamaica because they were
getting too friendly with the Cubans, and the Cubans were
too friendly with the Russians. Mercy knew exactly what that
was like because at school, when Shameem and Gina were not
talking to each other, if she got too friendly with Gina then
Shameem would persuade everyone else not to talk to her. So
she could only talk to Gina when Shameem wasn't looking. It
could all get a bit complicated.

Anyway, they had to put loads of bars of Imperial Leather
in the barrels. Mercy didn't understand why they didn't just put
in the Jayes green soap from the bathroom, but Mummy said it
would 'look too bad' if they sent the cheap soap.

Sometimes Miss Higgins sends letters and occasionally
photos. Mummy reads the letters out loud to them, and then
later Mercy sees dried water spots crinkled into the thin air
mail paper. She studies the black and white pictures of the
serious looking girls frowning into the camera, with the over
the top vegetation looming behind them. When she looks out
of the window of her house in Bradford she can see stone and
grey smoke. She wonders why Mummy and Daddy ever left
Jamaica. But according to Mummy, times were hard.

'When's she coming?' asks Janie.

'Next week,' says Mummy. Next week! Mercy wants to
know why she only just found out about this. Why didn't
Mummy tell her about it earlier because Mummy often tells her
things before the others. But it's exciting news anyway, a whole
new sister. Although it occurs to Mercy that she has enough
sisters to be going on with. She wants to know why Mona is

coming now, after all these years. Does it have anything to do with Tracy Barraclough falling off the midden?

'How old is she?' asks Mercy.

'She fifteen. She gwine help tek care ah unuh.'

Mercy is affronted. She is eight years old and she can take care of herself. She can wash her own clothes in the bath. She can make two (not three) Weetabix for breakfast, condensed milk sandwiches for lunch. She can boil an egg, and pick the bones out of a fish. They take it in turns to clean the house on Saturday mornings. Or rather the girls take it in turns, somehow Devon never has to do it when it's his turn.

Mercy thinks back to the birthday when he turned five. She presented Devon with the plastic step at the sink and told him it was his turn to do the dishes. Everyone else had to start helping when they turned five but Mummy just said, 'Unuh leff mi One Bwoy-Pickney.' Mercy was so outraged that she found it necessary to kick him when no one was looking. Devon is a horrible little boy, but then all boys are horrible. He ran screaming to Mummy and Mercy got beaten, but it was worth it.

'So,' says Mummy, 'we ha fi decide wheh wi fi call her.'

'What do you mean,' asks Mercy, 'Can't we just call her Mona.'

'Yuh can't just call her by her name! She is your elders.'

That's daft, thinks Mercy. Janie and Ruby are older than her and she just calls them by their names. Why does Mona have to have a different name?

'Unuh can call her *Sister* Mo,' says Daddy. And Mercy thinks of Sidney Poitier in that film where he says, 'they call me *Mr* Tibbs.'

'Sister Mo,' exclaims Janie. 'That's soo old fashioned.'

'Shet yuh mout', says Daddy. And it seems like the discussion is over.

That night when they are all in their bedroom they can't stop talking about Mona. What she's going to be like? Will they

really have to call her by a title instead of just her name? Mercy
wonders if she's going to talk funny like the other Jamaican
cousins and say *flim-show* instead of film and *axe* instead of ask.
Will she like Mercy? It would be nice to have a sister who is a
proper friend.

Ruby complains that Mona is only five years older than her
so why does she have to have a title 'like a flamin' teacher?'

Mummy tells them that Mona is going to sleep in the little
back attic bedroom, but no one ever goes in there because it's
so cold and mouldy because the roof leaks. On Saturday Daddy
sets off to Manchester Airport and the rest of them tidy the
house and get the bedroom ready for the new sister. It seems to
take all day for Daddy to come back, but eventually they hear
the front door slam. They all race up from the cellar to meet
the new sister.

Daddy is standing proud in the hallway on his best
behaviour. Next to him is a tall skinny girl holding another
suitcase. Her hair is plaited in cornrows. Her mouth is hanging
open and she has two very big front teeth, just like Mummy.
She's wearing a green dress with a big sailor collar and a
cardigan with a coat on top and ankle socks and shoes. But
she seems to be shivering even though it's still summer. Mercy
wonders if she is sick.

'Children,' says Daddy, 'Unuh come say hello to unuh Sistah
Mona.' Mercy wonders why he's calling them *children*. Usually
he just says *pickney*, if he means one of them, or, *pickney-dem*
if he means all of them. They come up one by one, in age order,
and shake Mona by hand.

'Hello Sister Mo,' they all say and Mercy wonders if she
should curtsy? Sister Mo nods and smiles her big-toothed
smile, but doesn't speak. She looks a bit scared.

Recently Mercy learned a new word for when people go on
and on about stuff in the past. It's called *reminiscing*. Mummy
and Daddy are at their happiest when they are reminiscing
about Jamaica. Mercy wonders if she will ever get to go to

Jamaica and visit Port Antonio where Sister Mo comes from, and eat avocado pear and guinep and star apple and all the other foods that Mummy and Daddy reminisce about.

Mummy hugs Mona and cries and calls her 'Mi baby gyal', but Mona stands stiffly and doesn't hug her back. Well they haven't seen each other for more than ten years. Mercy feels like she never really got over being in hospital for nearly a year with New Monya. When she came back she was different and so were they, like an old jigsaw where the pieces no longer fit. How bad must it have been for Mona? If there was ever a cord between Mona and Mummy it must have snapped a long time ago. How on earth can you make up for that amount of lost Mummy-time?

31

Industrial Action

Janie and Ruby carry Mona's suitcase up to the attic and she follows them holding on tight to the polished bannister. Mercy wonders what they are all doing up there and whether Mona likes her room, but Mummy seems a bit sad so she says downstairs near her. Later on they bring her down for dinner and she finally speaks with a low melodious voice.

That night, Mercy hears Sister Mo crying quietly and takes her an extra blanket because coming from Jamaica, the back attic room must be extra cold. Mona says 'thank you,' but it sounds like *tank-yuh*. Mercy is going to have to teach her the Queen's English or she'll get bullied at school, that's if they send her to school.

The next day Sister Mo fixes-up and comes down to help Mummy cook breakfast. The food that she cooks is lovely but it's spicier than Mummy's food and it makes Mercy cough. Sister Mo laughs at her because she can't handle hot-hot food. Mercy is not sure if she likes this new sister.

On Sunday, they all go to church and Mummy introduces Mona to everyone.

Sister Norman says, 'what a way she favour di fadda eh.'

Mummy says that Francine and Anita are too old to come now but Mummy is still hoping to get Baby Sonia.

Sister Mo has never seen television before and she has certainly never seen people kissing. They call her whenever there is a love scene and she rushes downstairs. Her eyes are locked on to the television when films like *The Big Sleep* come on. When Humphrey Bogart kisses Lauren Bacall she giggles and points.

The honeymoon is short; it turns out Sister Mo is worse than Mummy and Daddy, well no, nobody is worse than Daddy, but she slaps them for any little thing. And she keeps talking about how Hinglan Pickney is rude and faisty. She calls them 'Leggo Beast'. Mercy doesn't know exactly what that means but she knows it's not a compliment.

Sometimes when Sister Mo is not so angry, Mercy asks her about Jamaica and she talks about the food and places like Dunns River Falls and how this time of year, 'sun ah bun dung country'. She tells them that in Jamaica they didn't have a washing machine or launderettes, they had to take their clothes down to the river.

Mercy asks her if she misses Baby-Sonia and Sister Mo looks sad and tells Mercy a secret. The ticket that Mummy sent to JA was for Baby-Sonia. But Baby-Sonia said she didn't want to go to Hinglan and meet a Mummy that she didn't even know. Baby-Sonia said Miss Higgins was her mother now and she wasn't going to leave her. Was it Mrs Higgins who didn't want Baby-Sonia to leave? After all, she must be like her own child by now. Could you have a cord attached to a Mummy who wasn't your actual mother?

Sister Mo was happy to leave JA and go on an adventure to Hinglan because Mrs Higgins was way too strict. She doesn't say so, but Mercy suspects that Sister Mo is regretting her decision because looking after five unruly children (well four, because Mercy is *not* unruly) is not quite what she had in mind.

Mummy and Daddy complain about the man on TV who says there would be rivers of blood in the Tiber. Mercy knows all about the Tiber from the books at the Library. It's a river in Rome, but nobody wants to hear about that. Mercy has to live in ancient Rome all by herself; Dolly doesn't count because she's not very talkative.

Mummy kisses her teeth and said, 'and is dem same one invite we fi come build-up dem National Health Service. If we go back, who gwine cook dem food and wipe dem dutty batty?'

One day they are watching the news and all the workers are going out on strike. The newsreader says they are protesting about their conditions.

'I don't like *our* conditions,' says Evie. 'And we don't even get *paid* for cleaning the house. Sister Mo should bugger off back to Jamaica.'

Mercy remembers when Evie wanted to send Devon back to the hospital. But look at them now, foreheads together plotting and planning.

'Yes,' agrees Devon, sucking up to Evie, 'they should send Mona back.'

'I know what,' says Evie, 'let's go on strike.'

Mercy feels a bit sorry for Sister Mo but she doesn't like having yet another person in the house who can beat her. The others find bits of cardboard and sticks and they make placards and they paint them with signs, which say, 'Vote No for Sister Mo.'

Mercy watches as they make their placards and Evie gets them to practise in the bedroom walking around in circles shouting 'Vote no,' and waving their fists like the workers on the news.

They go downstairs and eat breakfast with too much pepper on the eggs. After Mummy and Daddy have gone to work, Sister Mo tries to get them to tidy up. They *down tools;* or rather, mops and brushes. They get out the placards and walk around the coffee table in circles chanting; 'Vote no for Sister Mo! Vote no for Sister Mo!' Mercy watches them but she doesn't join in because she knows what it's like to be the odd one out and even though she would like Sister Mo to go away, this is a bit too cruel. Mercy feels guilty about the strike, even though she didn't join in. She didn't try to stop them because they would have turned on her instead.

Then Evie starts another song that she makes up on the spot like on the football terraces. They watched Sunderland beat Leeds in the FA Cup. FA Cup programmes went on all day in the build up to the big match. Everyone expected Leeds to win but Sunderland, the underdogs, triumphed. Evie says they are the underdogs and they will triumph over Sister Mo.

She starts singing;

'Do ray me fa so la ti do
Sister Mo did kiss my big toe'

Sister Mo stands there with her big teeth and her hands on her skinny hips watching them and then fat tears fall and she runs up to her bedroom. Mercy feels sorry for Mona. After all, she didn't ask to come to England to be their babysitter. But Evie says, 'serves her flamin' right.'

When Mummy finds out that they went on strike, the placards are thrown in the bin and they're all beaten and she says, 'hungrateful little wretch unuh.' Mercy gets beaten as well even though she keeps telling Mummy that she *didn't* go on strike. Mummy tells them to show compassion to Sister Mo. Mercy thinks the compassionate thing to do would be to send her back to Jamaica.

*

A few weeks later Mummy says Sister Mo has been accepted on a secretarial course and she will be moving to London and living with Miss Judy in Kensal Green. Mercy is happy and sad at the same time because she's gotten used to Sister Mo and her spicy food, even though it still makes her eyes water. She hugs Sister Mo tight before Daddy takes her to the bus station and Sister Mo says; 'Behave yuhself Mercy, I will write yuh, becau' yuh is di only one ah dem have a drop ah sense.'

Even though Sister Mo didn't stay with them for very long, everything seems different after she leaves. Like a cracked mirror, the family reflection is slightly off. Mummy and Daddy seem to have lots more arguments, if that's even possible. Mummy still wants to send for Baby Sonia and get rid of the lodgers so that she can live on the ground floor but Daddy is dead set against it, because what's the point of spending big-money bringing another *hungrateful* pickney over who doesn't even want to come? Mummy cries a lot and says she would never have come to join him in Hinglan if she knew she would never see her other children again.

All this Mercy picks up from careful eavesdropping with the gaps in her knowledge filled in by Janie and occasionally Ruby. Some mornings Mummy's face looks swollen and she prays for God to 'strike him down ina him wickedness,'

On the news, the strikers walk backwards and forwards on the picket line chanting, 'the workers, united, will never be defeated.' Mercy wonders if Evie would be willing to unite and go on strike again. This time they could get rid of Daddy.

32

Shadow of the Valley

The Lord is my shepherd

Mummy is on her knees praying. She is wearing a pale pink nylon nightie with a wide scooped neck decorated with off cream lace flowers. When she is standing up, the nightie comes to just below her knees. Under the nightie she is wearing a slip, pale green and silky with thin satin straps. Under the slip she is wearing a vest, cotton with thick wide straps.

I shall not want.

No matter the season Mummy always wears a slip and vest under her clothes, even at night. During the day, she adds a girdle on top of all of this before she is ready to get dressed. Mercy loves watching Mummy put a foot up on the armchair in the corner of the room and attach her stockings to the loops at the bottom of the girdle. It is the most sophisticated thing she can think of.

He restoreth my soul

They are in the upstairs back bedroom. It is always dark partly because it is at the back of the house and partly because the curtains are always drawn. They are the same thick shiny dark purple with lilac leaves embroidered into them as they were when Mercy was born in this room.

He leadeth me in the path of righteousness

The bed takes up most of the room, or at least it seems to. It is piled with striped winceyette sheets, blankets and comforters and even more emergency blankets folded at the bottom just in case. Even in the so-called summer in England you can't be too careful, cold could strike at any time. In the corner is an ornate wardrobe big enough to hide a Lion and a Witch in. It has a matching carved chest of drawers, with scrolled feet in the shape of dragon's claws holding onto a ball. The top drawer is always open and the one below slightly more open and so on, until the drawers form a set of mini steps with clothes spilling out like a multi-coloured waterfall.

For his name's sake.

Mercy stands next to Mummy, holding her hand, squeezing it tight. Daddy is wearing his dark grey suit with the big jacket with the square shoulders and the baggy trousers with turn ups at the bottom. His shoes are the brown brogues punched with little holes in the leather. He is the Giant newly down from the beanstalk.

Yea though I walk through the valley of the shadow of death

They were in the bedroom when they heard the door slam. The others had already gone to bed but Mercy had pleaded with Mummy to be allowed to stay up just a little bit longer. Mummy agreed after some surprisingly light begging. Mummy was sitting on the little armchair in the corner of the bedroom reading her bible while Mercy sat on the carpet at her feet combing Dolly's hair. Dolly doesn't have that much hair left these days but Mercy would have continued even if it was just one strand. Dolly smiled, her painted eyes wide and happy, whatever happened.

I will fear no evil.

'Ah gwine kill yuh!'
The front door slams one floor below them, shaking the house like an earthquake.

When Maas D came over to help him pack, the air had been so charged that Mercy could feel the hairs stand bolt upright on the back of her neck. But instead of leaving, Daddy barged into the cellar living room. Mummy stood defiantly in the middle of the room. The others scattered like rats leaving a sinking ship, but, as usual, Mercy stayed.

He shouted at Mummy, saying all kinds of bad words. How it was his house and she should be the one getting out. Mass D stood behind him, holding the suitcase and saying, 'Long-Son. Come noh man.'

But then Daddy spotted Mercy peeping out from behind Mummy.

'Yuh!' he said pointing a long finger at her, 'I mark you off. If I evah see you pon street, I will *run* you down.'

He lunged at her. She tried to retreat behind Mummy but she wasn't quite fast enough. She felt the scrape of his nails along the side of her face. Later, when she touched the corrugated weals on her cheek, she was thankful for Maas D pulling him back, talking to him in low pleading tones, persuading him that no good could come of staying, and it was time to leave.

That was two days ago.

Usually after their rows it was Mummy who took them and left, but this time it was Daddy. But as Mummy always says; 'notting noh go soh'.

Mummy got the locks changed after Daddy left. So how did he back get in? He huffed and he puffed and he kicked the door down.

'Ah gwine kill yuh!'

Mummy jumps out of her skin and drops the Bible. Mercy jumps up reflexively; on guard.

'Ah we di blood-claat she ah change lock?' Mercy's eardrums rattle. 'Dis a fmi mi house,' he roars.

Mummy runs towards the bedroom door, pushes it shut and slides the bolt across. They can hear him on the stairs. It sounds like he is taking them two at a time.

For thou art with me

Mummy switches off the light. Now they are in the dark with just the light from the landing seeping under the door. There is an almighty bang as Daddy thumps the solid Victorian four panelled wooden door. Once, twice, three times, but the lock holds.

'Open the Rhatid door!'

Thy rod and thy staff they comfort me.

Mummy says nothing. Mercy stands on Mummy's left and takes her hand but Mummy hardly notices. Daddy is pacing and swearing outside the door. They can almost feel his breath huffing and puffing. Will he blow the door down? Then there are footsteps on the stairs. He is heading downstairs, is he leaving?

Thou preparest a table before me

Daddy never runs anywhere. His movements are always slow and economical, he's not going to waste any unnecessary energy; except when he is angry. Then he can move at lightning speed.

In the presence of mine enemies

Sound on the steps again; he's back. Crash. Something glints. There is a gash in the bedroom door. Then another and another. He is hacking at the door, methodically demolishing the top of the door with the machete until there is nothing but splinters left. The jagged edge of the bottom half of the door slices at the yellow tungsten light from the hallway as it invades the room.

Thou anointest my head with oil

He stands silhouetted outside the door and kicks open the lower part of the door which is still attached to the frame by one hinge, swinging at a drunken angle. He points the machete at Mummy, then at Mercy.

'I gwine kill yuh and dat-deh pickney.'

Mummy is breathing hard, her bosom rising and falling taking the hem of her nighty up and down with it, but Mercy can feel the shaking through her hand.

My cup runneth over

He steps closer, raises his bladed hand and the light from the hall bounces off the machete. Mercy had seen him open jelly coconuts with it. He holds the whole coconut up with one hand and slices chunks out of it with the other. As he slices, he throws the coconut slightly up into the air and it lands back in his hand slightly turned so that he can take another swipe at a clean part until he has whittled the whole top away and left a hole in the hairy flesh where the white of the coconut skull can be seen.

He takes a step forward. Mummy drops to her knees. Mercy keeps hold of her hand. The cord that binds them has become thin and sharp as piano wire, wrapped around Mercy's neck, strangling the life out of her. Mummy raises her face to heaven and starts reciting Psalm Twenty-Three.

Surely goodness and Mercy

Mercy locks eyes on Daddy like a Star Trek Tractor beam. She does not blink. She does not move. She does not breathe. The essence of her being is focused on him. Her molecules separate and float around the room, seeing him from each and every possible angle. In every single angle his right arm is raised up high.

Will follow me

Mercy calculates the trajectory. If he brings it down from there it will slice into her shoulder just to the left of her neck. Will it be her first then Mummy? How deep will the first slice go? How much will it hurt? Will it burn like the needle when they sewed up her head? What will it feel like to be dead? Will she go to heaven and see Joy or Tracy Barraclough? Tracy is probably in hell so maybe just Joy. No time for daydreaming now Mercy; keep the tractor beam locked on.

All the days of my life

Mercy is not afraid. She has left fear behind and is now just existing from one shallow breath to the next. She can feel her eyeballs drying out but she cannot blink. He does not seem to be looking at Mummy. He is looking at Mercy. Can he do it? The air is filled with the warm sweet richness of his breath. Martell, or is it Napoleon?

And I will dwell

She can feel the battle turning. Her forces are stronger. She doesn't know how or why but she knows he is weakening. But it is not done. If she blinks, if she moves, if she exhales in anything but the shallowest of breaths, the balance of power could tilt to him and all will be lost.

In the house of the Lord

Mummy's eyes are still closed, she is still reciting the psalm in a strangely calm low voice. She had disappeared into herself. Her words are all she has left. But Mercy knows that words are not enough against a machete. She wants to scream, to kick Mummy and to wake her up, get her to talk to Daddy, make him *see sense*. But Mummy is lost. Her only connection to the world is Mercy's hand, a frozen little bird's claw around the branch that is her mother.

For ever

Is he being polite? Waiting for the Psalm to end? Granting a last request? Mercy knows all the words because it's Mummy's favourite Psalm. All that matters is that she keeps her eyes on him; that she stays in the room, stays in the present. But parts of her keep splitting off, floating to the top corner to watch from the sidelines. She wishes that didn't have to happen but there is nothing she can do. She can't take her eyes off Daddy long enough to hold the pieces of herself together.

The dilithium crystals are breaking up Cap'n The machete doesn't matter. It isn't about that anymore. It's about his eyes. She has to keep her tractor beam locked on to his eyes. The room is dark so it's hard to see them. There is just a sheen of light from the bulb in the hallway. The reflection from that speck of light bounces off his eyeballs and into hers.

Mercy's skin, flesh and bones have been burned off by his gaze. Her intestines have fallen into the black hole that is his anger. It just grows and grows and spreads throughout the room like black ink. Mercy has stopped breathing as there is no air left; it has all burned to fuel his fire.

She is down to her last handful of atoms now. Everything else has gone, just her spirit fighting his, while Mummy intones in another universe. Can she hold out? After this she is going to have to start splitting her atoms.

And then, he just stops, like a conductor exhausted at the end of the concerto, the machete-baton hanging by his side. He can't do it. He doesn't have the strength. Her tractor beam held him in suspended animation just long enough. Mercy is just dust now hanging gravity free in space where time had stopped completely, but she is more than he is or ever will ever be.

She floats on her pyrrhic victory. She has been to the outer reaches of the universe, seen the stars and the planets forming. Her atoms drift back together as she reforms. But she is not the same girl she was before. He couldn't do it. Eight years old and she stared him down. It took her entire body, mind and soul but she did it. When slash came to burn, she sorted the girls from the men. Mercy the Magnificent, Mercy in her superhero costume with her superpower defeated Daddy the Dunce. She should feel triumphant, so she wonders why she feels such rage at his cowardice.

The clatter from the machete as he drops it on the floor sounds like a bell tolling inside her head. The little bits of light that reflected as it dropped to the floor were too weak to be any use to anyone. She rips her eyes from his to look down and see the cuffs of his trouser turn ups flip as he leaves the room. The door swings drunkenly on its solitary hinge behind him, saying good riddance. Mummy remains like a pillar of salt, kneeling on the carpet, silent as stone.

33

Rabbit

It's been three weeks since the machete and Mercy hasn't slept a wink. The others make fun of her more than ever now because she is so extra-jumpy. Mummy hugs her and keeps telling her that if it wasn't for Mercy, Daddy would have killed her, she would be stiff-stone-dead, stretched out on a slab. Mercy is ever so proud to have saved her mother but she feels sad that Mummy never asks her how she feels about that night, or what it cost her to keep the cord.

She can't stay awake watching and waiting for him every night but she can't sleep without machete nightmares either. She knows it's her job to look after Mummy but it would be nice to have a Mummy who could look after her.

At school, in assembly they sing;
Jesus wants me for a sunbeam,
to shine for him each day.

Mercy doesn't feel like a sunbeam. She's lost all her shine.

Walking home from school she makes a detour along Carlisle Road, heading for the library. She is so desperate to avoid going home that she forgets that it is closed on Wednesday afternoons. Still, she lingers outside the building. If she stands on her tiptoes she can just see in the windows. She peers into the gloom. These days Mercy stays in the library as long as she can, and the Mother-of-Books always has a kind-but-sad look in her big black-rimmed eyes when she says that they are closing and Mercy has to leave.

It's peaceful and quiet in the Library. No one shouts or throws things or hits anyone. If anyone talks, the librarian puts a finger to her mouth and tells them to shush. If this had been any other day of the week, she would have strolled in through the honey-coloured wooden doors, inhaled the delicious scent of old paper, sat on her favourite stool, in her favourite corner and read her favourite books, about Odysseus and Hercules and Helen of Troy. She would have shown Alexander how to untie the Gordian knot properly, instead of using brute force and just slashing it with his sword. She would have lived in Ancient Greece for a thousand years.

She spent ages trying to work out how to pronounce Clytemnestra, the woman who kills her husband. Mercy should tell Mummy about her. But that whole family, ended up killing each other, which is a bit much. Today, as she heads slowly home, she is Sisyphus, rolling the rock up the hill, only she is strong enough to get it right over the top. She frightens herself silly with images of Prometheus, strapped to a rock for the eagle to peck out his liver. But in her version she breaks her bounds and strangles the evil eagle. She is Icarus but with more sense; Achilles, without the dodgy heel; a Cassandra who everyone believes.

She recognises it immediately. The Hillman Avenger, lean, green, low-slung with wing mirrors on stalks like ant antennae. He is at the wheel in his trilby. His wide-suited shoulders seem to take up the whole of the inside. Mercy's heart smacks her chest and her legs lock like a bicycle with a slipped chain. Her stomach constricts itself around the half-brick as her throat squeezes her windpipe, choking off air. The only senses left are her eyes and ears.

Since that night, dread walks beside her. She is constantly looking over her shadow's shoulder, clinging to the sides of buildings, not venturing near the edge of the pavement unless she absolutely has to. At crossings she stops, looks and listens, again and again like the Green Cross Code Man says. Then she scurries across, a lone wildebeest crossing a river full of crocodiles.

And now there he is, behind the wheel of the Avenger. She is rigid and rooted like a dead tree. Only her eyes retain the power of movement, widening as the olive-green vehicle inches closer. She sees his eyes glint in recognition.

If I see you pon the street, I will run you down.
There is no use in trying to outrun The Avenger.

She is not even a Catholic but Mercy remembers the prayer. If she is going to die she had better get her affairs right with God, like how she plays with Dolly too much and prefers her to real people, or she lives in ancient Greece too much instead of the house on Hill View in Bradford. But surely God can understand *that*.

Pray for us sinners
Now and at the hour of our death.

Now back to the dying; she can almost feel the crunch of metal on flesh, feet flattening, kneecaps split by the chrome bumper. She can see the last triumphant gleam in his eyes as she disappears under the wheels. The last thing she hears is the crack of her pelvis under the axle. It's almost a relief to experience the real thing after all the nightmares. The leg bone is no longer connected to the hip bone. If Joy got to be a nurse in up heaven, she can put Mercy back together again.

But he doesn't run her down. Mercy has to climb out of the deep dank well of living dream, and emerge into the grey light of the present. He drives on by, laughing, eyes gleaming. He keeps the Hillman Avenger on the road and leaves Mercy on the pavement, all turned to stone, except for the little trickle of pee down her legs.

34

Great Britannica

Daddy has been coming round late at night and roaring and banging on the doors. On the third night Mummy chucks a pot of hot water out of Devon's bedroom window and she gets a direct hit. Mercy likes this Mummy, the one who fights back and doesn't just kneel down and wait to die. But Daddy comes back with the police.

'Yes,' says Mummy, slapping her chest with the palm of her hand, when they ask her if she threw boiling water on him. 'Yes mi do it!' And Mercy wants to slap her and tell her that sometimes it's okay to lie, because the water wasn't boiling it was only hot. And what about the machete and him nearly killing her and Mercy, and the time he dragged her out of Mr Aziz' shop, why doesn't she tell them all about that? The policeman talks about assault and grievous bodily harm and Mummy just smiles, a scary smile, like she doesn't care if she is arrested and sent to prison for the rest of her life; she wants the world to know that Ornette Hanson finally fought back.

*

A white taxi comes to pick them up. Mercy has never been inside a taxi before. Turns out it's just a car with a driver they don't know, an Indian man with a moustache as thick as a broom.

He says, 'No no no! Too many,' pointing at them. 'I can't take. Overcrowd. I lose licence!' Mummy has to argue with him to let her bring everyone. Mercy scowls at him.

'Well okay,' he says frowning, 'but cost more because I lose licence.' He won't let her put Devon on her lap in the front, like she usually does, so he has to sit on Ruby's lap in the back.

Ruby is not happy about that. She knows she can't pinch him because he will scream blue murder and Mummy will get mad and the taxi driver will lose-licence. The rest of them have bags piled on their laps, they are all squashed in like a tin of angry anchovies.

Mercy realises with a sharp shock, that in all the rush she forgot Dolly. Her heart drops into her shoes. She can't leave Dolly behind, who will she tell all her secrets to? With Joy gone, now she has no one. Tears form as she twists around to look out the back window of the car as it pulls away from their house on the hill. She waves, hoping Dolly can see her, hoping that she will get her back one day.

'Stop wriggling!' Janie shoves her. She shoves Janie back. A VW Beetle passes them on the other side of the road and Janie punches her on the shoulder and says 'Punch-a-car!' Mercy fumes; she was too busy thinking about Dolly to get the first punch in. She will get her own back on Janie. She keeps her eyes peeled for VW Beetles.

The taxi drops them off outside a rickety Victorian house on Lumb Lane. It doesn't even have a garden; the front door just opens straight on to the street, like something out of Charles Dickens. But Mercy doesn't care because it's just them and Mummy and this time, please God, *this time*, she really and truly won't go back. Mercy is good at hoping. She's had lots of practice because Daddy always manages to sweet-talk Mummy into going back. But after the machete? *Surely* not after the machete?

Mummy knocks on the door and a skinny man with a big belly opens it. He's white like a slightly soiled sheet, the sort of colour Mummy describes as looking like sick-chicken. He has a moustache too but it has very little hair in it. Mercy wonders if he is going to have a baby because he looks ready to pop.

He takes one look at them all and says, 'not on your Nelly. Yer never said anything about five bloody kids.'

'My children is very well behave,' says Mummy, in Speaky-Spokey. Ruby elbows Janie and Mercy and they stand up straight and slap big grins on their faces, like when they walk into assembly.

'No can do,' he says, crossing his arms, standing with his feet far apart blocking the doorway.

'They will be very quiet,' says Mummy and Mercy knows that's a big lie because although Mercy knows how to be quiet, Devon has never ever been quiet for more than a few minutes in his life, even around Daddy. The man says nothing.

'But we noh have no-weh fi go,' pleads Mummy.

'Not my bloody problem,' he says, looking at each one of them in turn. Mercy is furious at this horrible little pregnant man, swearing and arguing with them on the street, like they are so much rubbish. She wants to tell him that they have their own house, and it's loads better than this one, with a proper garden and everything. But he will tell them to go back to their own house then Mercy wishes it was just her and Mummy. If it was just the two of them he would let them in.

Mummy asks him to spare some, 'milk of human kindness.'

'What yer on about?' he says

Mummy suddenly looks very tired, her shoulders slump, she drops the bags on the pavement, kneels down and starts crying and says, 'In the name of our Lord and Saviour Jesus Christ. Do, please I beg you.'

The man looks around, eyes shifting guiltily, and says, 'Alright, alright, just stop yer crying will yer. Don't know why your lot get so bloody aereated.' Mercy balls her hand into a fist ready to hit him but she can't lose her temper or else he won't let them in. She feels like her head will explode and she glares at him, but he doesn't seem to feel her fury.

Mummy says, 'God Bless you and cause his face to shine upon you,' and she wipes her knees and then her nose with a cotton hankie from up her sleeve.

Mercy is worried that Mummy will start proper-praying and speaking in tongues like she sometimes does when God has worked in mysterious ways, and that might scare the man off.

But he says, 'Gonna cost extra 'cos kids cause damage.' Mummy has to pay more rent and she has to pay it there and then on the doorstep, in cash, before he will let them in. People are walking past and looking at them and Mercy feels all embarrassed. She can't believe how many different emotions she has felt in the few minutes they have been standing there. But the overwhelming one is fury. Fury at Daddy, the taxi driver, at Janie (there were no more VW Beetles) and now this pot-bellied, thieving, little pig of a man.

Mercy thought they were getting the whole house, but it turns out it's just one room, the downstairs one at the front. There are no curtains so passersby can just look straight in. It makes Mercy think of that song, *How much is that Doggy in the Window*. There's no furniture in the room either, not even a carpet, just scratchy bare wooden floorboards and one big lumpy mattress. It has a pale yellow stain in the middle with a dark brown border that makes it looks like a map from *Treasure Island*. The fireplace is boarded up and there are shelves in the alcoves at either side. Where are they all supposed to sleep? She's used to sharing a bed with her three sisters but Devon and Mummy make six, and that really is too many.

Mummy gets food out of one of the bags and goes to the kitchen at the back of the house which is even smaller than the tiny one at home. She makes some sandwiches with hardo bread, butter and jam. Mercy helps by slicing the bread.

Mummy says, 'Puppa Jesus, yuh no see poor mi gyal,' as she pats the side of her face.

There's no bathroom in the house, just the sink in the kitchen. So Mummy brings a bowl of water into their room and they all have to get washed with a cloth. There's an outside loo in the backyard but it's slimy with moss and flaking paint

and they have to share it with all the other people who live
in the rest of bruk-down house. They can't play out because
it's not safe. Skinny women with hollow eyes and bruised legs
totter up and down the street. Cars slow down and men lean
out and argue with them. Mummy says they're fallen women
and she prays for them.

There's no light in the privy and it smells of concentrated, stale
poo. The chalky paint comes off on your hand when you touch
the wall. Mercy would rather wee in the yard, but you can't
do a number-two in the yard so she holds her nose, says 'yuk',
and squats over the broken toilet seat like Mummy told her
to. Then she pulls off a square of newspaper from the string
attached to a hook on the wall to wipe her bum.
    Mummy sleeps in the middle of the bed, Ruby and Janie
on one side, Evie and Mercy on the other and Devon is turned
crossways at the bottom, so at least he's easy to kick. It's not
very easy to sleep on a mattress with your whole family and
Mercy dreams that they are shipwrecked like the *Swiss Family
Robinson*, and the raft is sinking. She thrashes about in her
sleep, trying to swim. She wakes up when Evie shoves her off
the end of the mattress.
    'Stop kicking me you bongo.'
    The next day Janie's eczema is worse and Mercy has to
practically suck on her inhaler like a lollipop in order to breathe.
Mummy tells them that they will have to go to a new school.
Mercy is not happy about this because she was just getting used
to White Abbey Primary, reading in assembly, and her very
own desk. And what about Gina and Shameem, they won't
know where she is?
    'I know the way to White Abbey, Mummy,' she says. 'It's
not far. We could walk there, couldn't we Ruby?' Ruby looks
doubtful.
    Mummy says, 'don't cross-question me,' and Mercy knows
that that's the end of that. Ruby tells her that if they go back to

their old school Daddy might find them and Mercy thinks of the machete and how long it would take to boil a pot of water. But then she can't imagine Daddy setting foot inside White Abbey Primary; the School Secretary would send him packing, machete or no machete, even if he brought a signed note saying he was allowed to chop up Mercy.

Green Lane Primary is just around the corner. They have to wait in the corridor while Mummy goes into the Headteacher's Office. The corridor smells of polish and a bit of pee. Mercy doesn't like Green Lane, it's all modern and flimsy and a lot bigger than White Abbey and the kids look scary. A big heffalump of a boy goes out of his way to accidentally-on-purpose bump into Mercy as he passes them in the corridor. She rubs her shoulder, stares at him and says 'Ow!' expecting him to say, 'sorry.'

But instead he says, 'What you looking at, monkey-face?'

'Billy Bunter,' says Mercy, quick as a flash.

He takes a step towards her with his fist raised and a wide grin on his flat, freckled face.

Ruby steps up and says, 'better leave my sister alone or I'll flatten your nose some more, spoonface.'

He steps closer and says, 'You and whose army?' And all four of them, Ruby, Janie, Mercy and even little Evie take a step towards him. He squares his shoulders at them and they all take another step forwards with perfect telepathic timing, like they planned it. Then he looks frightened and scuttles away. They grin at each other.

Mummy comes out of the Headmistress's Office and Mercy can see that she's been crying and wonders what the Headmistress said. Did Mummy have to beg for them to be taken into the school. She hopes Mummy didn't have to pay extra for having too many children. Because if this carries on, they'll have no money left. Mercy just wishes she could stay at one school long enough to get used to everything.

She is put in Standard One, Janie in Standard Two, Ruby in Standard Three and Evie and Devon are in the Infants. Mercy puts her hand up and answers all the questions, because they're a doddle. At breaktime she is asked to stay back. The teacher gives her a spelling test. Mercy gets everything right; Easy Peasy. So the teacher gives her another, she gets all of that right too; Lemon Squeezy. So the teacher takes her by the hand and takes around to Standard Two.

She says to the Standard Two teacher, 'Got a right clever little one here. Going to have to move her up.'

And that's how Mercy ends up in the same class as Janie on her first day at Green Lane. Because they're both new they get to sit together but Janie is not happy that Mercy is now in her class. So Mercy lets Janie copy her on the spelling test and tells her which hand goes where on the big cardboard-clock. Then Janie doesn't mind so much about having Mercy in her class. Whenever the teacher asks a question Mercy's hand shoots up because she knows the answer. The capital of France is Paris. The capital of Italy is Rome.

Mercy is the only one who knows that the capital of Mexico is Mexico City. Mercy thinks everyone should know that because they only just had the Olympics in Mexico. The two men in berets bent their heads and held their fists up with the black gloves and Mercy wished she lived in America and she had leather gloves and enough Black Power to keep Daddy away for good.

The Standard Two teacher takes Mercy by the hand and leads her down the hall to Standard Three. She explains to the Standard Three teacher, 'Got a clever one here, we're going to have to move her up a year.' Mercy smiles at Ruby who is sitting at the back, and hopes Ruby won't mind if she sits next to her. But the teachers have an argument. Not the kind of shouting, throwing, argument that Mummy and Daddy have but the kind of furious, polite argument that white people have where you can only tell that they are angry because they stand up straight and press their lips together and narrow their eyes after they speak.

She hears the Standard Three teacher say; 'Oh no, no, no, Janet; not in a month of Sundays. You're not palming her off on me.' So Mercy is taken back to Standard Two to sit with Janie. She wonders why nobody wants her. What did she do wrong?

Every afternoon they go back to the one room on Lumb Lane. The Library on Carlisle Road is not that far away, she can almost see it around the bend of the road. But she might as well be looking at the Himalayas from the foothills. She dare not go there just in case Daddy sees her, changes his mind and decides to run her down. They sit cross legged on the bed to have the dinner that Mummy manages to cook on the little wonky stove in the tiny, grubby kitchen.

Devon cries his loud boy-crying and says he misses 'My Dadaay,' and he wants to go back home. What on earth is wrong with him? How could anyone miss Daddy? Splinters from the scratchy bare floorboards and six to a mattress is better than being scared stupid all the time.

On the third evening Mercy is looking round the empty room and she spots the corner of something just peeping out off the highest shelf. She gets a chair from the kitchen, but she still has to stand on her tiptoes to grab it. The huge book nearly falls on her head. Bigger than A4, with a hard cover, it is white with raised ribs on the spine and swirly gold lettering. It says *Encyclopedia Britannica*. Mercy knows that the *Encyclopedia Britannica* contains all the knowledge in the world.

A sweaty salesman, with a too-tight tie once came to the house trying to sell it to Mummy. When she said no, he said it was a valuable investment and that she could pay in thirty-six easy monthly instalments. But Mummy told him that she had The Holy Bible, which was God's word, and that she didn't need no *hinvestment* or *hinstalments*. He retreated backwards down the garden path when she started praying for his soul.

The *Encyclopedia Britannica* is made up of enough books to fill a whole bookcase and Mercy would have given her right arm, or at least Dolly's right arm, to have it in the house. But she didn't dare argue with Mummy because she knew that it was Out of the Question, because Mummy isn't Made of Money and it doesn't Grow on Trees.

This is just one book though, the back end of 'R' and the first part of the letter 'S'. It's definitely better than the Bible, which is full of lots of begatting and thou-shalts and thou-shalt-nots, and it doesn't just have one story like Janet and John. It has all of the facts about all of the things, as long as they're in the back end of R or the first part of the S.

From now on, Mercy is a girl on a mission. She doesn't miss the Library any more and spends every evening reading. She tried sitting on the third step from the bottom in the house on Lumb Lane but the other tenants shouted at her, and one even kicked her accidentally-on-purpose as he went past. It wasn't the same without Dolly to talk to anyway, so she had to sit in a corner, next to the fire under the shelves.

She learns all about Russia, about Catherine the Great and Rasputin and the Revolution and how Russia doesn't exist anymore because it's become part of the USSR and that they are *Communists*. Mercy slurps up knowledge like water in a desert. The bare room with just a mattress on the floor dissolves and in its place Russia materialises, complete with Serfs and then the Anarchists and the Bolsheviks. She is shocked to discover that they shot their King (the Russians called him a Tsar but it's the same thing) and his wife and all their children and one of them was called Anastasia and nobody is sure if she's actually dead. She tried to tell the others about the Tsar and Anastasia but they don't believe her, and they're not interested in reading it for themselves. Part of her is glad though because she doesn't actually want to share the Encyclopedia.

Rowing is a way of racing boats using oars which are a lot bigger than the ones in Manningham Park. The most famous race is the one between Oxford and Cambridge universities. Mercy looks at the drawings of the University buildings which look like enormous palaces and wishes she could go there. They probably have huge libraries, bigger than the one on Carlisle Road. She's willing to bet that *they* have the whole set of the Encyclopaedia Britannica, not just the letter R and the first part of S.

She thinks about what it would be like to live in a house with the whole of the Encyclopaedia Britannica in it, with every bit of knowledge that is or ever will be, at her fingertips. From Russia she skips forward to the Sahara, the biggest desert in the world and she thinks about the film *Lawrence of Arabia* and his adventures. Will she ever have adventures? Running away from Daddy all the time is her biggest adventure so far, but she wants to go further than the other side of Bradford.

In the distance she hears someone call her name, but they are far, far away because she is on a camel in the Sahara helping Lawrence of Arabia defeat the hordes on horseback.

Eventually, she looks up and Mummy is standing over her and saying, 'Mercy! Me ah call, call, call you. When dis pickney nose deh in a book she blind to di whole world,' says Mummy smiling.'

She closes the book and feels a woosh of air as the world inside it slams shut.

35

New Start

A lady from the council comes to visit them. She has a clipboard and a clipped voice. She wears a navy-blue gabardine coat, tightly belted at the waist and a matching navy blue beret. Her dark curly hair makes her look a bit French but when she opens her mouth she's definitely from Yorkshire.

She takes one look at the room on Lumb Lane and says, 'Utterly disgraceful!' Mercy isn't sure what the disgrace is. They tidied their clothes onto the shelves either side of the fireplace and made the bed. It's not their fault that all six of them are living in one room with no curtains or furniture and just a mattress on the floor.

Mummy sends them out in the yard to play while she talks to the lady. The yard at the back really *is* utterly disgraceful. Evie and Devon huddle together playing marbles. Janie and Ruby lean with their backs against the house trying to look all sophisticated, chatting about Michael Jackson versus Donny Osmond. Mercy tries to join in but she is bored to tears in seconds. And anyway, Janie does not appreciate Mercy's humble opinion that *Puppy Love* is the most *utterly* pathetic song ever recorded. She leaves them to it and heads back inside. By standing in the corner of the kitchen, she can just about hear the conversation between Mummy and the council lady.

'Why didn't you tell the police about the machete attack?'

'Well,' says Mummy with admirable logic, 'he never actually *chop* me with it.' No, thinks Mercy, he just chopped up my sanity. Scaring them silly with a machete might not be as bad as chopping them but it's still pretty bad. Mercy knows that there are bits of herself that she will never get back.

'And the police cautioned *you?*'

'Becau' him tell whole heap a lie pon me,' the Speaky-Spokey was slipping.

'Not to worry, Mrs Hanson, there is no moral judgement here. I'm just trying to get to the facts behind your current housing...er... situation.'

'Mmmm,' says Mummy. Mercy can hear her voice cracking. She tiptoes away, not wanting to hear the rest.

*

A few weeks later, in the middle of the Six-Week holidays, they are moving again. This time it's right over to the other side of Bradford to a 'council estate'. Mummy says it like it's something shameful. It's called Newlyn Square. Their two-storey house is called a maisonette, which is basically a house with another house on top of it, but no garden.

Sister Mo comes back from London to help them move. Mercy almost doesn't recognise her because she looks so different now. Instead of plaits, her hair is hot combed all straight. She swishes in wearing lipstick and a fake fur jacket and Mummy doesn't even say a word about it. She has finished Secretarial College and got a job in the typing pool of Woolworths Head Office on Baker Street near Sherlock Holmes' *actual* house. She has proper bell bottom jeans and a funny London-Jamaican accent. She says, *innit* a lot.

Mercy asks her what London is like and Mona tells her about Piccadilly Circus and the shops in Kensal Rise where you can buy Jamaican food and go to Blues. Although she makes Mercy promise not to tell Mummy about the Blues because Miss Judy is even more Christian than Mummy and doesn't like her going dancing and other sinful things. She only stays for the weekend. Sister Mo says Bradford is dull as dishwater and she will never come return to live 'back ah country'. Mercy asks if she can come to London to visit and Sister Mo says 'maybe, if yuh good'. And now Mercy has somewhere else to dream about and London is more achievable than Ancient Greece; *innit.*

The Newlyn Square house is very boxy and modern with three bedrooms: one for Mummy, one for Devon and all four girls are shoe-horned into their own room. No change there then. But at least this time they have two sets of bunk beds. The furniture has come from *Govament Hassistance.* Mummy says that like it's embarrassing as well. She had to leave all her good-good furniture in the Hill View house.

The walls are hollow so the house is echoey. Mercy never thought she would miss the big draughty house on the hill, but she does. Here there are no nooks and crannies; no cellars or sloping attics, no huge pieces of carved Victorian furniture to hide in. Lions and witches would turn their noses up at the flimsy wardrobe in the girls bedroom. And there is no Dolly.

But there is one welcome difference: this house has central heating. The windows have double glazing instead of rattling, cracked, glass, and every room has a radiator. No more huddling around the fire getting chilblains. She can sit on the third step from the bottom all day long because even the hallway is warm. Mercy knows that she should be happy they have a nice toasty house but she still misses the house on the hill with the cellar and the bannister with its shiny handrail which they liked sliding down when Mummy and Daddy weren't watching. She wonders if Dolly is alright and shudders to think what Daddy might do to her with a machete if he finds her. She could ask Mummy for another Dolly for her birthday but then she is eight years old now, and that's much too old to be playing with dolls.

It's a long walk to Carlisle Road Library, over an hour, but as it's the summer holidays Mercy doesn't mind walking there and back. She hopes Daddy doesn't see her. If he does he might torture her to tell her where Mummy is living before he runs her down, but she is *utterly* resolute, *innit.* She would never, ever crack under pressure. She feels like a secret agent in enemy territory, breathing a sigh of relief whenever she gets inside the doors and slides safely into a book. Her heart beats slower and she stops the asthma-wheezing. The other children and their chatter melt away as she straps on her sandals, girds her loins and helps to nail wooden planks onto the Trojan Horse. Late at night she climbs inside it with the other soldiers and waits for the invasion of Troy. She never sees herself as Helen or Cassandra, she is always a soldier, a fighter or an adventurer, Athena god of war.

Mummy is at least happy that she doesn't have the big old house to clean anymore.

'Tank God fi small mercy,' she says. But now she has to take two buses to work and two buses back. At least they are old enough to make their own breakfast and get themselves to school. But every evening when Mummy comes home, she looks a little more tired and Mercy is worried that she can't manage.

A new house means a new school. This time they will be starting at the beginning of a term not just plopped in halfway through. What is this one going to be like? Will the teachers tell her off for being a clever-clogs; putting her hand up too much and blurting out the answers before they finish asking the questions? Will she get moved up a year and then back down again? She promises herself that she'll just be quiet and see how things go and hope that she can make some new friends at Newlyn Primary School.

Mercy gets up early every morning and makes breakfast for everyone: scrambled eggs, toast and tea. When it's all done and laid out on the little dining table in the kitchen she stands at the bottom of the stairs and shouts, 'breakfast is ready!'

They all come tumbling down like a herd of buffalo. No one ever says thank you but Mummy says 'yuh such a good girl Mercy,' and kisses her on both sides of her face, and that has to be enough.

Newlyn Primary is very different from all the schools she's been to before. For a start there are lots of Black children and most of them seem to be Jamaican. She's still in a minority but it's a bigger minority than she has ever been in before. Here nobody asks stupid questions about her hair or sneakily tries to touch it. It's bad enough when the other children did it at White Abbey, but when the teachers did it as well that was too much. They pretended they were just patting her on the head but Mercy could tell they were really feeling her hair because you don't squeeze your fingers like that when you are just patting someone on the head.

There are a few Dominicans and some from Trinidad but Mercy knows not to call them *Small Islanders,* because Mummy got in trouble for that with the Dominican lady who lives next door but one.

Mummy takes them down to the Education Office and they get a grant for new school uniforms. This time the new uniforms are *actually* new and not worn clothes that somebody has washed and handed back. Mercy feels very proud in her brand-new uniform. There's a light blue blouse and navy skirt, a royal blue V-neck jumper and a tie with diagonal stripes in yellow and blue.

It turns out that Newlyn Primary doesn't believe in moving children up a year, so Mercy is moved back down and has to redo all the stuff she learned at Green Lane. It's very boring but she occupies herself by explaining things to everyone else in the class, which is a blessing and a curse. She doesn't mind explaining but she doesn't like it that now everyone *expects* her to help them with their homework. It's one way of making friends, but the thick kids are not the right kind of friends.

Mercy counts twenty-eight children in her class and twelve of them are Black. It's obvious that the Black kids *run-tings,* because they're cool and they know about music and clothes and they can dance. It's also obvious from the first lesson that the coolest person in the class is Shelley Lindo. She has short-

short hair shaved close to her scalp, amazing cheekbones and a megawatt smile. But there is something about Shelley's sharp almond shaped eyes and blinding smile that tell Mercy that it would be better to have Shelley as a friend than an enemy. Glenda sits next to Shelley. It looks like they are best friends because they're always heads bowed, deep in conversation about something or other.

Mercy wishes she had a best friend, but she's been to so many different schools that she doesn't really see any point in making friends because she'll have to leave them behind soon, or, like Joy, they die. Life can get very lonely without friends, best or otherwise. Especially now she has lost Dolly. Mummy could not be persuaded to go back to the house on the hill for 'dat *chupid* piece a plastic,' no matter how much Mercy begged.

36

Bully for you

The PE teacher is called Mr Cavanagh. He's short, and a bit stocky with jet black wavy hair and blue-blue eyes which look a bit odd to Mercy. He has a funny accent but it's not as hard to understand as Mrs Kaplinsky's. He bounces on his toes like he's got ants in his pants. Mercy wonders if he ever learned to sit still. If Miss Kaplinsky had been *his* teacher he would have got the ruler every day. He lives in a red track suit with three white stripes up the sides of the arms and legs and scruffy white trainers. He's always joking with the other teachers. He's not Black but he's definitely cool.

When they get out onto the sports field he takes out a large wooden wheel thingy to measure the hundred metre track. Mercy wonders why, as it already has neat white lanes painted on.

'What's all this about, Sir?' asks Shelley, marching up to him like she owns the place.

'Sent our times to Yorkshire Athletics but they didn't accept them.'

'Why not, Sir?' Shelley shakes out her long, lean, thighs like the athletes on TV.

'Say the times are too fast, so they are. I'm double checking the measurements.' Mr Cavanagh makes some notes in a notebook and then the headteacher, Mr Ramsbottom, comes out and signs the notebook. There seems to be a lot of kerfuffle about getting the track measured properly. Mr Cavanagh says the original measurements were right but they are going to have to do timed runs again just to be on the safe side.

Mercy is a good little runner so she is looking forward to it. They jog slowly around the field a couple of times to warm up and then they do some stretches. Mercy has never done *stretching* before. Then they jump up and down on their tip toes and do high-knees. This is proper athletics. Mercy feels like she is practically ready for the Olympics. There is a buzz about the playing fields as they line up. Mr Cavanagh even has starting blocks like the ones on telly.

Everyone else knows how to do it already but he shows Mercy how to use them, with one foot in front of the other and hands splayed out just behind the starting line. Shelley rolls her eyes, making out that Mercy is a bit thick. Mercy clenches her teeth but says nothing.

'On your marks,' Mercy feels her thighs tense up, Shelley and the others straighten their knees and push their bums up in the air so she does the same. It feels funny though, like she's about to do a forward roll.

'Get set,' they all look up. Shelley glances from side to side and grins.

'Go!' Mr Cavanagh fires an actual starting pistol which Mercy hopes has blanks in it, or else he might be overdoing it. She sets off as fast as she can. A good race is important in the making-new-friends stakes. Shelley is not going to be impressed by a slow-coach. Mercy gets in front of Glenda but Shelley sprints off like a turbo-charged gazelle, a shimmering blur of gleaming brown arms and legs. She crosses the finish line long before anyone else and keeps running to slow herself down, stopping only because the race has finished and not because she actually wants to. Now Mercy knows why Yorkshire Athletics thought the times were wrong.

Afterwards, Glenda tells her that Shelley is not just the fastest runner of the girls, even the ones in the year above, she's the fastest runner in the whole school, boys included. Mr Cavanagh pats Shelley on the back, Shelley beams like a Queen overseeing her Queendom. Mercy tries not to look too impressed but fails.

She knows that she still has to make friends with Shelley. If you can make the bully like you then you're safe-(ish), for a while anyway. If you can't beat them you have to join them, or at least get them on your side. But she's still not sure how to do it. Some people are funny and can get the bully laughing. But Mercy knows that she's not funny. At afternoon break she hovers near Shelley and the rest of her gang in the playground.

Shelley says they should do a dance. Mercy smiles to herself, she definitely knows how to dance. Shelly and Glenda start working out the moves to *Baby Love*. There are only two of them, and you definitely need three to be *The Supremes*. Mercy edges a little closer and starts half copying the moves. Shelley narrows her eyes at her and Mercy stops dead in her tracks.

Then Shelley smiles her big smile, 'Wanna dance?'

Inwardly Mercy jumps for joy, but she tries to play it cool and saunters over.

'Course.'

Shelley even lets Mercy put in some of the moves and by the end of playtime they've worked out a routine that the three of them perform. The rest of the playground, well, all of the girls and one girly boy, gather round to watch them do the dance and they even get applause.

Shelley lives in Newlyn Square as well, two streets down from Mercy. About half of the children at Newlyn Primary live in the council estate; some, like Glenda, live in houses which their parents actually own. Mercy quickly works out that there is a hierarchy. The children whose parents own their own houses look down on the ones who live in the council houses in the square. But the kids in the square are cooler and more streetwise.

Mummy says she doesn't like Newlyn Square because it's like living in a *blasted fishbowl*. But Mercy knows that the real reason she doesn't like it is because Mummy used to own her house, but now she has slipped down the *hierarchy*. She warns them not to chat her business to 'all and sundry'. Mercy knows that she means all the stuff with Daddy and the police and the one room on Lumb Lane.

Glenda tells Mercy that Shelley's mother died of cancer. Glenda pats her non-existent breasts with both hands so that Mercy knows where the cancer was, without her having to say the word 'breast'. After that her dad just gave up and *went to seed.* He didn't even know how to plait Shelley's hair so he just cut it all off. He just goes to work, comes home, plays reggae and drinks Mackeson Stout. Shelley and her little brother are Leggo-Beast and can do whatever they want.

Mercy is bored in class. Explaining the lessons to the others can only stave off the *ennui* for so long. PE is now her favourite subject. Mr Cavanagh calls them *athletes* instead of children and although he jokes with all the other teachers, when it comes to PE he takes everything really seriously. He 'pulls strings' and gets them some really good kit and he even drives the school minibus when they go to away meetings. Mercy wonders if he has time for anything else except being a PE teacher, she's sure he just lives in the minibus in his red tracksuit.

Mercy likes Rounders. She is not very good at hitting the ball but she's quite good at catching so she makes the team and gets put at Fourth Base. Shelley, of course, is brilliant at rounders. She's an all-rounder. She can bowl like a bullet, run like the wind, catch the rock-hard rounders ball one handed and when she is batting, she whacks the ball high and hard every time and races around all four bases without even breaking a sweat. With Shelley on their team Newlyn are at the top of the League and Mercy imagines playing rounders for Bradford, then Yorkshire, then England and finally, the Olympics. She's not sure if they have rounders in the Olympics but they should.

Being clever doesn't seem to count for much at Newlyn Primary School. It's all about sport; running, rounders, long jump and netball. Mr Cavanagh even manages to get some proper javelins from somewhere. He says they will only find out what they are good at by trying everything. Of course

Shelley plays Centre in netball. Mercy isn't very tall so she gets put at Wing Attack which is okay because she can run up and down and pass the ball to Shelley whenever Shelley shouts for it; which is all the flaming time.

This week, the girls Rounders Team is playing at home against West Bowling Primary. Newlyn are at the top of the league and they almost always win. But not today. They were close but Mercy never managed to hit the ball so she didn't score any rounders. She is *disconsolate*, she feels like it's all her fault. She hangs her head and slouches to the back. Afterwards Mr Cavanagh asks her if she knows whether she is right or left-handed.

She says, 'I don't know, Sir', which is a bit of a silly answer but it's the truth.

'At my other school, Sir, I got hit with a ruler if I used my left hand.'

He shakes his head and says, 'we'll not be having any of that nonsense here, Mercy,' and she is delighted that he remembers her name.

After West Bowling have left, Mr Cavanagh asks everyone to stay back and do some more practice. Shelley bowls to Mercy who holds the bat in her right hand. She tries to calm down but she swings and misses.

'Don't you be worrying yourself, try again,' says Mr Cavanagh. Mercy can feel herself getting all het-up. She wishes she could relax enough to actually connect with the ball even if she can't hit it cleanly. She swings too soon and misses again, Shelley smirks.

'Right,' says Mr Cavanagh. 'This time, with your left hand. Relax your shoulders, bend your knees slightly. Don't look at the bat, keep your eyes on the ball. Off you go.' He nods at Shelley.

Shelley fires the ball so fast it feels to Mercy like it's coming out of a machine gun. But she relaxes like Mr Cavanagh told her to and swings her left hand at the ball. She misses; again.

She is crestfallen. She's just not the sporty type. But what was that 'bop' sound?

Mr Cavanagh is clapping and she wonders why. She looks down to the floor to see where the ball has dropped but it's nowhere to be found. Glenda runs over and slaps her on the back.

'Wow!' She says. 'You wanged it right out of the playing fields.'

It is only then that Mercy realises that, for the first time ever, she has hit the ball clean, on what Mr Cavanagh calls the 'sweet spot'. The reason she didn't see it was because it flew so far so fast.

'There you go,' says Mr Cavanagh, coming over to shake her by the shoulders, 'didn't you just know it, another star is born.' Mercy knows that she is bright. Everyone tells her that she is clever, but she assumed that there was a rule. If you are good at academic stuff you couldn't be good at sports as well. Well this is a different rule book. Everyone is patting her on the back and telling her well done. Everyone except Shelley.

37

Cross Country

After rounders practice, Mr Cavanagh says everyone who wants to stay on the Rounders team has to run in next week's Cross Country race because it will help with their stamina. He looks at Shelley when he says that and she mutters under her breath that he is picking on her.

'Rubbish,' he says and Shelley jumps because she didn't realise that he heard her.

'Nothing could be further from the truth, Shelley Lindo,' he says as Shelley pouts. 'Coloured kids can run long distance,' he adds, 'you're not just sprinters.'

Shelley turns to him triumphantly and folds her arms. 'We're not *coloured*,' she says, 'we're Black.'

Mr Cavanagh turns almost as red as his tracksuit. He takes a deep breath.

'Okay,' he says evenly. 'What is it you'd rather be called?' All the girls on the rounders team are Black. He looks at Mercy and raises an eyebrow.

She squirms. Even Mummy says 'coloured' sometimes, but the cool people on the news, with the big afros, leather jackets and *attitude* all say 'Black'. She thinks back to the two men and their Black Power gloves at the Mexico Olympics; they got into so much trouble for it but they did the right thing. She doesn't want to upset Mr Cavanagh but, for once, she thinks Shelley is right.

'Black,' she says firmly, biting her bottom lip and looking down at her plimsolls.

He looks at Glenda: 'Black.'

Everyone else says, 'Black.'

'Okay athletes,' says Mr Cavanagh. 'My apologies. From now on, *Black* it is.' And that is the end of it. Mercy isn't sure who has won the argument. Shelley got her way but Mr Cavanagh doesn't look like he's lost. Mercy didn't think children were allowed to challenge Big-People and get away with it. She was sure they were going to be sent to Mr Ramsbottom and get the cane for being disrespectful. But Mr Cavanagh gave in and did it with such style that he seems to have won.

Mercy has no idea what Cross Country even is. Shelley makes out that it's worse than climbing the Himalayas. Glenda says it's three miles of running without a track across fields and stuff and that Mr Cavanagh does it in his spare time. The race is up at Odsal Top where it's always windy. Mr Cavanagh drives them there in the school minibus giving them a pep talk all the way there.

'Just do your best athletes. Nothing ventured, nothing gained. Find a pace you are comfortable with and stick with that. Now you just be running your own race and let everyone else run theirs.' He seems to be at his happiest when he is giving them pep talks. Mercy wonders what it would be like to have a dad like Mr Cavanagh who praised her all the time, instead of one who couldn't wait for her to do something wrong so he could hit her and sometimes the only thing she did was to look at him wrong. It's drizzling and the course is hilly and muddy. Mr Cavanagh has borrowed spikes for them to help them grip. Mercy's are a bit too tight but she doesn't complain.

'Stick with me,' says Shelley, as they gather at the starting line. 'I'll slow down for you.' Mercy is grateful because she doesn't want to trail in last. They set off and in less than five minutes Mercy's chest starts to hurt. She wishes she had brought her inhaler. She hasn't needed to use it since they moved to Newlyn Square and she thought she had finally grown out of her asthma. She doesn't want to have an asthma attack and die up on the Yorkshire Moors. It feels like Swimming Lessons all over again.

But then something very strange happens; after the first mile marker she gets used to the pace. Her chest still hurts but it's bearable. She manages to get her feet in time with her breath and the rhythm of her feet hitting the ground. The pumping of her arms and legs feels good. She is not running from anyone, or to anywhere, she is just running and the half-brick that lives in her stomach feels a little smaller today. The fear that accompanies her most days gets left behind, like she is finally outrunning it. She doesn't need Shelley to slow down for her anymore, in fact she wants to speed up, and see what will happen if she tries to run her own race and not Shelley's.

'Can we,' puff 'go a bit,' huff 'faster,' she says to Shelley between breaths. Shelley glances over at her and raises a disapproving eyebrow.

'No.'

It dawns on Mercy that Shelley hates Cross-Country not just because she doesn't like running up and down hills, but because she isn't very good at it. She can't do long races. If it's not easy, Shelley Lindo doesn't want to do it. Mercy has no idea what kind of runner she is because she's never done much running and she has definitely never run more than a mile before, but she knows that she feels better going a bit faster.

'Okay,' she pants, 'I'm gonna speed up a bit. See you at the finish.'

'Whatever,' spits Shelley. Mercy picks up her pace. She wants Shelley as a friend but she also wants to know how fast she can run. She wouldn't like herself very much if she gave in just to keep in with Shelley. Today, she's had enough of holding herself back just to keep other people happy. The race is hard but she finds that if she simply keeps her head up and synchronises her legs with her breathing she can do it. Her natural high-step helps her to skip over the stones and the bounders.

Mercy's whole life has been learning to skip over stones and boulders while still staying on her feet. She is agile and nimble, like the first Greek messenger who ran to Marathon, although she hopes he doesn't drop dead like he did at the end of the race. She can see Athens in the distance, the sun dancing on the surface of the Aegean Sea; smell thyme, marjoram and lavender on the Mediterranean breeze; feel her sandals on the pale rocky Greek ground her feet become winged and she is flying, almost.

As she runs, she gradually overtakes all of the other Newlyn girls, ticking each one off like a shopping list. She feels high as a kite, Icarus looking back down on the earth. She does not know what is happening but taking long deep breaths feels good, getting totally absorbed in the running feels good.

She counts her steps and every fifty she speeds up, just a fraction, to see if her chest can take it and, guess what; it can! It wasn't asthma after all, it was just her lungs waking up. It takes her over half an hour but she finishes with a bit of puff to spare. Mr Cavanagh is jumping up and waving at her from on the finish line

'Mercy, you're a marvel so y'are,' he says, 'you're the first girl from Newlyn to finish.'

Mercy is shocked that she has done it. She almost hugs him but catches herself and waves her arms in the air instead. Just like the left handed rounders, she has done it. She has found out what she can do by pushing herself. She has beaten Shelley Lindo in a race. She makes a fist and yells 'Yay!' She knows that it's mean to be almost as happy about beating Shelley as running well, but she doesn't care. Today she is going to be mean. They have finally escaped and she won't have to see Daddy ever again. She feels like she is actually at the Olympics, on the podium getting her medal with her Black Glove in the air, waving to her friends, Romans and Countrymen.

She stands next to Mr Cavanagh, doubled over with her hands on the thighs catching her breath, an unfamiliar warm glow of pride seeping into her chest. She cheers the other Newlyn Primary kids as they trickle in, jumping up and down beside Mr Cavanagh shouting herself hoarse. Shelley finishes in the top half of the race but she's the last of the Newlyn girls to cross the line. She looks ill and has a thunderous scowl on her face.

38

Heat of the Night

'Therefore,' booms Mummy, 'what God hath joined together let *no man* put asunder.' Her voice actually sounds like thunder. Mercy is supposed to be doing her homework but it wasn't difficult, she raced through it in less than ten minutes and now she is sitting on the new Mercy Step eavesdropping, which is also not difficult as Mummy doesn't have the quietest voice in the world.

Mercy likes Miss Mary. She is a very gentle woman (which is more than can be said for Sister Norman) although she has never been the same since Joy died. These days she's like a half-deflated helium balloon that keeps trying but failing to get back up into the air, and gets a little more battered and frayed each time it hits the ground. Miss Mary looks after the Pardner Money for everyone, which is like their own little bank, because the proper banks are too *bad and teef and wicked* and they won't lend money to Black people.

When Mummy and Miss Mary get together, Mummy generally does most of the talking. Miss Mary smiles and nods and says 'mmm,' and 'yuh so right,' and 'in Jesus name'. She's basically punctuation for Mummy's monologues. Mummy is cooking, although from the sound of it she's kneading the dough for the dumplings harder than necessary. *Flop*, it lands on the counter, she lifts it up and, *slap* it lands again.

'My have fi get down on mi bended knee and ask Massa God forgiveness.'

'Mmm,' nods Miss Mary.

Mercy wonders if any of this has anything to do with the *nocturnal* visit.

*

Two days ago Mercy got up in the middle of the night to go to the toilet. On the way back from the loo she was presented with an apparition in the hallway. She was still sleepy so it was hard to tell the difference between waking and dreaming. Her panicked mind ricocheted and backwards and forwards between reality and imagination not knowing where to stop. She hadn't dreamt of him in ages, not while she was sleeping anyway. He would pop into her mind when she was wide awake and she had to shake her head hard to get him out.

This time, when she saw him, her body didn't move. But her spirit reared up like a horse on its hind legs neighing in terror. Her heart clenched in her chest cutting off the blood supply to her limbs and if she hadn't just been to the loo, she might have wet herself.

In her waking dreams he is in his baggy, grey suit with the trilby and a lit cigarette bobbing at the corner of his mouth, its red tip the only colour in the picture. She knows this vision is real because he is only wearing a white string vest and a pair of blue and white crumpled, cotton underpants. The hallway is dark. His pale clothing makes him hover like a spectre looming out of a lake. The more pressing, and immediate problem though, is that he is blocking the way back to her room. The stairs are also blocked off by his presence, there is no means of escape. If he was a fire, she would be toast.

She stands there, staring at him. She wishes her brain could work faster, that it was not so scrambled by his presence, real or imagined. Then slowly his lips part and his face creases into the cousin of a smile. The gold tooth winks at her in the darkness. She feels like an onlooker at a car crash, unable to turn away as the vehicles pile into each other and steel crumples and creases.

There is no fat either on Daddy's body or his face so his smile looks like a mechanical manoeuvre. She can make out the muscles, tautening as they slowly drag the corners of his mouth upwards and outwards. In some ways the performance is spellbinding, only trouble is, she does not want to be bound to him by spells, witchcraft or anything else for that matter. She should scream and wake everyone up; but screaming requires working vocal cords.

Then, very slowly, he turns sideways to let her pass. But to do so she will have to venture closer to him. She inhales, flattens herself against the wall and creeps sideways holding her breath as she comes within millimetres of him. She dare not meet his eyes so she looks down. His feet are ashy and his toenails long, like an eagle or what's that other long-toed bird she read about in the library? A Cassowary. With a swift kick he could disembowel her.

She can smell his sweat along with something slightly more acrid underneath as she slides along the wall. She is inching along a mountain pass with a sheer drop to certain death below. Time inconveniently slows to below a crawl as Mercy feels herself drawn into the diamond shaped holes created by the string of his vest. His abdominal muscles are tight and taut like a hunter ready to pounce on prey. Just keep going, it's not far. You will get there in the end. Why does traversing her father take so long? She feels like a mountaineer tackling Everest after previously only walking the Pennines.

It takes a few lifetimes, but she makes it past him and into the relative safety of the bedroom. Hers is the top bunk, but there is no strength left in her legs to climb. She sinks down at the bottom of the ladder feeling the cold steel of the rung across her shoulder blades. She tries as best she can to wrestle her breathing back to normal. But her heart is still doing back-flips and her stomach has knotted itself into a butterfly loop.

Why?

Why is he here? How did he get into the house? She is a light sleeper but she did not hear a knock on the door. Did he break in like a cat burglar? The obvious answer is so terrifying that for a while she can't even consider it. But once her brain

alights on it she can no longer deny it. Mummy must have let
him in.

And what's more, they arranged it so he would arrive well
after the pickney-dem had gone to bed. Her stomach ties itself
into a figure eight. If she had more courage she might have got
up, stormed into Mummy's bedroom, stood at the foot of the
bed, legs wide, hands akimbo and screamed, 'After everything
you said? After everything he did? After the machete? How
could you?'

She wants to hit Mummy, kick her, slap her, batter her to
a pulp. She clenches her teeth, digs her fingernails into her
palms and screams into the emptiness of her skull. Betrayal
burns through her veins like acid. Tears roll down her cheeks
and plop onto her nightie. She feels the wetness seep through
to her skin. She nearly died to save Mummy, she went to hell
and back. And now Mummy goes behind her back? Mummy is
Judas Iscariot.

The gentle synchronised snoring of her sisters slowly calms
her down. She considers waking them up and telling him then
that Daddy is here. That is definitely what motormouth Janie
would do. Evie would tell no one, but she would launch herself
at him like a heat-seeking missile and he would laugh as she
hammered on his chest, fully understanding her anger because
they both knew she missed him. And Devon? Devon would
lose his tiny, carrot-faced mind. Ruby would be wary, not as
wary as Mercy but she would hang back and carefully assess
the lay of the land before sidling up for a hug or a pat on the
shoulder.

She exhales slowly, so as not to wake anyone. She doesn't
need to ask herself what it is about him that terrifies her, but
what was it about *her* that he hates so much?

As she sits there, her brain whirrs and chirps like the huge
banks of computers on *The Man From Uncle*. To her certain
knowledge Daddy has never visited the maisonette in Newlyn
Square. How did he know where they lived? Mummy said she

had a Court Order so he wasn't supposed to come near them or he would get arrested. Should she call the police and tell them he's disobeyed the Court Order so they must come and lock him up?

When her legs begin to cramp she stretches them out, wriggling and straightening her toes and finally she climbs back up into her bunk. She lays watching shadows gradually appear, lengthen, and creep across the ceiling as it slowly gets lighter. At around six a.m. she hears hushed steps on the stairs and the front door clicks open and then gently shut. Mercy peeps out the window.

She sees him open the door of the Hillman Avenger, then he turns and takes a last long look up at the house. Mercy ducks, hoping he hasn't seen her. A couple of minutes later the car backfires once, then it, and he, are gone.

*

'Mi ah tell yuh', says Mummy, 'mi have to use douche fi wash out weh him do to mi.'

'Yuh so right,' replies Miss Mary.

'And after all a dat,' said Mummy, 'him want me fi sign paper-dem.'

'In Jesus name,' says Miss Mary.

'I tell yuh', says Mummy, 'de man come nice-nice me up fi get me fi sign divorce paper.'

'What a wickedness!'

'Supposed to pay two pound a week maintenance for each of the pickney-dem. I don't see one red cent from him.'

'Mmmm.'

'But him ah live with dat Jezebel and people see him ah buy ice-cream fi her pickney-dem.'

Mercy hears a splash as the dumplings drop into the boiling water.

So what Janie had been telling her was true. Mercy is nine now and they have been living in Newlyn square for almost a year and all that time Daddy has been living with Jessie aka Jezebel. She heard Devon and Evie talking about going to see him but she thought that was just their imaginations. Apparently Jessie doesn't live too far from Newlyn Square, just the other side of Manchester Road; far too close for comfort.

The key to eavesdropping is to know when to leave and Mercy has heard enough. She tiptoes back upstairs to try and digest this new and disturbing information.

39

Breaking Eggs

Mercy gets up earlier than everyone else. Sometimes Mummy is already up and in the living room praying, but usually she has gone to work. Mercy loves the silence in the morning before the house starts banging to the sound of her siblings. She can pee and clean her teeth in peace with no one barging in. Then for a few precious moments she can have the living room to herself. Even so, for some reason she still prefers her step.

Now she is going to make scrambled eggs on toast for everyone like she does every day. She pops the fluffy white Mother's Pride in the toaster and puts the kettle on. She checks in the fridge, staring with complete bewilderment at the one solitary, speckled, egg. There are supposed to be at least four. Where have all the others gone? She searches the fridge and the food cupboard but that's it; just the one.

What is she going to do? They have scrambled eggs every morning; they absolutely have to. Mercy makes a plan. She takes the one egg and breaks it into a small bowl, mixes it up with a fork and adds a little bit of milk. If she's very careful she can make five miniscule omelettes. It takes a lot of doing to make sure that they are all equal in size and all perfectly circular, but she manages it.

Then she spreads margarine on each slice of toast. The omelettes look like tiny yellow islands on vast golden seas of bread. She adjusts them so that each one is right in the middle. If she had a ruler she would check, even though she knows that would be a bit over the top. The kettle boils and she makes a pot of tea; it's easier to put the milk and sugar straight into the pot as everyone likes their tea sweet. She pours five chipped mug-fulls. Heading out to the hall, she places her left hand on the bottom of the handrail and her left foot on the Mercy step and sings out.

'Breakfast is ready!'

A stampede of siblings tumble down the stairs like they have been waiting for their alarm-clock of a sister. Devon looks at the tiny omelette stranded in the middle of the slice of toast and says, 'what the 'eck is this?'

'Is an omelette, carrot-face,' says Mercy.

'Is it 'eckers like,' he says, poking the toast.

'There was only one egg,' says Mercy, 'had to make it stretch.'

He sneers at the paltry offering, lifting the side of his lip in a bad Elvis impersonation.

Ruby clouts him over the side of the head, 'shurrup Devon your big bongo,' she says. 'Ignore him,' she half-smiles at Mercy but doesn't say thank you. None of them ever do. Everybody eats their tiny omelette on toast in silence. Mercy feels like a failure. She doesn't know why she gets up early and makes breakfast every day. Nobody ever asked her to, she just knows that it's her job. And today she couldn't do it. Today's breakfast did not cut the mustard.

It took her so long to make the omelettes that she doesn't have time to do her hair properly before school. Her stocking-foot came off during the night so her plaits are all over the place with bits sticking out at the sides and peppercorns at the back.

Devon and Evie skip off in front of her but she doesn't feel like skipping today. She feels the weight of the earth, and the entire solar system, on her shoulders. Shelley runs past her just before she reaches the school gate and slaps her on the back of her head.

'Picky-head!' she yells. Payback time for the Cross Country race, but it barely makes any difference to Mercy as she is already beyond sad. By the time she gets to school, the weight is pressing the air out of her lungs and she finds that she is crying.

At first it's very quiet and no one can tell. Her shoulders just heave gently. She has learned to cry quietly because crying loudly means getting something to cry for. It will be okay, she will stop soon, before anyone notices. After all the things that have happened in her life, the lack of eggs for breakfast is not exactly the worst.

She manages to hold it in a bit during assembly but after they get back to class it gets worse. She wonders if it's like having the hiccups. If she drinks some water through the wrong side of the glass will it stop? But in class, instead of just her shoulders heaving, tears start falling and she sees the classroom all wavy like it's underwater. And even though part of her is deeply embarrassed, she just can't stop it. She knows this is about more than Shelley calling her 'picky-head' because she had no trouble dealing with Tracey saying her hair was like a Brillo-pad

She starts crying out loud. It gets out of control and she starts howling like a starving baby. Everyone is looking at her, Glenda puts her arm around Mercy but that only makes it worse. Shelley just stares, ashamed on Mercy's behalf.

Mrs Jensen, her class teacher, takes her outside and asks her if she's okay. But her chest is full of tears and it's breaking open and spilling them everywhere. She can't stop crying long enough to say that she's okay. But she can't be okay. Someone who can't stop crying in the middle of school is not okay. Even if she *could* stop, what would she say? She can't explain what she feels because she doesn't know what it is. She just knows that there is sadness inside her, like an oil well. Someone has struck tears. It's gushing and she can't stop it.

Just then Mr Cavanagh turns into the corridor in his red tracksuit.

'Mercy is having a bit of a bad day,' says Miss Jensen. *Bit of a bad day?* Her world is disintegrating before her very eyes.

'Go one with you, Miss J. I'll look after her,' he says.

He takes her into the gym and sits her down on one of the long polished wooden benches. The gym is empty so at least that's something. Mercy cries and cries and her tears cry back at her bouncing off the echoey walls. It feels like there are hundreds of Mercys crying out their hundreds of tiny hearts. Gradually though it stops, the oil well has finally run dry. It just leaves her shoulders heaving and her breath coming in fractured gasps. The front of her royal blue school jumper is wet with tramlines. Mr Cavanagh says nothing. He just sits with her until her shoulders stop heaving and her breathing is almost back to normal.

'There now Mercy, any better?' he asks.

Mercy says nothing because she can't trust herself to talk. She might start crying again and if she does, God knows when it would stop.

He stays quiet for a while, then he gets up from the bench and squats in front of her so his head is at the same height as hers. He puts a gentle hand on her chin and tips it up so he is looking into her eyes. At any other time, attention from Mr Cavanagh would have been like basking in sunshine. But now all she feels is like she's drowning in a bathtub of shame filled with her own tears.

She finds it hard to look at him.

'Whatever is the matter, Mercy?

Silence.

'Sometimes it all gets too much. You can talk to me about it… if you want.'

Mercy still says nothing.

'Has something happened at school?

A tiny shake of her head. Shelley's 'picky-head' comment would be like water off a duck's back most days. It's only then that she realises that school is where she feels safe. There are rules at school and even if everyone doesn't obey them all the time, they all know what they are.

'Home?'

Mummy has told them time and time again not to chat her business, and anyway what can she say? How can she explain that all this is because there was only one egg? She knows that the problem can't be just one egg. Which came first; the chicken or one egg? The problem is that she couldn't work out a way to make it stretch so that everybody got enough. Part of her knew it was impossible to share one egg between five. But she is Mercy the Magical, Mercy the Munificent. But not today.

Mr Cavanagh is bouncing up and down on his toes like a little yo-yo. She wonders if his knees are hurting him as he has been there a while.

'I'm here, Mercy, I'm listening.'

Mercy doesn't know what to tell him. If she starts talking it will all come out in one huge, jumbled mess and she will never stop. Her brain feels like it's been smashed into lots of sharp little bits and they are all digging into her like so many splinters. One bit wants to tell him about Daddy and the machete and the half a brick that lives in her stomach. Another is still furious about all the times they ran away and all the times Mummy went back. Why is Daddy's Sweet Talk more powerful than Mercy's love? Afterwards Mummy is always telling her that she is right, that she is clever, that Mummy should have listened to her. But Mummy never does, not for long anyway. And then the one time Mummy fought back, they got chucked out of the house. God was lying; the meek didn't inherit the earth.

She thought they had finally escaped. A new start in Newlyn Square. But then, in the middle of the night, he was a nightmare made real, scaring her stupid and mute and she's back in outer space without any oxygen.

She's trying to get life back into herself but it won't go. It's like doing some weird long division, one into two won't go. Or rather many little jagged pieces of herself won't go back neatly into the box. She can't get the soul back into Mercy and, clever as everyone says she is, she can't explain to herself, never mind Mr Cavanagh, what's going on.

All she can do is stick to her routine. Get up, make breakfast for everyone, stand at the bottom of the stairs. Left hand on the handrail, left foot on the Mercy Step, sing-song 'breakfast is ready,' and then school. Do her homework; do everyone else's homework; do sports; do a dance; make friends, keep the friends; hope they don't die. But it's not enough. None of it is enough to keep herself together. She knows lots of words like 'amphibious', and 'cartilage' and 'Munificent'. But she doesn't have any of the words she needs to explain to Mr Cavanagh what is wrong.

40

No Blacks, no Irish, no Dogs

Shelley saunters into the classroom late, all glistening arms and legs. She has just turned ten but could easily pass for a teenager. Mercy would be lucky to pass for nine which is her actual age. She wishes she had longer legs and honey coloured arms. Shelley's cheekbones are so pronounced that she looks like a mannequin, so much more sophisticated than Mercy's round apple cheeks. If Shelley was an animal she would be a puma; Mercy would probably be a chipmunk.

Miss Jensen is talking about the Eleven Plus and when they are going to be sitting the exam which will decide what school they go to next. Grammar or Secondary Modern. Mercy likes the idea of a Modern school but something in Miss Jensen's tone suggests that the Grammar school is better. But why would Mercy want to go to a school that only teaches grammar? She already knows about commas, full stops and semicolons. She wants to do Art and History as well.

Mercy is sitting next to Glenda. Shelley stands behind them and says nothing.

'Hi Shelley,' says Mercy. This is not what Shelley wants, but she is sick of being at Shelley's beck and call.

Glenda looks up and smiles. 'Hiya Shelley.'

Shelley smiles a wide, and entirely false, smile back at Glenda. There is a short standoff which Glenda loses. Glenda shuffles uncomfortably in her seat and then moves so that Shelley can sit in the middle. Why does she need to be top dog in everything? She is already the fastest runner in Bradford in her age group and the one above as well. Mr Cavanagh is going to take them to the Yorkshire Athletic Trials and they know Shelley will get into the Yorkshire Under 11's Team. At playtime Shelley calls them over to their usual corner. Mercy thinks they are going to do a dance but Shelley had other ideas.

'Notice anything different about me?'

Mercy stares at Shelley. Her hair is still short like a boy's because her dad still doesn't know how to do girls' hair. Her clothes are the same, Mercy checks her shoes, nothing new there. Mercy shrugs her shoulders.

'Oh come on,' says Shelley, placing one hand on her hip and sashaying from side to side, 'there's something different.'

In all honesty Mercy doesn't have that much interest in knowing what, if anything, is different about Shelley Lindo this week, so she says nothing.

'New jacket?' says Glenda. Shelley doesn't wear a school blazer but instead comes in her own blue jacket from Chelsea Girl that is fitted at the waist.

'Had this one for ages,' Shelley tugs at her lapel.

'Trainers?'

Mercy looks down at Shelley's slightly battered plimsolls. 'Just tell us,' says Mercy.

'Well...' says Shelly, cutting her eye at Mercy and adding a last dramatic pause.

Mercy honestly can't say that she likes Shelley, this is a needs-must friendship, because Shelley's friendship also confers that of many others and so must be courted.

Shelley lets the pause draw out longer. Mercy resists the urge to kiss her teeth and walk away.

'I,' says Shelley, needlessly pointing to herself with her index finger, 'am not a *virgin* anymore!' She drips the word *virgin* with disgust; like saying that she's no longer an idiot.

Mercy's mouth drops open.

'Ketch up your lip,' says Shelley, flicking at Mercy's bottom lip with her index finger.

'Oh my God!' says Glenda.

'What!' Mercy is appalled, 'Shelley, you're only ten years old.'

'So what,' sneers Shelley. 'Ruben doesn't care.'

'Well he should care because it's illegal. How old is he anyway?'

'He's nineteen,' says Shelley, preening. Having a nineteen-year-old boyfriend makes her nineteen-adjacent.

'What was it like?' asks Glenda.

'It was amazing,' says Shelley, 'it hurt a bit at first but I feel like a woman now.'

'Shelley,' says Mercy, 'He's nine years older than you; it's a crime.' Mercy thinks of Cousin Bobby. She has done a lot of reading since then.

'It's a crime' says Shelley, mimicking Mercy in an extra-high voice. 'You are such a po-faced spoil-sport.'

'I'd rather be a spoil-sport than a...'

'Than a what?' says Shelley. 'What? Wot you calling me?' She puts both hands on her hips, legs apart, towering over Mercy.

Mercy buckles. 'Nothing,' she whispers.

'You what?'

'Nothing,' repeats Mercy slightly louder. 'I'm not calling you anything.'

'Well you better not be,' says Shelley. 'This is a secret right, you can't tell anyone.'

'Okay,' say Glenda and Mercy together.

'Cross your heart and hope to die,' says Shelley.

'Cross my heart and hope to die,' says Glenda.

Shelley swivels and brings her face close to Mercy, 'say it.'

'Cross my heart and hope to die,' says Mercy but it's her fingers that are crossed, behind her back.

Mercy doesn't know what to do with the news. There are words for what Shelley has done and none of them are nice. Slut, scrubber, slapper, tart. She has heard all of them and more in the playground at Newlyn Primary.

The next day the infamous Ruben comes to pick Shelley up after school. He's short and stocky but with a neat afro and very fashionable platform shoes and bell-bottom trousers. From a distance he is very good looking. But Mercy is sure that the most attractive thing about him is his Datsun Sunny. It's a bit old and orange and battered, nowhere near as dramatic as Daddy's Hillman Avenger, but it's still a car.

'Aren't you staying for Athletics?' asks Mercy.

'Oh puh-lease,' says Shelley, 'I've grown out of all that stupid running up and down, like *pickney*.'

Shelley waves to Ruben excitedly from the playground, then remembers that she's supposed to be all cool and sophisticated, she drops her hand by her side. Exaggerating the sashay of her hips she walks away from them. Ruben makes no attempt to set foot inside the school grounds.

Shelley turns around and waves cheerily at Mercy and Glenda. 'Bye *girls*,' she says. Shelley wants them to feel slighted and belittled, but Mercy doesn't feel any of those things. She just feels sorry for Shelley. Fancy throwing her running career away over a *boy*. When she reaches Ruben, Shelley puts her arms around his neck, but he looks around shiftily and removes them. Even with his platform heels Ruben is barely as tall as Shelley. Would she be interested in him if he didn't have a car?

*

'Now where's Shelley at?' Mr Cavanagh asks.

Glenda and Mercy glance sidelong at each other but say nothing.

'Sick is she?' he asks. 'I saw her in class earlier.'

'Don't know, Sir,' says Mercy. She likes Mr Cavanagh but she doesn't want to grass up Shelley.

After practice, Mr Cavanagh asks Glenda and Mercy to stay back. They look at the floor as he lectures them.

'There's a reason I'm going to all this trouble to get Shelley accepted into Yorkshire Athletics,' he says. 'It's not just because she's good but because the rest of you have improved by running with her.' He bounces on his toes with more energy than usual and that's saying a lot.

'If you know what's happened to her, can you please tell me. Running means the world to Shelley Lindo, this is not like her.'

Not anymore, thinks Mercy as she examines her plimsolls. They did promise Shelley that they wouldn't say anything, but then Mercy did cross her fingers. After practice, Glenda says she has to go but Mercy hangs around, she would rather be here than at home.

Mr Cavanagh tells Mercy that he'd like to enter her for the under-elevens Cross Country. She looks down and grinds her foot in some imaginary dust. She liked the running but it was very cold, although she did like beating Shelley. What Mercy does like, is Mr Cavanagh. He's like a little action man in his red tracksuit with the white stripes down the side, always cheerful, always jogging somewhere or encouraging someone.

'Or,' he says, sensing her reluctance, 'you could try your hand at hurdling. You run with quite a high step, Mercy, it might suit you. Fancy giving that a go?'

'Erm maybe, Sir. How long is the hurdles course?'

'That'll be a hundred and ten metres to start with.'

'Will, er, Shelley be doing the hurdles?' She tries to make the question seem innocent but Mr Cavanagh smiles conspiratorially at her. He can see that she wants something she can shine in.

'Doubt it, Shelley Lindo is a straight-up sprinter through and through.'

Mercy smiles, 'Yes, Sir.'

'Well, no time like the present. If you can stay a bit longer we can set up the course.' She helps him get the hurdles out of the shed and set them up at ten metre intervals.

'Sir?' she says as they manoeuvre the hurdles.

'Shoot.'

'Can I ask you a question?' Memories of Mrs Kaplinsky make her slightly nervous.

'Fire away.'

'Where's your accent from?' She is sure he won't hit her with a ruler for asking, but you never know.

'I'm Northern Irish, Mercy, Crossmaglen near the Border.' But the way he says it sounds like '*Norn Oirish*'.

'God's own country' he adds, 'but not a job for miles around.'

'Border to where, Sir?'

'The rest of Ireland. Should all be one country though, so it should.'

'So it's two countries on one island then?'

'Well that's a long story, Mercy, but Black people aren't the only ones fighting for Civil Rights at the minute.' Mercy is pleased he remembered to say *Black*. She thinks he would look good on a podium with his head bowed, a black glove on his raised fist.

'Is that why you came to Bradford?'

'Yup that's about the size of it. All we need now is a dog, Mercy, and we've got the Holy Trinity.'

Mercy laughs; she can't believe Mr Cavanagh told her a joke.

The hurdles are adjustable and he puts them on the lowest level but it still looks high to Mercy.

'You're left handed, Mercy, so you'll be left-footed as well.'

Mercy laughs again, she didn't know being left-footed was a thing.

He shows her how to measure her steps, push off with her right foot, lift her left foot high and then bend the right leg like a frog to get over the hurdles. She trips lots of times and bruises the inside of her trailing leg, but eventually she gets the hang of it. But even with the bruising and the tripping Mercy is having the time of her life. Mr Cavanagh is the one who makes her stop in the end. As they pack away he tells her about Ireland and The Troubles and why he chose to leave a country that he loved and it reminded her of Mummy and Daddy going on and on about JA. Mercy thinks The Troubles is a funny name for a war; like calling her pneumonia a cough.

'That's the Irish for you, Mercy,' he says, 'always seeing the funny side of everything.'

But Mercy feels comforted knowing that there are people in the world whose lives are harder than hers, and, like Mr Cavanagh, they can still smile and crack a joke.

'Your mammy'll be wondering where you are, so she will,' he says as she helps him dismantle the hurdles. But mammy/ Mummy is on an evening shift and she won't be home for hours and even then, Mercy is not entirely sure she will be missed unless breakfast doesn't appear as usual. Mercy doesn't want to go home. She wants to stay and keep talking about Crossmaglen and the Border, The Troubles, the Republican Army and Civil Rights.

There's a pause. At first she can't think of anything to say to keep the conversation going, and then, before her brain is fully in gear, she blurts out. 'Shelley has a boyfriend, he's nineteen. They are doing it. That's why she's not running anymore.'

41

Demons

Mercy sits on her step opposite the front door. It's not the same as the Mercy Step at Hill View but it's one space she can claim as her own. She doesn't have Dolly anymore but she has books from the school library; it's not like reading in the rarefied air of Carlisle Road Library but it's better than nothing. She can read well enough in the light coming through the pane of mottled glass in the front door.

Ruby and Janie are in the living room watching a TV programme called *Why don't you just switch off your television set and go and do something less boring instead?* Devon is still sleeping and Evie is playing out.

No sooner has she made herself nice and comfy, her shoulder wedged between the bannisters, than someone knocks on the front door. Well they don't knock, they bang on the door till it shakes. Through the bobbled glass Mercy can see the flat of a palm slapping. Are they going to break the whole door down? Should she open it or not? If it had been a nice friendly rat-a-tat-tat, she would have rushed over, done her bestest smile and gone to get Mummy, but this is not a friendly knock.

Whoever is on the other side of the door is not a happy bunny and she doesn't want them taking it out on her. No siree, no thank you. She hunches into the bannisters staring at the shapes as the hand lifts itself away and slaps again and again. She can tell from the outline that it is a man, short and broad in the shoulders: not Daddy.

'S'maddy answer di door!' Mummy shouts from her bedroom. Strictly speaking 'somebody,' includes Mercy and she is the closest to the door. What will get her into more trouble? A telling off from Mummy for not answering the door or opening it and getting a telling off from the stranger? She decides that whoever the stranger is, they are unlikely to slap her.

It is a furious Mr Patel from the corner shop opposite Newlyn Primary. She has never seen him outside the shop; she thought he never left it. Seeing him at their house is a bit like bumping into a teacher outside school. She doesn't actually know what thunder looks like, but Mr Patel looks like he is breathing it. His hair is slicked down from a side parting and he has a fat handlebar moustache so big it should be paying rent. He wears a white shirt rolled up at the sleeves and his belly hangs over his trousers. On his feet are brown plastic sandals instead of shoes. The whites of his eyes are actually red.

'Where the mother?' he asks.

Mercy stares wide-eyed at him.

'The mother!'

Mercy slowly backs away from the door, she shouts over her shoulder, 'Mummy, Mr Patel is here.'

'Who?' Mummy's voice trills back down the stairs.

'Mr Patel from the corner shop.'

'Mi ah come.' Mummy comes downstairs wiping her hands on a towel. She is wearing her blue checked housecoat over her day clothes and furry yellow heeled slippers. Her hair is tied back in a bun but wisps of it float out forming a halo around her face. No matter what she wears Mummy always look beautiful.

'Is what?' she asks Mr Patel.

'Thief. He thieving from my shop. He thinking I don't see.'

'Whe' yuh a chat bout?' Mummy frowns.

'The boy, he take sweet from my shop, many-many time.'

'What? Who? *My* Devon?'

So that's where Devon got the sweets from. Mercy had seen him furtively chomping away and refusing to share his bounty.

'Your boy, he taking sweets, I see where he running to.'

'Devon!' roared Mummy. 'Fetch yuh backside down yasso.'

Mercy sits back on her step. This is going to be interesting, she couldn't be happier if she had popcorn.

Devon clomps slowly down the steps, still in his pyjamas. His eyes get so wide when he sees Mr Patel that Mercy thinks they might roll clean out of his head.

Mercy folds the book on her lap so that she can get a better view of the proceedings.

'Did yuh teef from Patel Shop?'

Devon shakes his head but does not meet Mummy's eyes.

'*Deh*-von?' asks Mummy.

He hangs his head but says nothing.

'I gwine axe yuh *one* last time. Did you tek anything from Patel Shop?'

Devon looks up, his eyes brimming with unfallen tears. As he nods they trickle down his cheeks.

'Ah wheh you tek?'

He pushes his hands into his pyjama pockets, brings out a bunch of empty sweet wrappers and offers them to her like a sacrifice.

'Stolen!' says Sherlock Patel. 'You pay for this. You must pay.'

Mummy looks at Devon, and shakes her head slowly, disappointment dripping down onto her One Bwoy Pickney. Then she looks back at Mr Patel. 'Is how much?'

'I not sure what he take, but you pay me five new pence,' he says, obviously pleased with his detective skills. 'And he ban from my shop,' he adds, pointing at Devon. 'He not come in ever again.'

'Alright, alright,' says Mummy. She reaches into the pocket of her overalls and pulls out some coins. She peers at them, she's annoyed by this new decimalisation, but eventually she identifies the right ones and gives Mr Patel a five new-pence piece.

His fingers snap shut over the coin and he huffs and stomps off. 'He banned' he shouts over his shoulder.

Mercy smiles to herself, she wishes Dolly was here to witness the triumph. Devon's going to be in *big* trouble now. Mummy turns to Devon. He is going to get a good hiding and he deserves it too; especially for not sharing the sweets.

Mummy squats down so that her face is level with Devon's. His shoulders are heaving, he's putting on a proper show of contrition now, with tears and snot and everything.

And the Oscar goes to....

'Devon,' Mummy says softly, looking deep into his eyes, 'Is why you must make the Devil use you soh?'

Devon's shoulders hunch. 'I - I don't know Mummy.'

What? Mercy is apoplectic. The *Devil?* She's going to let him get away with blaming it on the Devil. If it was one of the girls she would be telling them in graphic detail about the hiding they would shortly be receiving. 'I gwine strip of de black skin left the de white. I gwine tan yuh behind. I gwine wring yuh lip till blood drop tip-tip-tip.' But Devon. Nothing, not even a slap on the side of his long carrot-face. He gets to blame it on the flamin' Devil?

'The path of the righteous man is beset on all sides,' says Mummy, still staring into Devon's eyes.

'I'm (sniff) sorry Mummy,' says Devon, tears still falling. 'I won't let the Devil use me again.'

Mercy can't help herself, she blurts out, 'Aren't you going to beat him, Mummy?'

Mummy swivels around, she has forgotten that Mercy is watching.

She places her fists on her hips, 'Yuh tink seh yuh is Big Woman ina disya house?'

Mercy says nothing, She turns and stomps upstairs clutching her book to her chest as Mummy heads towards the kitchen, pulling Devon behind her. The cord vibrates like an out of tune violin. Is it made of catgut? Mercy looks down at them over the bannister and thinks about spitting on him, but it might hit Mummy and then she'd be in real trouble. Devon

looks up, grins through his painted-on tears and sticks his
tongue out at her.

*

Mercy is in bed on the top bunk. She needs to pee. But she
doesn't like getting out of bed, especially not in the middle of
the night, not anymore. Her bladder, however, has other plans
and after holding it in for as long as she can she climbs down
and heads to the loo.

She can hear singing coming from downstairs. It's rather
late for Mummy to be having a prayer meeting but you never
know when the spirit might take her. She passes Devon's
bedroom door. It's wide open and she can see from the
streetlight filtering through the curtains that he is not in his
room.

She makes sure to tear the toilet roll exactly on the
perforations, just two squares; although to tell the truth Izal
toilet paper is the absolute worst kind of paper, worse than
newspaper, it hardly absorbs anything, you can easily end up
with pee running down your legs. She wishes Mummy would
buy Andrex, and perhaps a puppy as well. (*Mi noh have money
fi feed dawg!*)

Whatever is going on downstairs is getting louder. Should
she ignore it and go back to bed or go see what was going
on? She knows she should go back to bed but this is way too
interesting. She wants to be the one to tell the others in the
morning that she has seen something which they haven't.
The opportunity to be the purveyor of news is irresistible.
She tiptoes downstairs. She can hear women's voices. The
door to the living room is open. Mummy is there, along with
Sister Norman, Sister Wallwin and Sister Morrison. They are
standing in a circle; in the middle, Devon is kneeling on the rug
in his pyjamas.

Sister Norman still wears her bottle green coat and matching
hat. Her meaty hands are on his shoulders. It's hard to tell if she

is praying for him or holding him down. Sister Wallwin wears a navy gabardine coat with a bright red beret. When they are together Sister Norman and Sister Wallwin remind Mercy of Laurel and Hardy.

Mummy is barefoot, still in her overalls, speaking in tongues. 'Shan-talamah,' she says, 'Rekeh Shekeh, Hilosheh.'

Now Sister Norman has one hand on Devon's head, the other is holding up a Bible. As she prays, she trembles, and so does Devon's head.

'Thou art the Alpha and Omega, the beginning and the end,' she says, 'We beg of thee, cast out the Demon of Darkness from this thy young servant. Let your light and spirit enter his soul.'

Sister Wallwin hops up and down and saying, 'Get thee behind me Satan, Get thee *behind* me.'

Devon starts wriggling like he's trying to get away. 'I rebuke you Satan,' says Sister Norman gripping his shoulder tighter.

Devon tries to get up but in doing so he trips Sister Norman who loses her balance and falls right on top of him.

'Ouff!' Mercy hears every last drop of air escape Devon's lungs as he is flattened by a church-lady approximately five times his size.

When he manages to take another breath he yells, 'Gerroffa me!' But they know that is just the Demon talking. They all join in to hold him down. Mummy holds one leg, Sister Morrison the other; Sister Wallwin pins his arms, while Sister Norman stays laying flat out across his middle.

'And Jacob wrestled with the Demon all night,' Sister Wallwin shouts. They pray and sing and continue to speak in tongues. It is clear to Mercy that they are not going to let him up until every last one of his Thieving Demons has been cast out.

'Demon of Darkness,' says Mummy, 'I command thee to depart this child.' Mercy sits and watches for a little while more. It's not quite what she had in mind, but justice, of sorts, is being done. Then she starts to worry that they might spot her. She is fairly sure that she doesn't have any Demons inside her, but they might find some she doesn't know about. Is there a Demon that makes you hate your little brother? She wonders how long it will take to cast out all of Devon's Demons; he probably has quite a few. Mercy is not sure if she believes in Demons but the way Devon is carrying on, well, you never know.

Why doesn't he have the sense to just keep quiet and pretend they're gone? Or does he really have Demons that are refusing to leave? Mercy remembers one of Pastor Foster's sermons about Jesus casting Demons out of people and into a herd of swine. She doubts if Mummy has any spare pigs hidden about the house, but with Mummy you never know. She tiptoes back upstairs.

42

Mysterious Ways

Devon and his Demons recover pretty quickly and they're soon back to their usual annoying selves. When he's not jumping off the top of the wardrobe onto the bed pretending to be Batman, he loves riding around Newlyn Square on his red Chopper. It has long high handlebars, a big back wheel and a small front one, a bit like the Penny Farthings Mercy has been studying in History.

He's the talk of the town as not many of the children on the estate have bikes, and those that do just have ordinary bikes where both wheels are the same size. Devon thinks he is actually the Lord God Almighty because he has a flamin' Chopper.

When Mercy asked for new shoes, Mummy said she wasn't made of money. When Janie asked for a piano, Mummy said money didn't grow on trees. But when her One Bwoy Pickney wants a Chopper... Mercy knows that life isn't always fair, but she thought parents were supposed to make it a little bit fairer, not less. If she had an axe she would chop that Chopper to tiny little pieces.

It's the summer holidays and Mercy has been at Newlyn Primary for a full school year. She can't remember when she last stayed at the same school for a whole year. Last year Ruby started at Carfax Secondary. She came home every evening in her uniform, grey skirt, burgundy jumper and a striped burgundy and blue tie. She told them about subjects like English Literature and Economics, and Mercy was transformed back to four years old when she was desperate to go to school. Apart from P.E., Newlyn Primary School is getting pretty boring because she already knows everything. Shelley doesn't come to school anymore; Glenda says she has been taken into care.

Care? Mercy thinks that sounds fantastic and she wonders if she too can be taken into care. It would be marvellous to have someone whose job is just to care for her. They might buy books and toys for her, and a replacement for Dolly. She daydreams about having a bedroom all to herself. She knows that Mummy cares but her love has to be split five ways and there really isn't enough for all of them.

Now they have gotten away from Daddy, Mercy thinks life should be better for everybody. But Mummy seems sadder than ever. It's like she misses arguing with him; like she's more righteous when she is fighting with a real-life Devil. Could it be that in order for her to be a Saint she needs a Sinner.

She says the problem is the neighbours in Newlyn Square. They play music at all hours and they are a Godless People. As well as taking two buses to work and back every day, Mummy makes them all take two buses back to her old church on the other side of Bradford every Sunday, but thankfully, only for the four-hour morning service. On Saturdays when she is not working, Mummy joins Sister Norman, Pastor Foster and some of the other Church people to preach to the heathen in the City Centre. Mercy is mortified when Glenda tells her that she saw Mummy in Forster Square telling people to repent and be baptised because the end of the world is nigh.

Mercy is still getting up every morning and making breakfast for everybody and she feels like she is getting just as tired as Mummy. Although all six of them live in the house it feels like there are six separate little lives all wrapped up in their separate little boxes of bubble wrap.

Evie is the Cock of Year Four on account of fighting like a Tasmanian Devil; she's the Shelley of her year. Janie is everybody's best friend and Ruby, who was never much of a talker anyway, is wrapped up in being at Secondary School.

Now she's twelve, all she talks about is boys and clothes. She buys *Jackie* magazine with the money from her paper round.

Devon is running around like Leggo Beast with the boys from the estate. Every day there's a fight of some kind and sometimes he comes home with cuts, bruises and stories about how you should see what he did to other kid. One day he comes home minus the Chopper. He says that some of the white boys jumped him and took it off him. Mummy is not having that. She bought the Chopper on Hire-Purchase and she is still paying it off, so she gathers up her biggest Bible and they all head off to the house of Fergal, the Chopper-thief. Mercy knew something like this was going to happen sooner or later; getting Devon a Chopper was just *tempting fate*.

All of them gather outside Fergal's house. Mummy knocks on the door and explains to his mother in her best Speaky-Spoke, that Fergal has taken Devon's bike. Fergal's mum, who is skinny and sallow, with two of her front teeth missing, tells Mummy to, 'fuck off out of it'.

'We should call the police,' says Mercy, 'that's theft.'

'Yeah,' says Devon, 'like *they're* gonna do owt about it.'

Mummy starts to pray and sing in front of Fergal's house. She reads verses from the Big-Bible about how the wicked shall not prosper.

Fergal's mum plays loud music to drown her out. But Mummy goes home and gets the loud hailer that she uses when she is preaching in the town centre to convert the heathen. Mercy thinks Mummy has gone stark raving mad, but she dare not leave her alone. So along with Ruby and Janie they stay.

She starts singing;
'When we all meet Jesus
We will stomp and shout for victory.'

At first Mercy is really embarrassed but after a while they decide to join in with her. Janie is really good at singing so she harmonises with Mummy and she even brings a tambourine.

And before Mercy knows it they are all stomping and shouting with gusto for victory outside Fergal's house.

Fergal's mum says she's going to call the coppers.

Mummy says, 'Yes, you call them. Because we have God on our side.' She starts singing;

Joshua fought the battle of Jericho
Jericho, Jericho
Joshua fought the battle of Jericho
And the walls came tumbling down.'

Joshua and Jericho is one of Mercy's favourite Bible stories. She likes the idea that just by marching up and down they can get walls to fall. She imagines what it would be like to know that if you want something badly enough, the strength of your wanting could make it happen.

After only two-and-a-half hours of praying and singing, Fergal brings the bike out of the side gate. He says he was only having a laugh and there was no need for Devon to bring his 'mad mum' round.

Mummy says, 'God Bless you my *chile*. The Lord moves in mysterious ways, his wonders to perform.'

Devon grabs the Chopper and punches Fergal square on the nose. 'Yeah', he says as Fergal staggers backwards, 'mysterious ways.' After that Devon can't ride the Chopper outside the house any more as Fergal and his mates might jump him again. He tries to ride it around the living room and gets into a big fight with Evie after he runs it over her foot for the third time. Evie doesn't mess about, she punctures the tyres with the big kitchen knife and threatens to puncture Devon too. Then she gets a hammer and bashes in the handlebars, So the dead and disfigured Chopper lives under the stairs and Devon bawls like his best friend just died.

Mummy says that she has had enough of Newlyn Square and she is gonna get her family away from this cussed place, 'so help me Massa God.' Mercy hopes that they don't have to move again because even though the estate is annoying and they have to run home super-fast when the National Front Boys invade in their bovver boots, she has made friends and she would really like to stay put this time.

The next week Mercy overhears Mummy talking to Miss Mary. She tells her that after months and months of *lyad-lawyer* foolishness, she is going to get her share of the money from the sale of Hill View. She will put it towards buying a new house, then she won't have to live, 'in disya den of iniquity.'

Mercy is devastated at the news but part of her is pleased that she is the only one who knows; for now anyway. Apparently the Council Lady who visited them in the Encyclopaedia Britannica house on Lumb Lane told Mummy that she could have a three-bed house straight away or wait for a four bedroomed house but they didn't know how long that would take.

*

One Saturday morning Mummy asks Mercy to go to town with her. There's nothing Mercy likes more than an outing with just her and Mummy, she can't grab her coat fast enough. They get the bus to an Estate Agent's office near the railway station; it smells of dust and lemon air freshener. The reception lady glances at them as they enter the shop. Mummy says hello but the lady holds one finger up as if she's in the middle of something, so Mummy and Mercy sit quietly on the grey chairs in the corner. There are filing cabinets everywhere.

The reception lady is blonde with her hair in a ponytail and a pinched face, her mouth is pinched in a ponytail as well. She types loudly on the typewriter. Every so often she looks up at them but she does not offer to help. There is a small man in a brown suit in an office behind her, they can see him through the glass. He flips through lots of folders like he is trying to look important. Mercy thinks that they are being kept waiting on purpose.

Eventually the man bustles out and says, 'So sorry to keep you waiting, Mrs Hanson.' But he doesn't seem sorry at all.

'You're here about the house on Girlington Street.'

Mummy smiles and says, 'yes that's correct,' in Speaky-Spokey. She grips her handbag stuffed with papers tightly on her knees.

'Excellent. So have you brought the proof of funds?'

She fishes into the handbag, finds a tattered manilla envelope and hands him a tea-stained letter from the *lyad-lawyers* who have been doing the sale of the Hill View house. Mummy had asked Mercy to read the letter. It said that they are, 'holding the funds to your order'. Mummy didn't know what it meant but all Mercy knows is that they have Mummy's money but they can't give it to her until someone orders something. The problem, it seems, is that Mummy doesn't have a bank account.

She can't open one because women can only open bank accounts with the signature of their husbands, and Daddy isn't going to sign for her because Mummy is still refusing to sign the divorce papers. She has some savings with the Pardner Money because Mercy sometimes goes to drop it off for her with Miss Mary, but that is only enough for the deposit, not the house itself.

Why does Mummy want to stay married to somebody who doesn't want to be married to her? All this time she has been praying for God to, 'strike him down.' Isn't getting divorced from him the next best thing? Janie and Ruby say that he is still living with Jessie-the-Jezebel, over the other side of Manchester Road. Devon and Evie sneak off to visit him but Mercy would never dream of going. Mummy calls her, 'dat dyam Jezebel,' whenever she is talking to Sister Norman or Miss Mary.

Mercy considers offering to copy Daddy's signature like she did way back to go to the Panto, but that did not end well. And besides she has never seen Daddy's signature, she is not sure he even knows how to read and write.

'Thank you, Mrs Hanson,' says the estate agent. 'This is a substantial sum but still well short of the value of the property. And of course there are your legal fees to consider.'

'Well I did have a mortgage with my husband on the house at Hill View,' says Mummy, 'I was wondering if you could help me get a mortgage on this house?' Mercy hates the whiny begging tone in Mummy's voice.

'The difficulty is the same as the bank account,' he says, shaking his head like a funeral director. Mercy can't get over the feeling that he's putting on an act and not a very good one at that. 'Building Societies will not lend to women without a male guarantor and, unfortunately, you're not able to provide one.'

Mummy starts moving her lips but she doesn't say anything out loud. Mercy is worried that she might start crying, or even worse, praying. And then Mercy works out what she's doing. It's worse than praying or crying, she's *speaking in tongues*. It starts all quiet, it usually does, but it is going to get louder and Mercy can see that any minute now she is going to get on her knees and start shouting and waving her right hand in the air and then God only knows what will happen. But just then, God moves in a mysterious way, the man says:

'There could be another solution, Mrs er, Hanson.'

Mummy stops whispering in tongues, nods her head and brightens. The Lord has worked his mysterious ways very quickly today.

'We do have some private mortgage lenders.'

'Wheh yuh mean *private*?' asks Mummy.

'Well...' he says, drawing it out for effect like the Panto Dame, and Mercy thinks, *oh no you don't*.

'There are some individuals who are willing to lend to people in your, er, situation. As you have a deposit of well over fifty percent of the purchase price, I'm sure one of them would be willing to loan you the balance. However, I'm afraid the mortgage rate will be slightly higher than the banks or building societies.'

Mercy is good at maths so she says, 'Excuse me, Sir, but how much is the mortgage rate with the bank?'

He stares at her like she's a monkey who's just learned to talk.

'My daughter sometimes helps me with arithmetic,' says Mummy. *Arithmetic?* Mercy stares at her like she's a monkey who's just learned to talk.

'Oh I see, yes of course. The bank base rate is currently eight percent. So if you were eligible for a bank loan you would be paying around nine percent.'

'And how much do the private investors charge?' Mercy is delighted to *finally* be allowed to push-up herself in Big-People's conversation.

'That does depend on the circumstances of the buyer,' says the man looking confusedly from Mummy to Mercy, not sure which one he should be addressing. 'But for someone such as yourself, Mrs Hanson, although you are in employment, you do have five dependent children and this will affect affordability.'

'I supposed to get maintenance for them from my husband,' says Mummy. Mercy knows that Daddy is supposed to be giving Mummy two pounds a week for each of them but he hasn't paid a *red cent*. Mercy is getting annoyed, she just wants the man to tell them how much it will be, then they can work out whether or not Mummy can afford it. Why does he have to make such a song and dance about it?

She opens her mouth to speak but Mummy shoots her a look which she knows means she has done enough pushing-up for one day. He flicks through a folder on his desk and says, 'I do have one investor who is prepared to loan to somebody in, er, your circumstances. The interest rate will be,' he pauses and flushes slightly pink, 'sixteen percent.'

That's nearly double what the banks are charging! Mercy wonders why the world is so unfair. She looks across at

Mummy, but Mummy seems relieved. And she realises that Mummy would be willing to pay anything to own her own house again.

*

A few weeks later the sale is all completed and they all go to look at the new house. There is a little rock garden at the front which is nice because the maisonette at Newlyn Square didn't even have a front garden. The Girlington Street house is Victorian and the front door is painted a bright red, although not very neatly. It opens straight into a square living room with a high ceiling and a pretty ceiling rose. There is a proper fireplace as well, although some of the wallpaper is peeling and there is a bit of a mouldy smell. Through the door there are stairs leading to the first floor and a room at the back which is a kitchen and a dining room. This house also has a back yard which is another bonus because Newlyn Square didn't have one and people like Fergal could, and did, just walk right up and make monkey noises right outside their windows.

Upstairs there is a bedroom at the front above the living room which is going to be Mummy's room. At the back it's obvious that what used to be a bedroom has been split into two, one side is the bathroom and the other side is a box room which Mummy says is going to be Devon's. It's really annoying that he's going to get a room all to himself, again.

There's another set of steps up to the attic and although it's only one room, it's huge. Mummy says she's going to try to get a grant to turn it into two dormer bedrooms so instead of sharing with three sisters, Mercy will only have to share with one. And this house is not far from Carlisle Road Library so at least some good can come of moving yet again.

43

Slugs and Snails

Mercy has just had her tenth birthday. She didn't get a present from Mummy but she got one from school. It wasn't exactly a present but she got it at the end of term so as far as she is concerned that counts as a birthday present. It's a fountain pen, a Waterman and it's silver plated, nestling in its own red velvet box. She won the Under Elevens Poetry with her poem about the Wright Brothers and Kitty Hawk and the first ever flight. She just imagined that she was flying and the magic carpet turned first into a hawk (called Kitty of course) and then into a plane with wings.

She didn't even know that Mrs Jensen had entered her poem in the competition, but Mrs Jensen told her it was outstanding. And she is going to have another special trip this year, just her and no one else, so that's almost like another birthday present. She will be travelling alone on an actual train; she feels so grown-up. She knows lots of things about lots of things. Like how if you boil water it makes steam and if you freeze it, that's ice. Solid, liquid, gas. Atoms spread further apart or squeezing closer together but it's still the same stuff underneath.

Soon she will take the eleven plus and hopefully get into the Grammar School because it turns out Secondary Moderns are not for the academically gifted, which is what Mrs Jensen said at parents evening, the first one Mummy has actually come to. The way Mummy went on it looked like she was the clever one for producing Mercy. Every teacher heaped praise on her and especially Mr Cavanagh who said she could achieve anything she set her mind to (especially in athletics) and that she was a credit to the school.

Pastor Williams in Birmingham has asked for Mercy to come and stay for Christmas. He came to the church in Bradford when they had their Convocation. Mummy was very taken with him because not only is he a man of God, he is also very well turned out. He has a pencil moustache and wears a smart burnt orange suit with a handkerchief in the pocket and has a thin moustache like a film star; he reminds Mercy of Cab Calloway movies, although he doesn't sing and dance, well not to her knowledge. Mercy feels very special because she is the only one who has been invited, she didn't even realise that he noticed her.

He lives with his wife in a posh modern house, shiny with formica and red leatherette. They have no children, which is a bit odd. Mercy has never met a family with no children.

Mummy said something about a barren wife which doesn't sound very good. Mercy wanted to ask what 'barren' was but thought better of it. As soon as she got to Carlisle Road she looked it up.

On the day before Christmas Eve, (Christmas Eve's-Eve?) She takes a bus to Bradford Interchange then two trains to Birmingham, all by herself. She has to change at Leeds but she manages it. Halfway across the country all alone. Mercy the Maverick. Jason and the Argonauts had nothing on this, Birmingham New Street might not be the Golden Fleece but it comes pretty close. What an adventure!

Pastor Williams picks Mercy up from the station. She has never seen a train station so big in her life; she's glad he got a platform ticket and met her right off the train. On the drive to his house, he asks her about school and Maths and English and she talks about how she is top of her class in almost every subject and that she's going to go to the Grammar School.

They drive through a huge Junction which looks like a pile of rope, twisting and turning back on itself. It reminds her of the Labyrinth, she wouldn't be surprised if the bull-headed Minotaur suddenly popped out of the back of one of the lorries.

How anyone can find their way in or out of it is a miracle. Once they are safely through the Labyrinth she falls asleep, waking when the Pastor taps her on the shoulder to tell her they have arrived.

'Mrs Double-U,' he says, 'bring some tea for the pickney-chile.'

Mrs Double-U is a severe-looking, neat, slim woman who hardly looks at Mercy, which is not very polite. When guests come to their house in Bradford the family are all over them until they get shooed away by Mummy.

Mercy stands in the corner of the kitchen because no one has told her where to sit. The kitchen worktops are a mottled cream, the cupboards a shouty orange. The sink in front of the window has a mat on the floor where Mrs Double-U stands washing already clean dishes as she looks out over Handsworth. The wallpaper is the expensive wipe-clean squishy type, with imprints of kitchen implements; cups, saucers, knives and forks. A fluorescent strip light attached to the ceiling casts a science fiction glow across the room.

Mrs Double-U sends her to the sitting room, but it's so neat and tidy with doilies and plastic covers everywhere, that she does not know where to sit. So she just stands there, lost in the middle of the room. She is still marvelling at the modern house when Pastor comes up behind her with a mug of tea, sweetened to tooth-curdling levels with condensed milk. Mercy takes the mug of tea but it's very hot. She spills some of it on the front of her dress.

He picks up a tea towel and pats her. She has to concentrate not to spill any more of the hot tea. Pastor Williams leans in and his wiry moustache tickles her face. Before she realises what is even happening, his tongue invades her mouth, like a warm slug. She twists her head violently to the side, spilling more of the hot tea. The heat from the liquid transmits itself through the cotton though her woolly tights onto her thighs.

'Shhh,' he says, taking the mug of tea from her, placing it on the pale blue formica topped coffee table. It has graceful tapering legs darkening as they near the swirly red carpet. Mercy darts to the kitchen and stands stiffly next to Mrs Double-U, who completely ignores her. Later she is shown to a scarily tidy bedroom with a small single bed under the window. She can hear the telly in the living room and Pastor laughing at the Benny Hill theme tune. She is wondering why he did that with his wife in the kitchen; and why tell her to 'shhh' like it was their little secret? It's like Cousin Bobby all over again except Pastor Williams is a fully grown man. But Uncle Red was a grown man as well and he made her feel dirty.

With her heart in her mouth Mercy sneaks down to the hallway to where the bright red telephone is sitting on the table right by the front door. She knows her home phone number off by heart. She dials as carefully as she can, listening to the ratcheting click as the circular dial goes back to zero in between each number. Glaciers form and flow to the sea in the time it takes Mummy to pick up.

'Mummy?'

'Mercy? Everything h' alright?'

'Erm,' she's finding it hard to speak.

'Wha' wrong? Phone call hexpensive yuh know.'

'I want to come home,' she spits it out.

'Whe' you mean you want come home. You only just reach Birmin'am.'

'I don't like it here; I want to come home.'

'But is Christmas, Mercy!'

'I want to come home.' Mercy doesn't know how else to say it.

'Wheh wrong?'

'Please, Mummy, can I come back?'

'Puppa Jesus! Why yuh ah try mi patience Mercy?'

Her insides are churning with such deep shame and embarrassment that she cannot bring herself to say it. But if she doesn't say it, Mummy will not know what is wrong, and if Mummy doesn't know what's wrong, she won't let Mercy come home. She knows with utter certainty that Pastor will try again and that it will be more than just the slug. Mrs Double-U will not notice, or she will see and not see, or see and not care. Pastor is charming, he is suave, he is chatty, he has been kind enough to invite one of Sister Hanson's whole-heap a pickney-dem to stay for Christmas. Ungrateful wretch, how dare she complain. But she has to say something.

She is going to have to name the unnameable to a mother who never, ever talks about that kind of thing. A mother who lets Daddy come over in the middle of the night so that they don't know he's there. She is going to have to bring the night into daylight even if it kills her; and it feels like it might. But Mercy has faced death before, and she survived. The machete was worse than this, but only just.

She takes a deep breath. 'He, he touched me.' Mercy does not want to go into the details, she hopes Mummy can hear the panic rising like floodwater in her voice.

'Touch what, touch who?'

'Pastor...'

Her head is exploding. Her cheeks are burning, but this is the only way out. She can either implode or explode. She has to tell Mummy. She can't bear the slug again. But finding the words to tell Mummy feels almost worse.

'He put his...'

'Lord Jesus, Mercy, wha'appn?'

'In my mouth, he put his tongue...' She can't finish the sentence, because saying it, saying it out loud is like feeling it happen again.

It's done, it's out there; spilled, like so much vomit soiling the ground between them. There is silence just static and crackling and electricity down the phone line between Bradford and Birmingham. Mercy's heart is beating so hard that her vision is becoming bloody and blurred. Her temples are screaming and her skull is in a vice with the screws tightening every millisecond that Mummy does not speak. And then, almost like a record playing in reverse she hears Mummy say it.

'*What will people say?*'

Mercy is blindsided by the words. She has gone through the looking glass and entered an alternative universe into a world called '*what-will-people-say.*'

'Huh?'

'Wheh people gwine seh Mercy, if you come home early?'

Mummy can't have hear her heard her right. Will she have to tell it again; the slug, her mouth, the moustache, the tea, the burn, the dress.

'I want to come home, Mummy. Now.'

There is a long silence on the other end of the phone whilst atoms whirr and Mercy is lost in outer space where there is no air and where her molecules are sucked apart and reformed into a new different person. A person who has no one, absolutely no one to rely on.

'I want to come *home.*'

Mercy notices with wonder the new steel in her voice. She is not asking, she is telling. She is demanding, she's ordering. It's not like when she was little and she tried to sit Mummy down and tell her to leave, wondering why her bruised and bloody mother could not see that Daddy is a Bad-Man.

She becomes the parent, gently instructing her mother like a teacher would instruct a child how to write its name. Yes, that's how you do it, a circle with the pencil and then a stalk to create the letter 'a'. She can hear Mummy's mind ticking and working and calculating in the background and slowly but gradually coming to a conclusion. Mercy wins. Mummy will do the right thing. Mercy will get home. Merry Christmas to one and all.

'Put Pastor on the phone,' says Mummy.

44

Merry Christmas

Pastor Williams doesn't drive Mercy back to the train station. He calls a taxi and gives her a whole ten pound note to pay the fare, which is about ten times what it's going to cost. He says the change is for 'Christmas', but Mercy knows exactly what it's for. It's keep-your-mouth-shut-money. It's I'm-sorry-I-got-caught-money. It's Cousin Bobby and the Pear Drops all over again.

Mercy wishes she had been able to keep her mouth shut and then the slug wouldn't have gotten in, but she was taken by surprise. Boy-cousins are one thing, she didn't know she was supposed to be on guard around a Pastor. His severe wife frowns and says it's a shame that Mercy 'tek sick' almost as soon as she arrived and to have a safe journey and to give her *best regards* to Mummy. She gives Mercy a quick vice-like hug as Mercy gets into the taxi. Mercy gets the feeling that his wife is going to have to put up with the slug now.

The taxi driver is a genial bald round man who says, 'You going home for Christmas lovie?'

'Yes,' smiles Mercy, 'yes I am.'

On the long train ride home she buys almost all the sweets she can carry from the Buffet Car and pops them into her mouth one after the other. She reminds herself of Daddy and the way he uses the stub of one cigarette to light the next one so that there isn't even one millisecond when he is without nicotine. By the time she gets back to the shiny new Bradford Interchange she feels sick from all the sugar, but at least she can't taste the slug anymore.

Mummy hugs her when she gets into the house but doesn't ask anything about Pastor Willians and Mercy can't face bringing it up again so it just sits there, growing like a cancer between them.

*

Sister Mo is up for Christmas, all shiny, straightened hair, make-up, fancy clothes and wages. Her front teeth are still too big but they look all fashionable now, like a model. She brings presents for all of them, including a red fake leather mini skirt for Mercy which is too perfect to actually wear. She's nearly eighteen and says she's saving up for driving lessons and a *cyar*. Mercy hopes she doesn't get a Hillman Avenger. She doesn't have much time to talk to Mercy but she listens as she cooks and tells Mercy to *mick-ase* get out of Bradford. She doesn't stay in the house much though. She hangs out with the older cousins who still talk funny. They go to Blues together in their fancy clothes from Chelsea Girl, smelling of perfume and sophistication.

On Christmas Day the house is like a whirlwind fighting with a hurricane. Mona and Mummy cook up a feast, even if it is too spicy. There is turkey and roast potatoes and piles of brussels sprouts and for dessert Mona brings out a Jamaican cake which she made months ago in London. It has so much rum in it that they get drunk on the fumes just from unwrapping the silver foil. They eat until they are round like balloons, then they wait for their stomachs to deflate a bit and eat some more. Mona can chew turkey bones and spit out a pile of dust just like Mummy because they both have big strong Jamaican teeth, unlike Hinglish pickney-dem.

On Boxing Day morning Devon disappears for a while, then comes swaggering into the kitchen ostentatiously carrying a brown cardboard box.

'Whatcha got there?' asks Mercy, knowing, for a fact, that he is up to no good.

'Nothing for nosys, cheats and posies,' he replies haughtily, clearly glad that someone has asked.

'Come on, Carrot-Face,' says Evie, 'you know you wanna tell us. What's in the box?'

After everyone has inquired, Devon theatrically places the box on the floor in the middle of the kitchen and flings open the flaps. Inside is the world's most adorable puppy. It looks like an Alsatian but it's all black with long ears and huge brown eyes. It stares up at them looking like an orphan trapped at the bottom of a well.

'Where did you get it?' asks Evie reaching into the box to pick it up. Mercy hangs back. She doesn't like the way the thing pulls at her heartstrings.

Devon has been asking for a dog for ages, but Mummy always says, 'Mi cyan feed five pickney, never mind dawg.'

Devon starts boasting about how his friend's dog had a litter of nine puppies and his Mum allowed Devon to take the runt.

'You're the runt,' says Evie with her cackling witch-laugh.

'You're gonna be in big-big trouble when Mummy gets home,' says Mercy. And to make sure, as soon as Mummy sets foot in the door Mercy runs up to her. 'Devon's got a puppy. He's not allowed is he? Make him take it back Mummy, make him take it back.'

Mercy quite likes the puppy, but this is about the rulesMummy never makes Devon stick to rules but today she has to. Mummy has to finally put her foot down and make him take it back.

Devon hands the puppy to Mummy like it's a little baby. She takes one look at the puppy and melts. She pops it on her shoulder and pats its back, like she is burping a baby. She sways from side to side and starts singing, *'how much is that Doggy in the window.'*

Does the woman have no self-respect? Eventually Mummy recovers herself, shakes her head and hands the puppy back to Devon.

'First thing ah marnin' you must take di dawg back.'

'Why can't he take it back now?' asks an outraged Mercy.

She can tell that they are going to be stuck with the dog. She knows that tomorrow will turn into the next day, and the day after that. The puppy has already charmed Mummy and it's only going to charm her some more. Why is Mummy so easily led by Devon anyway? If one of the girls had brought it home, Mercy knows Mummy would march them straight back out the door with it.

The day after Boxing Day, Mercy finally gets to talk to Mona by herself, but that's only because she gets on the bus with her to Bradford Interchange to see her off to London.

'Can I tell you something?' asks Mercy as the bus trundles past the looming woollen mills on Thornton Road which smell of lanolin and grease.

'Wha'gwaan Mercy?'

Mercy looks left and right then tips her head close to Mona's and tells her all about Pastor Williams and why she came back on Christmas Eve.

Mona puts her arm around Mercy's shoulder, gives her a squeeze and says, 'yuh poor ting.' Then Mona tells Mercy a secret of her own. One of Mrs Higgins's neighbours back in JA, a man even older than Daddy, started bringing her little presents and saying she was nearly *ripe*. The presents gradually got bigger and better and Mrs Higgins started asking where she was getting things from and what she was doing for them. That was the real reason Mona jumped at the chance to take Baby-Sonia's place and come to England; she was running away before the neighbour came back to harvest her ripened fruit.

But Mercy has nowhere to run to. No one is offering her a plane ticket anywhere.

'Keep going Mercy,' says Mona. 'Study yuh books. Yuh will get out in the end. You can come live wid me in London when yuh finish school, innit.' It would be good to get away and go to London, even if she has to ride underground on a screeching tube train.

'Mona, are the tube trains really like the bowels of hell?'

Mona laughs with her big teeth, 'No, nothin' like dat. Dem loud but dem fast, and if yuh miss one, another one come along in a minute and de announcer seh "mind the gap"!' She says that bit in Speaky-Spokey.

'What gap?' Mercy is getting a bit worried about London and whether she could cope with tube trains and beggars but she needs to have something to hold on.

'In London, de world is yuh *hoyster*, Mercy.' Mona smiles a dreamy smile like she can't wait to get back to London and explore it. She talks about Piccadilly Circus and Speakers Corner where she goes on a Sunday after church to hear people stand on a box and talk about all sorts. Mercy has never seen an oyster but she likes the idea of adventures with Mona in a big new city. She can stand on a box and talk, and maybe people will listen to her.

The fancy new Bradford Interchange is sleek and smart like an airport. People bustle about importantly, there are echoey announcements over a tannoy system and buses glide into spacious tarmac bays with proper signs over the doors telling everyone where the buses and coaches are going. It smells all new of paint and diesel. Everyone is very proud of the Interchange because all the buses go to one place and you can change from a bus to a train really easily. Mona buys Mercy a Kit-Kat, gives her bus fare to get home and an extra big hug.

Mercy and Mona wave at each other, until the blue and white National Express Coach is out of sight. Then Mercy walks very slowly to get her bus back home. She leans her head against the glass on the journey back and manages not to cry. She is glad she talked to Mona about Pastor Williams but it's a long time to wait until she's sixteen to go and seek her fortune in London. How can she be sure there won't be more slug-pastors in London? She won't go to any churches, that's for sure; but Mona's neighbour in Jamaica was a dirty-old-man as well. How do you get away from them all?

45

Happy Bunny

No one notices her when she gets back from the Interchange because they're all too busy cooing over the new dog who is clearly staying. Devon decides to call him Bunny. He doesn't look the slightest bit like a rabbit, but it's hard to deny his cuteness and he purrs like a kitten when you stroke him. Devon puts an old blanket in the bottom of the cardboard box that Bunny came in and places the box under the TV stand.

At first, Bunny is timid, but he soon gets used to five sets of hands stroking him all day long. Mercy is determined not to be won over, but she does feel calmer when she is stroking Bunny, it helps banish thoughts of slugs and snails. Every evening when she gets home Mummy takes to picking Bunny up and carrying him around on her shoulder singing, 'how much is that doggy in the window,' and Bunny waggles his tail. It's been a very long time since Mummy sang to her. She wonders if the real reason Mummy had so many children is because she prefers babies to grown-up children.

At the Boxing Day service she overheard Mummy whispering to Sister Norman, 'why Pastor Williams must mek the Devil use him soh?'

'We gwine have fi fast and pray fi him soul,' replied Sister Norman, 'because from what I hear, is not di first time.'

Mummy's hand flew to her mouth. 'Yuh tink I should tell Bishop?'

Mercy wanted to go over and shake her by the shoulders and shout, *hell yes!* But she wasn't supposed to be listening, much less pushing-up herself in Big-People conversation.

*

Mummy might be fond of Bunny but she draws the line at dog food.

'Back home,' she declares, 'dawg eat leftovers. Mi nah spend fi mi good-good money pon dawg food.' So Bunny learns to like rice and peas and chicken and dumpling and fish heads and whatever they have for dinner.

Bunny is quick to realise that like the rest of the Hanson family, if he doesn't stand up for himself, he won't eat. When mealtimes come around, he nudges in at the dining table and stares up at them with his big round eyes. When no one is looking Mercy sometimes passes him the bones from the chicken-neck after she has sucked them clean.

Bunny's begging doesn't always bear fruit so he decides that any food which hits the floor is his, no taking-backsies. The natural extension of this theory is that any food which is about to hit the floor, or might conceivably do so, belongs to him. Bunny moves like lightning to catch stray food. There is now no such thing as retrieving a dropped sausage in their house.

It turns out that Bunny is a Retriever-Alsatian cross not a Labrador because his favourite activity in the whole wide world is retrieving things. If he can't eat it he will bring it back; shoes, coats, knickers, Bunny retrieves everything and then sits there looking ludicrously pleased with himself. Bunny is an idiot, but he can be a useful idiot when you need your slippers.

He grows quickly and now whenever he tries to get into his bed his frantic efforts to get under the TV makes it wobble. Mummy moves his box, but Bunny is still convinced that his rightful place is under the TV, probably because that is where everyone is looking at any given moment.

Mummy worries about, 'dis bloomin' dawg' damaging *Govament* property, because the TV is on hire-purchase. There's a metal box attached to the side into which they have to feed sixpences. Every month the man from Rediffusion comes to empty the box. Mercy works out that it will take them six years to pay for it. The TV has an annoying habit of cutting out right in the middle of their favourite programs like *The Generation Game.* Then there is uproar while they run around trying to find a sixpence. When it comes on again they've almost missed the conveyor belt, *'cuddly-toy, cuddly-toy, fondue-set!'*

Bunny decides to resume his rightful place, but as he can't get under the TV table any more he does the next best thing which is to sit right in front of it. They can hear the voice of Bruce Forsyth but all they can see is this large black dog with its tongue hanging out saying, *'didn't they do well!'*

Devon loves having a dog, but only for showing-off purposes. He doesn't actually take Bunny for walks or anything.

Mercy likes having a routine and, it turns out, so does Bunny. As soon as she arrives home from school Bunny insists on being taken for a walk. If Mercy is foolish enough to ignore him jumping around like a kangaroo, he goes to the hook on the wall where his lead is kept and, by standing up on his hind legs, can unhook it and drop it at her feet. The collar and handle are leather but the middle bit is a chain.

If Mercy ignores him, he picks it up and drops it again, this time on her feet. At the third time of asking, drastic measures are required, Bunny picks up the lead between his teeth and lashes Mercy around the ankles with it. Mercy has to shout at him to stop but he looks unrepentant, like it's all her fault. Although Mercy is annoyed, because being whipped with a chain is actually quite painful, she thinks Bunny is funny. If ever there was someone who made their every thought as clear as a bell, it's Bunny.

She wishes she could make *her* thoughts clear to Mummy. She is still angry with her about not reporting Pastor Williams. If praying for him was going to work it would have worked by now because surely praying is part of his job. Janie, who is the world's biggest gossip, tells her that all the girls in his church in Birmingham know never to be alone with him, but every now and then one gets caught and then they get teased for 'snogging the 'tache'.

Mercy likes to get out of the house and walk so she takes Bunny to Girlington Park. No one has taught Bunny to walk to heel and he wants to get to the park more than anything in the world so he practically yanks Mercy's arm out of her socket as he drags her all the way there.

As soon as they arrive at his sacred place, Bunny must find a stick. Her only job is to throw it as far as she can and Bunny races off like a rocket. He never gets tired of retrieving sticks and dropping them expectantly at her feet. She has to pick them up and throw them again before the beating begins. She finds herself laughing at his boundless enthusiasm. Not since Dolly has there been anyone she spent so much time with and Dolly wasn't actually real. When they get back, she sits on the new Mercy Step and Bunny lays his tired head on her lap while she reads.

The Hanson house is noisy and chaotic and so Bunny becomes a noisy and chaotic dog. He decides that it's his job to defend them from all comers, especially marauding postmen and sneak-readers of gas meters. After a number of unfortunate altercations the postman refuses to post letters through their door anymore. He just yells out, 'post for number nineteen,' and throws the letters on the doorstep, which Mercy is sure is against the rules.

Every now and then Mummy still likes to put Bunny on her shoulder and sing to him. They all think it's hilarious the way Mummy seems to have forgotten that he is not a puppy anymore as she tries to hoist a fully grown dog onto her shoulders. In Jamaica dogs live outside so Mummy decides that Bunny should be in a kennel as there are too many of them packed up in the kitchen-diner. The front room is for special occasions, but unless the Queen herself turns up it's going to stay empty.

Although when the Bishop came to see Mummy that time, they went in the front room. Mercy was sent upstairs so she didn't get to find out what they were talking about. But Janie was a good little spy and told Mercy that the Bishop said that Mummy had to bear some 'culpability' for sending her daughter 'like a lamb to the slaughter,' because Pastor Williams' 'proclivities' were widely known. The upshot was that the Pastors from all over the country were going to Birmingham for a big weekend of prayer and fasting for Pastor Williams' soul. Oh and Mummy would be promoted from *Sister* Hanson to *Evangelist* Hanson. Again, Mercy wondered why no one wanted to speak to her. Why was it all about the Pastor and his 'proclivities' and not the girls who were the actual lambs? How could they know all about him and still let him be a Pastor?

What was wrong with them, and what was wrong with Mummy for staying in a church like that? Probably the same thing that was wrong with her for staying married to a man like Daddy. Mercy can feel the cord stretched almost to breaking vibrating like a high-pitched scary note from a Hitchcock movie.

*

The backyard has no back wall so Bunny is tied to the house by a long chain, but he hates it because he can't retrieve anything. He howls like someone is murdering him and the neighbours complain. Mummy decides to solve the problem by getting a Polish man in to build a wall. He asks her how high she wants the wall.

She looks at Bunny and says, 'about so high,' pointing to her shoulder. It takes the man two days to build the wall, put flat stones on top and a gate in the middle. When it's finished Mummy is very pleased with the job and pays him in cash. He drives off in his battered blue van. They all stand and admire the new wall. It makes the backyard into a proper garden.

Mummy unchains Bunny from the back wall and says, 'Goh play Bunny.'

He takes one look at the wall, backs up a few steps, runs and jumps over it on the first go, triumphantly walking back around to the gate to be let in again. He's found the perfect activity; he can retrieve himself.

46

Ten going on Eleven Plus

They are all queuing up outside the hall waiting to go in and take the exam which will decide whether they go to a Grammar School or a Secondary Modern. Some of the others are nervous but Mercy is still and calm like a lake on a windless day. She actually likes exams because, for an hour or so, there is peace and quiet and no nasty surprises.

To keep Glenda happy she pretends to be nervous too, although she finds it hard to gauge exactly how nervous to pretend to be. The thing with feeling so different from everyone else is that she is always acting, never really being herself. Mrs Jensen walks along the line and puts a hand on Mercy's shoulder. She jumps, her elaborate charade has been discovered.

'Mercy, can you go and see Mr Ramsbottom.'

'Why, Miss?' Mercy's confidence pops like a bubble. Why is she being singled out?

'He'll explain,' says Mrs Jensen. Mercy cannot decipher the look on her teacher's face, but she is sure Mrs Jensen is hiding something. Now she is worried. She walks down the corridor to Mr Ramsbottom's office. The polished parquet floor gleams at her, saying, *you're in trouble*. She racks her brains, but can't think of anything she's done which might lead to a visit to the Head's Office. She takes a deep breath, tries to compose herself and knocks on the door with two, timid, taps.

'Come in,' Mr Ramsbottom's voice is grave.

'Have a seat, Mercy,' he says. She does not want to sit down. She wants to go back to the hall; the exam will be starting soon and she'll miss it.

The low green chair means she has to look up at Mr Ramsbottom who sits behind his shiny oak mountain of a desk. He wears tortoiseshell glasses, his dark brown hair has a floppy fringe which he pushes out of the way, but it just flops back down again. She can see the hairs growing out of his nostrils.

'Now then, Mercy.'

'Yes, Sir?' She wants to scream at him to stop faffing about and just get on with it.

'I've received a message from your mother. There is an... er... yes, a problem at home. You are to collect your things and go home immediately.'

'Yes, Sir.' It doesn't occur to Mercy to ask what the problem is. If a teacher tells her to do something she does it, no questions asked. Now that they are living in Girlington she has to get two buses back home. The first one arrives quickly but the second one takes ages so she hops on another bus that is heading toward home. All the way she drums her fingers on the windows, trying to work out what is so important that she has to be dragged out of school. She gets off at the top of Girlington Street, a long cobbled hill that gets steeper and steeper as it rises. The houses step down the hill, each one leaning against its neighbour for support. The numbers at the top are up in the three hundreds and Mercy's house is number nineteen. It's a long walk down.

The wooden gate is rotting at the hinges, so it hangs at a slight angle, neither fully open nor closed. The front room is usually full of furniture but empty of people, but today everyone is in there. Janie is marching backwards and forwards in front of the gas fire, her school tie adrift around her neck. Devon is draped over a chair in the corner wailing worse than he did when the Chopper died. Evie is lying flat out on her back on the floor; chest heaving, sobbing her heart out, tears falling sideways into her ears. Mummy is sitting in the middle of the sofa with Ruby next to her, a protective arm around her shoulder.

What strikes Mercy more than the sight of her family, is the sound. Everyone is crying. There is snot coming from Mummy's nose, Ruby is trying to wipe it up but she can't see what she is doing because she's crying too. Bunny is locked in the kitchen howling because he has been left out, Devon is making that unearthly noise, the long loud 'ahhh's' and Janie is actually shrieking. What the hell is going on? It's like that Bible verse about wailing and gnashing of teeth. Mercy's ears feel like they are being battered. Whatever it is, surely, they don't all have to carry on like this.

'What's happened?' she asks. No one hears her.

'What's going on?' she says, louder this time. Everyone stops, all eyes turn on her, like they forgot she existed.

'Daddy's dead!' Janie's eyes are red-rimmed. She says it angrily, like Mercy should have worked it out from all the commotion.

Mercy looks at Mummy for confirmation. Mummy nods into her hanky.

'Is that all?' Mercy has barely taken one step into the house. She turns on her heels and walks right back out again, 'I'm going back to school,' she says, shutting the door on the wailing and gnashing behind her.

There is a bus coming along Thornton Lane and she has to run to get to the bus stop but she makes it, thankful that she has a bus pass to pay for all these journeys. She stares blankly out of the window on the way back to school, wondering firstly if she will get back in time for the exam and secondly if she is supposed to feel anything.

She has missed lunch and the afternoon classes have already begun by the time she gets back to the polished corridors. She hangs up her coat and makes her way to her classroom. Everyone is out doing P.E. Mrs Jensen looks up, her mouth drops open in surprise.

'Mercy! Are you alright? Have you been home?'

'Yes, Miss, but I don't want to miss the test. Can I still do it?'

'Are you sure you want to stay in school? Don't you want to be with your family... at a time like this?' So Mrs Jensen *did* know why she had been sent home. She could have told her and given her the choice of avoiding two miserable wasted journeys.

No, she thinks, *I do not want to be with my family at a time like this. I want to take the test and get into the Grammar School.* But she doesn't say any of this. She just stares at Mrs Jensen with a determined look which says she will fight if challenged.

'Well, wait here, Mercy,' says Mrs Jensen eventually. 'I'll have to go and check if it's okay.' Mercy is left in the empty classroom all by herself, but she knows, with a dogged certainty, that they will let her take the test she will pass. Mercy is very good at shutting out the outside world. All her life she has had to block out things that might make her sad and find another nicer world to live in: one without Daddy and the constant worry of when she might step on his many land mines.

The half-brick in her stomach shrinks, just a little bit, but someday it might disappear altogether. She will not cry a lie. This time she will not pretend to feel what she does not. Mrs Jensen comes back and tells her that she can sit the test after all, but as everyone else has already done it, she will have to sit in Mr Ramsbottom's office so that he can invigilate.

She raises her eyebrows at Mrs Jensen. 'What does *invigilate* mean, Miss?'

'Supervise, he's going to watch to make sure you do it all by yourself.' For the second time in one day Mercy goes to the Head's Office, but this time she is in charge. Mercy is in her element, lost in knowledge. This is her world and she wishes the test could take all day and all night so that she can put off going home forever and ever Amen.

47

Lying in State

Mercy makes sure to come in through the back door today. There is no way she's coming in through the front door as that leads straight into the living room because *he* is in there. The kitchen is jam-packed. Even though the room is small, there seem to be dozens of people in there. Mona has arrived from London in a cloud of perfume, an afro, black polo neck, chunky gold crucifix and a black leather trench coat. She looks like *Shaft*. Her big front teeth really suit her now, like a proper 1970's model. She hugs Mercy, gives her a lipstick kiss on the cheek and tells her to keep up her spirits.

Mona doesn't seem very sad that Daddy is dead, but then why would she? She hardly knew him, but if she had stayed in Bradford longer he would have grown tired of being on his best behaviour and shown her his true colours. She goes back to chatting to the Jamaican girl-cousins and Mercy notices that her Jamaican accent comes back really strong when she hangs out with them.

*

Mummy is at the sink filling up the kettle. Water is pouring out of the tap and welling up in her eyes. She seems to have gotten shorter than her five foot nothing in the last week. She wears her nylon blue overalls over a red pleated skirt and a flower printed blouse with collars that rival the wings of a Boeing 747. Ruby and Janie call it Mummy's 'style and fashion.'

She slowly lifts her face, managing barely a half smile. Mercy wants to hug her but there are too many people in the room. The golden autumn light streams in through the big kitchen window illuminating the shimmering tears forming in Mummy's eyes.

The water overruns the kettle but Mummy doesn't seem to notice. Mercy gently takes the kettle from her, nudging her aside and pours out some of the water before clicking it onto its stand. It's electric but designed to look old fashioned; steel, round and shiny with a snout with a whistle which screams the house down when it boils. She wants to tell Mummy that she got her results today. She passed. She will be going to the Grammar school, not Carfax like Ruby and Janie. But today is not a 'good news' day.

'It's okay, Mum,' says Mercy. 'You go sit down, I'll make the tea.'

Mummy looks around distractedly for somewhere to sit but every sittable surface is taken up by the considerable bottoms of her friends, and their assorted children. Sister Norman wears her olive green wool coat which she never takes off, even when she is inside, along with the matching turban hat. The curls of her shiny black wig peek out of the sides. The massive cheeks almost overwhelm her gimlet eyes. She is wedged in between the dining table and the wall. A seat close to the gas heater is not to be given up lightly on a cold September afternoon. The prattling of people talking is irritating; they are all making the right noises but not actually doing anything.

'The Lord giveth and the Lord taketh away.'

'Yea, in the midst of life we are in death.'

'Bear up, Evangelist Hanson. The Almighty nevah gi' you more than you can bear.'

'We is put on this earth for just three-score years and ten.'

'Him was only fifty-four,' says Mummy, a tear dropping onto her overall pocket.

They aren't helping Mummy at all. Not one of them has hugged her or even put an arm around her shoulder. *This is our flamin' house*, thinks Mercy. *Why don't you lot just bugger-off?*

But she knows full well that they are not going to leave. There are three more days to go before the end of Nine Night. Three more nights of the house full of people 'comforting' the bereaved family, which actually means just eating them out of house and home. Mercy is well and truly fed up of being sent to the shop to buy more biscuits. And it can't be any own-brand foolishness; she has to get proper McVities chocolate digestives. Mummy is going to be bankrupt by the time Nine Night finishes.

Mercy makes sure to put an extra sugar in Mummy's tea and give her two chocolate biscuits. These remain untouched on the side of her plate, but not for long as Bunny manages to wobble the plate so that they drop and, in an admirable feat of agility, he catches them both before they hit the floor. She also has to offer tea to all the Church Ladies. Everyone says yes to a cup of tea and everyone gives strict instructions on how it is to be made.

'You put in one sugar? No, I said half!'

'Is how far you stand throw di milk?'

'Dat ah white sugar, you noh have demerara?'

'Yuh use yuh baff hand mek dis?' Why tea made by a left-handed girl was bad, no-one ever explained, could they really taste the difference? They think nothing of sending Mercy back to remake tea which is not finished to their exact specifications.

'Dis will ha fi do,' is the highest compliment she receives.

Last night when, finally exhausted, Mercy had gone up, she found Lilly, sister Norman's daughter, asleep in her bed, so she had to get in and sleep head to toe with her.

Bunny jumps up at her.

'Hello Funny-Bunny,' she tickles him behind his long ears and he smiles at her. Mercy's after-school appearance means one thing and one thing only. 'I'll take Bunny for a walk,' Mercy says as an excuse to get out of the madhouse.

Bunny, hearing his name and the word 'walk' in the same sentence, jumps up and starts wagging his tail vigorously in the

faces of the children on the floor who make a huge kerfuffle.
Then he darts over to the hook where his lead is kept and
sits directly under it thumping his tail like an amped-up rock
drummer.

'What!' says Sister Norman, 'at a time like dis?' She stands
up sharply. 'Yuh father is in the front room. Yuh noh even go
pay yuh respec'.'

Mercy looks at Mummy but Mummy just looks down.

'Walk dawg? Whe yuh mean walk dawg? Go seh Goodbye
to your fahdah.' She manoeuvres her bulk surprisingly quickly
to grab Mercy by the shoulder, her fingers digging in just
above the collarbone. She almost frog-marches her prisoner to
the front room, shoves her in unceremoniously and pulls the
door shut behind her.

'Pay yuh respec'!'

The front room is always dark, partly because of the heavy
velvet curtains, partly the criss-cross leading in the window
and partly because it faces east, so after lunch it gets no light.
Family pictures adorn every wall, some at a rather jaunty angle.
Some have one or two additional pictures jammed in outside
the glass held by the frame. No two frames are alike. Mercy
doesn't even know who some of the people in the pictures
are. The ones she likes best are the old-timey ones in black
and white with the unsmiling Jamaican sisters in their white
ankle socks staring out into the future. The furniture has
been pushed to the side. The red leatherette three-piece suite
covered in pale cream antimacassars and the splay legged coffee
table look like they are in a second-hand furniture showroom.

In the middle of the room, on a shiny metal trolley with
rubber wheels, is the coffin. Dark mahogany with six brass
handles, and, as Daddy is - was, six-foot-six, it's huge. Mercy
stands with her back against the door which leads back to
safety. How is she supposed to pay her respects? She feared
her father but she never respected him. She feels nothing but
dread clawing at her. From where she stands, she can see the

pleated white satin but not the body. The muscles in her neck are aching from hunching her shoulders.

He's dead, she tells herself. One of Mummy's sayings comes to mind. *The dead have no dominion over the living.* Mercy isn't too sure about that. There's barely any air in the room, he has sucked it all out. It was chronic bronchitis they said; the Capstan Full Strength can't have helped. Mercy doesn't have any memories of her father without a cigarette between his fingers or bobbing at the corner of his mouth; he always lit the new one from the stub of the old.

Her feet grow roots and anchor her to the spot; will she ever be able to move again? After it feels like the earth has revolved around the sun a few times, she sways slightly, managing to snap the roots and lift one foot, placing it carefully in front of the other. Three agonising steps later she is close enough to see.

He is wearing a dark suit, his white gloved hands are folded across his chest. She hauls her eyes upwards toward the face. In life his cheekbones were prominent but now they jut out like cliffs, trying to escape from his face. His eyes are closed and sunken so far back into his skull that they resemble dark pools. He does not appear to have any eyelashes. The skin is an ashen, unnatural black-grey and the lips are thin and stretched into a tight grimace.

She leans ever so slightly forward and then; it happens.

He sighs.

She hears it clearly. A long low 'uuhh,' like he is surprised to discover that he is dead. The blood in her veins freezes as her heart goes on strike. An image of Lot's Wife pops into her head and she can no more move a muscle than a pillar of salt. Is he actually dead or is he just pretending, so that he can lure her close and reach out a bony hand to clutch her by the neck. Then it begins. Her skull starts peeling back to allow her to float out. The climbing out of her body towards the ceiling starts.

No.

No, she tells herself. Not this time. *Please don't leave me here by myself.* She manages to hang on like a fallen mountaineer clutching for dear life to the ankles of a companion. And this time, for the first time, she stays. As she sinks back into herself, the skin of her scalp unfurls itself back onto her head and zips shut with a thrumming noise. She knows she's back because she begins to feel woozy. She has not breathed since he sighed, since he stole all the oxygen.

She lets out the air from her burning lungs as slowly as she can manage, so as not to disturb him. And then she tries again. Do it, Mercy, take another breath. She still has not moved. The muscles in her back, tight as tent ropes, trying to hold her upright.

Her body is back under control now, sort of. Her left hand reaches forward and she watches her fingers touch his face. It is clammy, like meat from the fridge. She pulls her hand back, under her own control now.

Daddy is dead.

She can see it with her own two eyes, feel him cold under her fingers. He will not be there to terrorise her ever again. She will not have to look over her shoulder wondering if and when he will make good on his promise to run her down with the Hillman Avenger. The half a brick of tension that lives in her stomach will someday dissolve and disappear, and she can have a life free from the corroding fear that kept her company ever since she met him. She will become Mercy Whittington in London with Mona.

She can hear her own breathing now; her lungs are working again. She thinks of the time she drew him. The way he swooped down like an eagle on a lamb to take the notebook and laugh at the fact that she had caught his likeness. Even then she couldn't tell if he was laughing at her or with her. Her brain is working overtime trying to decipher what she feels.

It is not grief, like when Joy died. It is not indifference like with Tracy. It is the loss of something she never had. The loss of possibility. There will never be another chance to have the father she wanted. One who would be impressed by her skill with pencil and paper; one who might marvel at the fact that aged seven she could capture his portrait; one who might be proud that she has passed the exam and is going to the Grammar School. A father who might take them to Chester Zoo and not lose his temper.

All those years she longed for him to cast a loving glance in her direction, the way he looked at Devon or Evie. She did not want to hear him tell her he loved her, that was ridiculous, beyond the realms of possibility for Irael 'Sonny' Hanson. But a look, a smile, a sigh even, some microscopic sign that he was happy to see her.

48

Morning

The funeral was almost a month ago. It's early morning and everyone is asleep. Everyone except Mummy and now Mercy. She tiptoes downstairs and peeps into the sitting room. She can just see the back of her mother's hunched shoulders as she sits crying softly on the sofa. Mercy doesn't want to be heartless but surely by now it is time for Mummy to stop weeping and wailing and fix-up. She didn't even *like* Daddy. The two of them had spent the eleven years Mercy was on earth fighting like cats and dogs.

All the times Mummy tried to escape. When Mercy had been the hero of the hour persuading her to pack a suitcase and run for her life. Mercy's blood curdles as she thinks about the night of the Long Knife, Mummy kneeling meekly like a sacrificial lamb and saying her last prayers. That will never, ever happen again. Mummy should rejoice.

Mercy knew with absolute certainty, while they were down there, in the shadow of the valley of death, that had she not locked eyes, horns and every fibre of her being with him, they would never have lived to tell the tale.

Mercy can't think of a time, place or a universe in which she will miss her father; in which she will miss the, now shrinking, half a brick of tension that lives in her stomach.

But here is Mummy crying like her world has been cracked in two, and all the king's horses and all the king's men can never put it back together again. Mercy thought she understood Mummy, knew her inside out. The cord that linked them may be invisible but it was strong, wasn't it? But if she did not actually know her mother then what did she know? She thought she knew what was good for Mummy and being away from Daddy was it.

The important thing, the thing that Mummy should be thinking about, is that it's over. She can understand Devon getting a bit hot and bothered; as the One-Bwoy-Pickney he had been ridiculously attached to Daddy and his carrot face has gotten longer every day since Daddy left. Evie is the same, it's like a part of her left home when Daddy did.

Mummy snorts loudly into her handkerchief and Mercy takes this to mean that her tears are beginning to abate. She gently pushes the sitting room door all the way open and goes to sit next to her mother. Even though she knows Mummy has no reason for feeling the way she does, Mercy also knows that it's necessary to tread carefully. She takes Mummy's hand in hers and strokes the back of it. Mummy looks at her with far-away, watery eyes.

'Hello, Moom,' she says mournfully.

Mercy strokes the back of her hand for a little longer before shyly looking up at her mother's worn out face. 'Mummy,' she says, tentatively, 'can I ask you something?'

'Yes, Moom, is what?'

'Well... You've always said Daddy is the Devil and I heard you praying lots of times for God to strike him down. So why are you so upset now that he's dead?'

Mercy holds her breath. She really doesn't want to offend her mother but she desperately needs to understand what's going on.

Mummy sighs like she is trying to empty her body of air, and finally says, 'I did love him.'

In just four words Mummy manages to shatter Mercy. Again. The words hang in the air, poisoning it like the Mustard Gas Mercy learned about in World War One.

What the hell do you mean you loved him?

Of course she doesn't say the words out loud. Mercy doesn't swear. But the shock of hearing her mother use the 'L' word in relation to her father is worse than when he tried to kill them. She had hoped, now that Daddy was gone, to get Mummy to herself. What kind of hollow victory is this? She has Mummy in body but not in spirit because her heart belongs to Daddy. But how can Mummy love someone who could treat her as badly as he did? If Mummy loves Mercy, then how could she also love someone who treated Mercy so badly? If she loves *him* it can only mean that she doesn't really love Mercy. If what Mummy is saying is true then it is not only Mummy's world that is cracked in half, Mercy's is broken too.

Pastor Williams was bad enough, but this? This latest betrayal is worse. The rock of certainty on which her childhood was built is being smashed before her very eyes. That certainty was that once they got Daddy out of their lives everything would be fine. And now he is out, gone for good, and everything is not fine. Mummy is a tearful, blubby mess, mournfully admitting to being in love with a man who never showed anything remotely resembling affection to her mother, and barely any to his children.

When Mummy said to Miss Mary that marriage was an institution made by God and what God had brought together let no man put asunder, Mercy thought that she had to refuse the divorce because it was part of her religion, not because she actually *wanted* to stay married to him. But here is Mummy admitting it, in broad daylight. She loved him.

Mercy loves her mother but the nature of that love is changing, hardening into something she does not like. Mummy wants to leave her children and climb into the grave beside her dead husband and Mercy can't forgive her for that. She doesn't say the words but she feels herself shrinking inwardly away from her mother, the cord may still be there but she doesn't feel for it.

49

Duppy Conqueror

It's Halloween, autumn leaves fall in flurries, yellow and orange outside, whipped by the wind. It is the eerie, quiet part of the night, around three in the morning, and Mercy is asleep in the attic bedroom she shares with Evie. Their single beds (which used to be the bunk beds at Newlyn Square) are parallel to each other, against each wall of the dormer bedroom. In between, each has a small chest of drawers. The room is rattling and boiling in summer and rattling and freezing in winter, on account of the builders not putting any insulation in the wall when they built the dormers. The air is steamy with their breath and sweat.

Deep in her sleep Mercy hears deep kettle-drums along with strange warbling, or is it shouting? There are shapes dancing but she can't tell if they are animal, mineral or human. It is one of those times when she knows she is dreaming, so she decides to wake herself up and check. It takes a few attempts but she manages eventually to surface and wrench her eyelids open. It is still dark but the thin curtains let in weak light from the lamppost outside. When her eyes have adjusted to the dark she can see that Evie is still sleeping, one leg inside the covers, one out.

But the noises are real, and they are coming from downstairs. What is going on? She crawls out of bed, pulls her dressing gown from the nail on the back of the bedroom door and heads out. The door creaks. She checks, Evie is still asleep. Opposite her is the door to Ruby and Janie's attic bedroom. She listens, gentle breathing from Ruby and bear snoring from Janie. Tiptoeing down the steps from the attic to the first floor she can hear that Devon is still in his room because he snores even louder than Janie. So who is downstairs and who are they talking to?

One voice is definitely Mummy's. The other? Not so sure. It is deeper, gravelly, like some kind of alien. Mummy is praying but it's different from any prayers Mercy has heard before, more desperate, more intense. Mercy sits on the top step just outside Mummy's bedroom looking down and straining to hear.

'Get thee behind me Satan!' Mummy's voice is clear and echoey like a gong. There is a growl in response. Who, or what, is down there with Mummy? Mercy can stay on the step and guess or tiptoe down and have a look. But what if she doesn't like what she sees? What if Mummy gets angry that she has come down and beats her; or worse, makes her pray? What if it's one of those mythical creatures she has been reading about in Carlisle Road Library, with the legs of a goat, the torso of a man and the horns of a devil?

'The Dead,' Mummy says, stamping on each word, 'have no dominion over the living.'

Murmuring and growling in reply.

Mummy keeps on praying and speaking in tongues. Curiosity nips at her toes and Mercy begins inching down the steps on her bottom. The kitchen diner on the left is in darkness but there is a light on in the front room to the right. The light is coming from the floor. She can see that the room is illuminated by a lamp. The round glass shade is broken but the bulb still works, surrounded by a skeleton of wire. Some of the pictures on the walls are askew and one is smashed. The frame containing the wedding picture of Mummy and Daddy is broken. The picture itself is torn down the middle, with Daddy removed and just Mummy on her own in her tiny waisted wedding dress. The coffee table is upended like a dead animal with its legs in the air.

'I rebuke you,' says Mummy. 'I rebuke you in the mighty name of Jesus Christ my Redeemer and Saviour.' She is holding

a glass in her left hand and the Big Bible in her right. It is covered
in soft black leather with the words 'Holy Bible' embossed in
gold on the front and again on the spine. The leaves are so
thin they are almost transparent and the edges of the pages
are dipped in gold. This is her main Bible. She has others, the
travel Bible for when she is going on long journeys, the Church
Bible that she takes with her on Sundays, and another little one
which was always kept in her handbag, just in case. Every room
in the house has a Bible secreted somewhere, because, well, you
never know when you might need to cast out some Demons.

The half pint glass with a faded image of a crown on the
front is half empty. Mummy throws great gobs of water into
each of the four corners of the room. Mercy watches each
of them as they arc through the air catching the light of the
broken lamp before they hit their target: window, door, carpet,
curtains.

'I am,' she splashes water onto the sofa, 'the Alpha and
Omega,' she splashes again, 'the beginning and the end,' splash.
'No man comes to the Father but through me.'

'You,' Mummy points into a corner of the room with the
Bible, 'shall not enter here.'

She starts speaking in tongues again, stamping in small
circles in the middle of the room to the beat of an unknown
drum. Each time she exhales it's loud like a chant. 'This kind
goeth not out but by prayer and fasting.'

Mercy knows she has to go in. If nothing else Mummy
needs help in her fight against The Unseen. Mummy lives in
a different world to everyone else. A world of Demons and
discerning and destruction. Whatever she is fighting, she is
struggling. If Mercy is with her that will help.

She stands up and the cold sweat that has been gathering
under her armpits trickles down her sides. There is also sweat
between her legs; for a second she thought she had wet herself.
She pushes the door to the living room fully open.

'Mummy?' she whispers, and then more loudly, 'Mummy?'

Mummy's eyes swivel in their sockets towards her. It takes a few blinking seconds before Mummy recognises her. And in those seconds the deadly fury in Mummy's eyes petrifies her.

'Come,' says Mummy, still half-in-half-out of her spirit state. 'Come pray wid me.'

Mercy tiptoes over broken glass to stand next to her mother.

'You see him?' Mummy asks.

Mercy can't see anything but she nods anyway.

'Yes!' shouts Mummy. 'Out of the mouths of babes and sucklings.' Mercy is rather offended at being called a babe and suckling but now is not the time to point that out.

'Yuh dead!' screams Mummy. 'You dead, dead and bury. Get thee back to hell.'

'Dead,' whispers Mercy.

And Mercy knows who – or rather what – it is. For one last time she slides into Mummy's head and looks out at the world through Mummy's eyes. She can't stay in there for long; it is too hot, the fires of hell are actually trying to consume her mother. She can see Daddy trying to come back. His long bony fingers trying to claw his way back into the world. The sunken cheekbones and the eyes rolled back into his skull. The suit jacket hung off his bones. He still has his trilby. A cigarette is clamped between his teeth but instead of ash at the tip, it pours lava. Where his fingers touch the furniture blessed with holy water they dissolve and drip like melted, orange wax.

He can't cross holy water, because Mummy has blessed it good and proper. Mummy is living in the Book of Revelation where it is the end of days; the sun has turned black and the moon has turned to blood. Are they going to keep fighting for eternity? Mercy has to choose. She can't stay and fight or she might never get back out again. Whether he is alive or dead doesn't matter anymore. She can choose to leave him there. He has no dominion over her at least, not anymore.

She slides back out of Mummy and into her body which has been waiting patiently on the sofa. She slowly turns her head from side to side and rolls her shoulders to fix herself back in.

He is dead, isn't he? She touched the body. She saw him lowered into the ground and his friends cry and sing mournful songs as they ruined their good suits 'molding' the grave. She has to convince herself that there is no way he can come back. It's not easy, all that science she is learning at school means nothing in this house. Not in this room with her mother fighting to send Daddy back to Hell. If her teachers had asked her right here and now if she really spent half the night helping her Mummy to fight Daddy's Duppy she couldn't deny it.

It doesn't matter what she believes. What matters is Mummy. If Mummy believes it then so does she. But does she have to believe what Mummy believes? Maybe there isn't a God. Or if there is, he (or she) isn't all about fire and Brimstone. Mercy feels a growing certainty that she can't articulate, that her world does not have to be the same as Mummy's.

Then growling again. It is coming from Mummy. Both voices, his and hers, are inside Mummy. They rage at each other. Mummy is tearing herself apart trying to cast demons out of her own body. Can it be done?

Then, suddenly, Mummy slumps onto the sofa with her chin on her chest. She is mumbling, speaking in tongues. She goes quiet and then hums and gradually comes back to herself like she has just run a long hard race. The glass of water is empty and the glass is in smithereens at the front door. Mummy is breathing more gently now. Mercy sits close to her, close but not quite touching.

50

It's squid-ink black, warm and quiet. All the outside sounds are muffled. The winter sunlight shines yellow, orange, then almost red, dimly filtered under the soft heavy crimson blanket, trying to sneak its way under her eyelids. She squeezes them shut, tighter, wanting to stay under the covers for just a little bit longer, before she has to come out into the cold and face the music, or more accurately the lack of it.

Curled up in the foetal position, she is half-awake half-dreaming of long-lost Dolly and their endless conversations about what they were going to be when they grew up. Eyelid squeezing does not help, the effort just wakes her up some more. Evie is not quite snoring in the bed opposite, the low rumble just loud enough to make her sister's presence felt if not heard.

It is a snow-cold Saturday in the middle of December. She doesn't want to come out and face the world because she knows what is out there. A family who are variously mad and, whether dead or alive, will no doubt have forgotten that today is her eleventh Birthday. Well, the most dangerous one is gone now but he might as well still be here, stalking the house with his Daddy long legs as far as Mummy is concerned. Mercy is beginning to wonder if Mummy is actually better off with him dead than alive. He seems to be taking up even more space in her head. Now that he doesn't have a body, his spirit roams everywhere. Mercy knows he's not real but Mummy doesn't.

There will be no present, Mercy has gotten used to that now, and probably not a bigger one at Christmas either. She will make her own present: a day in the Library. Despite their madness and badness Mercy loves her family; but she is not sure if she likes any of them, or if they even like her. Mona said she would send a card with something special in it, but it hasn't come yet, perhaps it will be in the second post. Mercy hopes it's a ticket to London.

Could it be the nine months she spent as a baby in hospital with pneumonia, alone and lonely, working so hard to cling onto life. Did something in her break and she doesn't know how to fix it. The bit of her that should have known that there was a warm and loving family waiting for her, wasn't so sure. It could all be whisked away any minute. You don't get to choose your family do you? You get the Mummy you get, and all the sisters and the One Bwoy pickney and that's that. No cross-questioning. Mercy has never felt secure. She had too much time to think and consider in the hospital. She couldn't just be, she had to strategize to stay alive. I think therefore I am. If she stops thinking she no longer is.

Something invades her thoughts. It's a deep, soft churning pain in her belly. It aches like she has eaten something that disagrees with her. Is it Marley-gripe or fluxy-complaint? She feels somehow different. Somehow more and also less whole than she was the night before. She rubs her belly in circles but the pain does not go away. It clenches like fingers slowly curling into a fist. Waves like the contractions she felt long ago when she was on the inside, wash over her. Intestines complaining as they slide over each other, velvet viscera ill at ease. Dis-ease.

She slides her hand further down. Feels damp, then wetness. Has she wet the bed? No, not Mercy, never. She's way too old to be wetting the bed. So what is wrong? She slides her hand between her legs; slippery. Rubbing her thumb against her fingers she knows this is not pee. She sniffs her fingers; iron filings. And then slowly, through treacle it dawns on her it is 'P' but not the kind she thought.

They learned all about it in biology at school, the girls all nudging each other and giggling. They were shown all sorts of contraception and someone stole the pill; good luck to them

with just the one. Mummy never said a word to her, even after
Ruby and Janie started theirs. Janie reported that Mummy's
only comment after thrusting a pack of Kotex at her was, 'no
badda bring belly in a disya house,' and as far as the birds and
the bees were concerned that was that. Women's business is
never mentioned in this house full of women.

Mercy is ripe now, but ripe for what? She doesn't want
anyone picking her fruit no matter how many presents they
give her. Has she become a grown woman and what is the
difference between this and being a child? She has never felt
like a child anyway so maybe she is just growing into who she
was always meant to be. But she is still nervous. Mercy has to
tell someone, but she's not sure who. Mona isn't allowed to
use the phone at Miss Judy's house except in emergencies. Is
this an emergency? But what can Mona do from all the way
down in London? She's going to need things, sanitary towels or
tampons or whatever.

She heads to the bathroom, standing stock still for a while
staring at the blood on her hands. Is she really a ripe fruit now?
Will anyone be able to tell? What if Pastor Williams asks if
she can come and stay in Birmingham again? She knows how
babies are made now and she will not be bringing any belly
anywhere. She will definitely run away to London if Mummy
tries to send her to Birmingham.

One of Mummy's scripture verses from Revelation comes
to her. *I am washed in the blood of the lamb.* She runs her fingers
under running water, until the red turns to pink, then clear.
Then she stuffs a load of toilet paper into a clean pair of
knickers. Thankfully none of the blood of the lamb got onto
the sheets so she won't have to take them to the Wash House.
Mummy hasn't gone to work yet so now is the time to go and
tell her. Mercy feels embarrassed, like she did when she told
Mummy about Pastor Williams; like somehow, at some level,
this is all her fault. How dare she grow up?

Duelling in her mind with school's normal and natural is Mummy's dirty and sinful. She heads down to the kitchen with the unfamiliar wodge between her legs. The words are quite simple. *Mummy, I've started my period.* But she can't bring herself to say them out loud to her mother. So in the end she walks into the kitchen and holds up the bloodied knickers.

'Mummy,' she says, 'look.'

Mrs Hanson looks up and lets out a short, shocked gasp as she sees her daughter's menses.

'Alright,' she says, eyes narrowing, 'wait.' Mummy disappears upstairs and comes back with a pack of Kotex, each one the size of a small house brick. She gives Mercy the pack but no information or instructions on how to use them. She doesn't look Mercy in the eye as the contraband is handed over. Mercy turns over the large soft package.

'Mummy?'

'Is what?' Mummy answers with a note of irritation in her voice.

'Can I have Tampax instead?' Mercy would rather not waddle around with one of the house bricks.

'You what!' The conflagration that Mercy has sensed building behind her mother's eyes detonates. 'I rebuke you in the name of Jesus!' she shouts 'Dem tings is de work of the Debble. Is sinful to push tings up inside a yuh. Only dutty gyal would use dem tings.'

'No.' Mercy stands her ground, the knickers still gripped like a bloody sword in her left hand. She doesn't have any money so she can't buy Tampax herself. If Mummy doesn't buy them for her she won't be able to have any, but she's not going to be condemned for the mere suggestion.

'I am not dirty.' She fixes her mother with a stare that surprises even her. If she was Jewish, her teacher said, she would be getting a Bat Mitzvah, a celebration of reaching womanhood, a ceremony and a big party. But something tells her Mummy will not be throwing any parties any time soon.

'You think seh yuh is big ooman in a disya house?'
'No,' says Mercy, 'I only asked for Tampax.'
'Don't use that blasted word before my face.'

Something that has been slowly stretching inside Mercy
finally reaches breaking point, becomes gossamer thin and then
snaps. Mercy knows something has happened, but not exactly
what. She almost falls backwards with the recoil, winning an
eleven year tug of war when the other side suddenly gives in.

She's taller than her mother now and from what seems like
a great height, she looks at a frightened little woman, who like
King Canute is trying to keep the modern world at bay: trying
to keep her girls from growing up to enter a world where men
like Pastor Williams put slugs in their mouths. But ignoring it
will not stop it happening. It breeds in darkness.

Mercy knows that Mummy's way has served her well. God
and the Devil, Saints and Sinners, Demons and Angels, the
binary which has helped her mother make sense of a world
which treated her with contempt at best and outright violence
at worst. But it will not be Mercy's way. Not all bad things can
be prayed-away. Mercy, for all her fantasies, is choosing the
world of the mind over the spirit. The cord has finally snapped,
Mercy feels like she has just given birth to herself.

She heads back upstairs to get dressed.
'Noh badda turn yuh back pon mi,' says Mummy.
'I'm off to the library.'
'Book-learning? You need God's learning.' She softens her
tone slightly, 'come pray wid me, Mercy. Dis is a time for
fasting and prayer.'

There has been no mention of her birthday, the blood has
washed away Mummy's memory of this day eleven years ago
when Mercy slithered into a winter so much colder than this
one. Mercy stares at her mother, the corners of her mouth lift
into a shadow of a smile. She will not stay and pray.
'I'm going to the library.'

'Book-learning!' Mummy explodes again, 'is book-learning ah bring you ina mi face axe fi dem disgusting things.'

For almost all of her life Mercy has believed her mother to be good and true and honest and righteous. But now, married to Daddy in life, shackled to him in death, Mummy is lost in a world from which Mercy cannot save her. Even though Mercy once stood firm before a man with a machete, willing to die for her mother, it is with a heft of sadness that Mercy realises that although she loves her mother, she cannot abandon reason for her. She cannot do what her mother is always asking, which is have faith, blind faith.

God will provide. But God, in the shape of Pastor Williams, only provided slugs and snails and puppy dog tails. Mummy wouldn't defend her; the woman for whom she would gladly have laid down her life could not pick up her voice for Mercy. It's not that she no longer trusts her mother, it's that the absolute blindness of that trust has gone.

Mercy turns and heads upstairs. She swaps the loo roll for the sanitary towel, which is marginally more comfortable than an actual breeze block. She gets dressed in a skirt and socks rather than trousers because now she has *accidents* to worry about. Just as well it is a Saturday morning and she doesn't have to go to school, this might be an awkward day otherwise.

When Mercy comes back downstairs. Mummy is praying loudly for her soul, imploring the Almighty to deliver her from her book-learned, own-way, wickedness. Mercy hesitates. She *could* stay, she could try and get inside Mummy's head again. She can see the little door above Mummy's temple, the crack with the red orange light seeping through. It would be so simple to just slip out of her skin and crawl inside. See what she sees, hear what she hears, but Mercy is not going to go in there again. Something tells her that she may never get out again. She has spent her whole life trying to save Mummy. It didn't work. So now she has to save herself.

   She opens the front door quietly and slips out into the
sharp, winter sunshine. It will take her fifteen minutes to walk
to Carlisle Road Library. And as she walks, the pain in her belly
slowly recedes.

Tee hee hee

The process that started eleven years ago is finally coming to an end. I have been slowly chewing through the umbilicus and finally severed the cord.

From now on I will have to breathe for myself, suck in air, strip the oxygen and spit out carbon dioxide. I'm on my own on the outside. I have learned to walk and talk, and fight dragons and slugs. I speed up my walking, feeling the gentle rolling of my pelvis as my weight transfers from foot to foot. The pain in my belly subsides with movement so I break into a run, like I'm doing Cross Country at Odsal Top, overtaking everyone else on my way to live my life.

Pace yourself, I say to my legs, you've got a long way to go. I will keep on running, not running away but running towards, toward a future that I construct for myself, with my own bare hands. One day, Mummy will be proud of me the way Daddy never could be. He could only see a wiley child with a brain which could outwit him but not out-hit him. Maybe one day Mummy will come to see a clever daughter as a blessing not a curse.

But in the end it doesn't really matter. In the end I'm on my own. We're all on our own, coming into this life kicking and screaming, ready to write a letter to The Times about the indignity of it all;

the blood and the guts, the squeezing and the pain. I can write now,
I can walk and talk and I can tell my own story.

> *Mummy and me?*
> *No, just me.*
> *Tee hee hee.*

--- The End ---

Marcia Hutchinson

Marcia Hutchinson was born to Windrush generation Jamaican parents in the UK in 1962. She was the first pupil from her comprehensive school to go to Oxford, where she gained an MA in Law. She worked as a lawyer before founding the educational publishing company Primary Colours, which she ran until 2014. She was awarded an MBE in 2011 for services to Cultural Diversity.

Moving to Manchester in 2012, she became a community activist and was eventually elected as a Labour Councillor in 2021. She is now a full-time writer and an active member of the Black Writers' Guild. She is the co-author with Kate Griffin (under the pseudonym Lila Cain) of the historical fiction novel *The Blackbirds of St Giles*, which was published by Simon and Schuster in 2025.

The Mercy Step is her literary debut as a solo writer, and was selected as one of *The Observer's* Best Debut Novels for 2025.

For all media enquiries please contact Sophie Goodfellow at FMcM Associates on sophieg@fmcm.co.uk